beholden

CORINNE MICHAELS

dedication

To the men and women who serve their countries and the families they leave behind.

Especially my husband for his years of sacrifice and dedication.

prologue

Catherine

I STAND BEFORE the mirror in my knee-length, black dress. My hair is pin straight and I've opted against eye makeup. Not even waterproof mascara can withstand the torrent of tears I've shed lately.

I'll see him today.

I'll somehow handle looking at the man who's no longer mine. The one who forced me to love again, give my heart to him—then forced me to be alone. He's gone and I won't get him back.

I'll need a miracle to get through this.

Giving myself another once-over, I'm as content as I'll ever be. What does it matter anyway? Who gives a shit what I look like in the grand scheme of things? I'll be wrecked by the end of today—again. There will be no coming back. I'm in hell—no, purgatory. I walk around living, but feeling dead inside.

"You ready?" Ashton whispers behind me, placing her cool hand on my shoulder.

"Yeah, sure. It's not getting any better than this," I reply without any emotion.

I feel hollow.

He took everything from me.

"Okay ..." she trails off and leaves the room to let me finish up.

Once I'm done, I head out to the living room. We gather our belongings in silence and head to the car. Ashton drives without the music on, giving me time to do nothing but sit and think of Jackson. I see his face, hear his voice, feel his hands on me, but it's not real anymore. Phantom feelings for a man that isn't real. None of it was real. I sometimes wonder if I just made it all up in my head. Made it into something it wasn't.

As we pull into the metal gates of the cemetery, I stare out the window wishing I were anywhere but here. I don't know how I'll make it through this.

The car stops and Ashton places her hand on mine. "Cat, we don't have to do this. If you can't be here ..." She stops and bites her lip. "No one would judge you." The empathy swimming in her eyes rips through my heart, tearing me apart.

I glance at the tent set up at the gravesite. The people starting to filter around to bid their final goodbye to a man they loved. I sit here—frozen. Trying to piece together the parts of my heart that are no longer beating. I hear the remnants thumping erratically in my chest, but I feel nothing.

"I promised I'd be here, Ashton," I say with an air of finality.

I may not want to, but the bottom line is, I love him. I gave my heart to him and I made promises—no matter what, I won't break them.

We exit the car and start to make our way to the sea of black. The dark hearts in pain and sorrow surround the area. My heels puncture the soft grass while the gaps in my heart grow larger with each step. The smell of fresh grass fills the air. I can feel his presence. Every part of my body is tingling in awareness. The tears pool in my eyes blurring my sight and I stumble, but Ashton keeps me from falling.

"Ash ..." My voice quivers as I will myself to keep from falling apart.

"I won't leave your side." Her deep, blue eyes are filled with her vow.

I nod and draw my strength from her.

She's here and won't let me fall.

Keeping my head lowered, I continue moving while she holds on to my arm. I don't want to see faces. I focus on the beads of dew hanging on the blades of grass. I take in each one as if they're tears from God. Tears because none of this is okay. If I can keep my eyes down, I won't have to see the urn that sits on top of the tombstone. I won't see the friends and family with tear-filled eyes. I can pretend this is an awful dream and none of this is happening. I don't want to hear the words telling us we should be thankful for the time we had, because there's never *enough* time.

"I'm right here with you," Ashton whispers and wraps her arms around me.

I nod, not trusting my ability to speak. I'm barely hanging on.

Silence falls upon the crowd as the preacher speaks, talking about heroism and sacrifice. Opening my eyes, I take in the scene before me. The four sailors stand off to the side dressed in their dark blue uniforms. Ribbons and medals hang from their chests. I glance at the American flag folded next to the urn, the gift for his ultimate sacrifice. I listen to the words and the quiet sobs of people in pain.

When the reverend stops speaking, the sailor moves and the bugle blares playing "Taps." Each note shreds through my body, penetrates my bones, and shatters my heart. Tears stream down my face unabashed. The uniformed sailor walks over to the front row placing the folded flag in delicate hands. He kneels before her speaking as she nods and trembles. The sounds of her loud cries break through my fragile façade.

"Shhh, Cat," Ashton murmurs in my ear. "You're shaking." She rubs her hands up and down my arm trying to warm me.

If only I was shaking because I'm cold.

I turn into her when a hand ghosts up my shoulder, "Catherine." His deep voice echoes in the eerie quiet.

The sound of his voice is my undoing. A sob breaks through my chest as Ashton catches me while I fall apart.

CHAPTER ONE

JACKSON

"**K**ILL 'EM AND let's go!" Mark's loud voice bellows over the zinging of bullets raining around us. "Up on the ridge there's another one!"

I return fire trying to shoot my way to safety. Screams and gunfire are all I register through the chaos. The dust flies with each bullet hitting the dirt.

"Muff!" Mark calls out as my vision starts to fade.

The metallic taste of blood floods my mouth.

"Motherfucker! Move!" he yells, trying to get me out of harm's way. Opening my eyes, I see Mark's face contort as he continues to shoot.

Using my arms, I try to crawl closer. It fucking hurts. The pain is everywhere as a bullet rips through my abdomen, stopping me from moving. I lie here out in the open ready for my fate.

I look over at Mark as he returns fire and rushes towards me.

"Mark," I croak out, my vision hazy as he approaches me.

I close my eyes and succumb to the black. I don't want to wake up. The pain is too much. Besides, Catherine is here in the dark. Hearing her voice makes me want to try, but I'm losing my will.

"Jackson, you have to fight!" Her voice is thick with emotion.

"I'm too tired, baby. I want to stay with you. It doesn't hurt so much here. You make me feel better," I tell her, content to see her face and hear her voice. I know she's not real—but I want to stay here.

Her eyes close as a tear falls down her beautiful face. "You'll hurt me more if you stay. You have to go back. *Please.* For me," she begs.

I'll do anything not to hurt her again. I'd give her everything just to stop the look of suffering on her face. I open my eyes and the piercing torture jolts me back to life while the bullets slice through the air around me.

Mark hoists me over his shoulder as I hold back a scream from the impact against my injured shoulder. The pain radiates from my head to my toes, reminding me I'm still alive. If I can still feel, I can fight.

"We have to go. Now!" The tone of command conveys the urgency of the situation.

I'm thrown in the back of the Humvee and the jolt causes me to cry out. "Holy shit! It fucking hurts!" I can't hold back. My vision fades again and I'm not sure if it's from the pain or if I'm coming to the end.

"Muff, can you hear me?" The doors slam closed as we take cover in the Humvee and start to move.

Mark hovers over me. We continue to take fire but the protection of the vehicle allows us to get the hell out of here. Each bump in the road is pure agony. They drive frantically trying to get back to the base as one soldier radios in my injuries.

"He's been shot three times. Get the HELO on standby!" Mark yells out to him as we take a sharp turn, causing me to shift.

"My fucking leg," I cry out.

"Put your hand over your shoulder." He presses my hand over the bullet wound, trying to force me to put pressure on it.

"I have to deal with your leg, so you have to hold it."

I try to hold on but I can't feel my arms, every limb is heavy. My hand starts to slip. "I can't—" I start to say.

"You don't have a choice, you son of a bitch!" Mark yells in my face. "Shut the fuck up and hold on to your shoulder!"

Mark grabs a needle from the medic bag and injects something in my arm. Everything becomes foggy and numb. I'm so tired. The smell of sweat, blood, and fear filters through the Humvee.

Something slaps my face forcing me to open my eyes. "Eyes open, you fuckbag! Don't close them!" Mark's eyes are wide and focused. I feel my pants rip. "Muff, this is going to hurt," he says calmly before he clamps his hand around the bullet hole in my leg, pushing down.

"Fuuuuuuuuuck!" I scream out as a hot fire spreads through my veins burning everything in its path.

The pain is taking over and I can't fight the black.

He pushes again as my eyes fly open. "I told you. Keep. Your. Eyes. Open!" He turns to the driver. "Faster!" Mark ties something around my leg creating a tourniquet. His voice is harsh but I hear the undertone of fear. We both know this isn't good. The blood loss, the multiple bullet wounds, and the fact that we're not close enough to the base is the reality we face.

Mark rips open my shirt and sees the blood around my abdomen as his hands tremor in terror. My hand falls again and he positions himself to put pressure on my stomach and my shoulder.

"Be there in three," the driver calls back to us.

"You have three minutes to tell me all the reasons I should keep you from bleeding out. You close your eyes, I'll fucking push harder. Try me, motherfucker." He grips my face making me focus on him.

"Tell her—"

"Not a chance. Tell me."

"I love ..." I pass out from the agony.

I awake to the constant stream of beeping behind me. Where am I? I feel something warm in my hand but I can't open my eyes. The weights holding my eyelids closed are too heavy to lift. I hear mumbling and I swear it's Catherine and Mark, but that wouldn't make sense.

Attempting to get my limbs to cooperate, I try to lift my arms but they won't move.

"Jackson …" I hear her call to me. "Please wake up. I don't know if you can hear me, but God, I hope you can."

Catherine.

She's here.

She takes a deep breath and lets it out, clearly upset. "Mark called and I … I just … come back to me." I hear her sob and the need to comfort her overwhelms me. I want to wake up and tell her it's okay, but everything is locked. Every part of me is heavy and unwilling to cooperate.

"God, there's so much to say. You have to be okay, because I c-can't. I can't live with knowing this w-was all we h-had." Catherine's voice tears through me. "I'd give anything to go back and never let you leave my house that night. I'd barricade you in my damn room. I-I'm so s-sorry, baby. Please be okay."

She has nothing to be sorry for. I did this to her. I was a chickenshit. I created this doubt of how I feel about her because I chose to walk away. I didn't want to destroy her, yet that's all I've done.

"I wish I would've called you. Or come to you that night. Shit. But as soon as Mark called I came. I ran … to you, Jackson." She lets out a shaky breath. "I love you and I'm here now. I just want to see you open your eyes, baby. It's been too long since I've seen your eyes. I miss your smile, and your voice. I miss you being an ass, and being charming. I miss it all. Please,

Jackson. Wake up, dammit!" she begs and sobs.

The sounds of her cries echo in the room. Each hiccup guts me. I can't speak. Hell, I don't know how long I've been out for. I'm obviously alive, but am I really? If this is death—I'm being robbed. There's no white light or anyone calling me to another side. I'm lying here. Trapped in my own body, listening to people around me.

"Cat, come on. You need to sleep. It's been two days and you haven't moved." I hear Mark's voice. "He'll wake up. He's too much of a dickhead to die." He laughs and her half laugh makes my heartbeat accelerate. The monitor beeps louder and they both stop talking.

This is complete bullshit.

"It's been a while, Mark. Plus, I don't know if I ..." She trails off sounding hurt. *Fucking eyes—open!* "The doctors said his leg is in bad shape. What if he has to have another surgery? He barely made it out of the last one."

"He'll be fine. Remember who we're talking about. Trust me, he's been through worse than this. He's just going to make us all suffer for a while," Mark says, trying to reassure her.

"What if he doesn't want me here?"

I shouldn't have left, but I couldn't stop. Rage consumed every part of me. My failure was all I could see. Catherine would be next and I will *not* allow it. I'll break myself apart before I let anything happen to anyone else.

"Listen, Kitty, he wants you here. I know you guys haven't been together that long, but he cares. I wouldn't have called you and gone through the red tape if I wasn't sure what you mean to him."

"You weren't there that night." Her voice cracks and so does my heart.

"You have to understand him—he's an idiot. A big, giant, fucking moron."

Catherine's soft laugh stops her sniffles.

"I'd bet on him, Cat. He'll wake up." Mark is comforting

her and I'm here helpless. I hear her muffled sobs and each part of me tears open—I hate hurting her.

I feel something against my bedside. It's torture to hear and know what's going on but not be able to talk or move.

Mark begins to speak in the distance. "I think you should get some rest at the hotel. Ashton leaves today, you could go with her—"

"No! Not even an option." I feel her hands touch my hair and guide it to the side. "I'll go to the airport to drop her off, but I'm not leaving until he wakes. And if he wants me to leave … I'll … well, I don't know, but I'm not leaving until he throws me out." She sounds strong and sure.

I try again to open my eyes, give her a sign that I'm alive. But they won't budge. Fuck this. I'm going back to sleep. Then I can stop feeling so weak.

I listen to the beeping, counting each one as my mind replays the shooting. Remembering the feeling of metal shredding my skin, the smell of death in the HELO, the blood staining my clothes and skin. I have no idea how bad my injuries are.

"Of course he wants you here. Why do you keep saying shit like this?" he asks.

He doesn't know I walked away from her like I did. He doesn't know the pussy I was and the dick move I made when I got the call. I went there and things happened so fast. I was ready to tell her everything. We were going to talk and figure our shit out. Then I got the call from Mark and I lost it. The failure of not being able to save someone else weighs on me.

"You don't understand. When he left—"

"Knock, knock," an unfamiliar voice says.

"Is everything okay? The last nurse was just here." Catherine's voice is strained.

"We're going to give him a little more meds to keep him comfortable," an older woman's voice comes through. "He's been having some irregularity in his heart rate."

"Is he okay?" Catherine asks, sounding scared.

I'm fine. Just pissed off.

"Yes, we're going to make sure he's not in any pain," the nurse explains.

"Jackson." Catherine's small hands caress my face. "I'll be right back. I have to take Ashton to the airport." Her lips press against my cheek and she leans in close to my ear whispering so only I can hear her. "I love you. You're it for me, so don't go anywhere." I feel her lips press against my face again as the meds drag me into the black.

"He's crashing!" The helicopter noise drowns out most sounds but I hear them frantically screaming. "Stay with us, Cole. Only two more minutes."

Two minutes. I can hold on for two minutes.

My eyes fly open as they work on my chest and inject something into my IV. Jesus Christ, I can't take much more. The fighting and trying to hang on is exhausting. I want to be done. I want the fucking black and numbness because there's no pain there.

"Give him another round of epi," the medic calls out while he stabs something into my chest.

The sound of my gasps and gurgling is horrifying. I'm going to die. I feel it in every bone in my body. The blood loss from the three gunshot wounds I sustained is too much. Even in this state I feel pain. It runs from head to toe and amplifies with each second that passes.

"Hang on, buddy, we're almost there," he yells in my face trying to make me focus.

The helicopter touches down and I'm moving before we stop. The colors of light flash quickly as I'm being pulled out and thrown on a gurney. The sun is blinding and each part of me feels heavy as they run toward the hospital. I want to scream out—yell at the top of my lungs to let me die. I don't want to feel any more. I close my eyes and I see her again. I see her dark brown eyes glaring at me. I hear her quiet cries and it tears at my soul. Her face is contorted in pain. The tears are filling in her eyes as she refuses to break contact.

"Don't leave me," I hear Catherine call out but her voice is fading.

"Prep him for surgery. Now. Trauma one." There are voices all around yelling different orders. Trying to get control. People barking numbers but I can't focus. I open my eyes and only see the bright light above. Either God is calling or it's one of those bright ass lights they use in the hospital.

I moan and try to move my arm but someone clamps it.

A man in a blue mask comes into view trying to get me to focus. "Stay still, Cole. We're going to take you into surgery. You need to calm down. Knock him out. Now!"

Calm? He's fucking joking, right? I can't calm down.

"Catherine!" I scream out.

CHAPTER

TWO

ANOTHER FUCKING FLASHBACK. I can't determine what's reality anymore.

I'm tired of being tired. When I'm in this awake but paralyzed state, I'm battling my mind and my body. I want to tell Catherine what I think and feel. But my goddamn body won't get with the fucking program.

Then the fucking nightmares exhaust my mind. Haunting me with the shooting—forcing me to recall everything over and over. Either I see the bullets ripping through me or I see the aftermath. I'd rather go through Hell Week again—at least there we had fun crawling through dirt and mud.

"It's been four days and he still hasn't woken up, Mark." Catherine sounds weary and worn.

"I know, Kitty."

"You know I hate that," she replies and I imagine her eyes rolling.

"Yeah, well, since I don't have Muff here to give shit to ... you're the next best thing." His laughter is short and forced.

I've known him long enough to hear the fear. It's the voice we used when we were on a mission and things were going south. Full of lies but the words we needed to hear to get through it. Sometimes you need reassurance things are going to be fine even though you know they're not. He's doing his best to hold out for her. I must be in worse shape than I imagined.

The small hairs on the back of my hand move when she breathes. The ability to feel it gives me hope I'm coming around.

Maybe soon I can open my damn eyes.

"I'm happy I amuse you, Twilight." That's my girl. Give it back to the fucknugget. "When do you have to head back to the States?"

"Soon. I have to make sure the rest of the contracts run smoothly and are under control, but ..." A chair scrapes across the floor. "I can't leave yet, Cat. I know I need to, especially with Aaron gone, but ..." He trails off and takes a deep breath. "We only have two other guys who know this shit like we do. I've been with him since day one. This company may have his name, but it has all our blood, sweat, and tears."

Another chair grates making a loud sound. "Is the company in trouble? I can try to do some press stuff from here. Manage the story as much as possible. You know this is what I'm good at. Plus it's my job. I can't fail him." Catherine seems anxious to help. She speaks quickly trying to get him on board.

She must be going out of her mind. Everything in her life stopped so she could be here. I have to wake up. But when I do, will any of it matter? I'll be injured at the very least, and we're broken.

"No, we're okay for now. We have the contract in Afghanistan that's still not in a good place, but I have a liaison in place. What about Raven?"

That stupid company. It's tied to me and bringing me down. If I get rid of it, there's a part of *her* that goes. If I don't, there's a part of *me* that will lose everything. Of course, there's the fact that Catherine knows nothing of my past and what it all means. Who the fuck even knows if she'll understand once everything comes to light? She may bolt and I don't know if I'd blame her.

I remember how I felt when that prick, Neil, showed up at her house saying he was her fiancé. The idea of her being tied to anyone that closely ripped me apart and made me see red. I'm aware other men have had a place, but I still hate it.

"Raven is good. Danielle's handling things well. I've

released a few updates about his condition, and the shareholders seem to be staying put for now. There hasn't been a dip in the stock either. I have a few people with ears to the ground if anything comes up. I cancelled my meetings with the press for next week. And pushed the launch off." I feel her fingers brush my hair back. "I guess it's a good thing he's my job." Catherine's short laugh is followed by a sob. "God! I just sit here and look at him and ask the same question over and over. Why? Why is this happening? I'm so scared he's not going to wake up. That we won't have a chance to make things right and I c-can't!"

"Shhh, it's okay," Mark murmurs, and her sobs destroy me.

Even though I can't move, every piece of me is in pain.

I fucked up.

"It's not okay. None of this is *okay*," she sniffles. "I thought we were going to find our way, Mark. I was ready to fight everything for him. Then he ripped me apart and he *left* me! He fucking left and didn't look back. I know he had to leave to handle the situation with Aaron. I wasn't against him leaving for that … just him leaving *me*! There's something else. I know it." Catherine's voice shakes in anger.

My mind is slipping as I try to keep up with their conversation. I struggle to focus but the sounds are blurring together. I'm fucking drained.

"He has his reasons, Cat. You may not like them. Fuck, I don't like them."

"What reasons?" She sounds small and scared.

The exhaustion is overtaking as I fall back asleep unable to know what Mark will tell her.

Pain. The pain is back. It travels through me as I try to process what is going on.

"Okay, motherfucker, I've been patient. I've let you lie here and not said shit. I've held her while she cried. I've called your family. Done everything waiting for you to man up. But I'm done now, Muff. Wake the fuck up!" Mark's voice interrupts my foggy sleep.

Oh, I'm awake now, dickhead.

"I'm so mad at you! You go and get shot in front of me. You always have to be the fucking martyr. You couldn't take cover like I said to? I told you to watch your six. Now look, you're fucking half dead." Mark's voice cracks on the last word.

"I'm not going to be the only one left here, asshole. You think you're the only one here who lost them? I fucking lost them too. So, what? You're going to quit and make me carry all of it? No, you wake up and you deal with this shit too. I was on the same mission! I watched them get carried out. I heard the same fucking sounds and lived the same hell. You weren't the sole person responsible for them going into that village. I was there too," he stops and exhales.

"I could've said we should stay together, but it was risky either way. Selfish fucking asshole you are. I've let you be this self-sacrificing prick for long enough. You don't get to be the only one allowed to hurt. There were six of us! Six of us who walked into that fucking village and only three came out. There's not a day I don't think about them. I remember walking into that fucking funeral watching Melissa grieve. Watching Crystal hold on to that flag. Now there are only two. So who carries the fucking guilt if you die? Huh, you selfish son of a bitch? That's what I thought. Just lie there and let me deal with this alone. God, you're such a pussy." Mark breaks off, drawing a few deep breaths.

I want to scream, choke, and claw my way out of my own skin. Selfish? Fuck him. He didn't send them to their deaths. He wasn't the one who had to make the call. I did. When I get out of this coma, I'm gonna kill him myself.

"And then what? You're going to walk away from her too? Why? You need to get your fucking head straight. I was there for that too, you know. I watched her almost ruin you. But Catherine isn't Maddie. And if you're going to do this to her then you don't deserve her. She loves you for some stupid ass reason. She didn't hesitate for a second to come running when I told her you were hurt. She jumped on a plane. Maddie wouldn't have. But you don't see that because your head is shoved so far up your ass. You forget the bad and focus on how this was somehow your fault. You're not responsible for all the bad shit that happens in life. I swear to God, Jackson, you die and I'll fucking find you in the afterlife and kill you myself." His own emotions become too much as I hear his breath catch.

I hate him in this moment because he says all this when I can't defend myself. There's no chance for me to tell him to shut the fuck up. I don't want to hear what he's saying about Madelyn or Catherine. They aren't the same, but he wasn't there. He didn't see it. He didn't know that once again my decisions had consequences. No, instead he wants to tell me how I'm wrong? Mark better pray I don't come around right now.

After some silence, Mark's breathing returns to normal.

"Hey," Catherine's voice is close and soft. "You okay?"

"No. I'm not." Mark sounds empty.

"Yeah," she pauses and lets out a deep exhale. "Me either."

How long have I been out? It's like I'm in some alternate universe. Some Tim Burton movie where you think you're being drugged. I'm waiting for dancing ponies or a talking pumpkin to appear.

"How long have you been standing there?" Mark questions.

"Just long enough to hear you threatening to kill him yourself. Which I'm sure if he can hear us, he's ready to choke you for." She gives a small half-hearted laugh.

"I'm sure, but at this point I don't give a shit. Hopefully I pissed him off enough to wake up. I thought by now ..."

"Mark, it'll—" Catherine's voice is low.

"Sorry, Kitty. Come here."

She sighs and I imagine he has her wrapped in his arms. Holding her close while I lie here and get to picture it. Why the fuck am I not waking up? The idea of Catherine in any other man's arms is enough to make me want to tear my heart out. I know Mark would never cross that line, but I'm going out of my mind. I need to touch her, hold her, and let her know it's all going to be okay.

"You know, I keep hoping I'll wake up and be back in my apartment and all this will be a bad dream," Catherine says with a shaky voice.

"He's always been that guy in the group who wanted to prove everyone wrong. I hoped I could get him angry enough that his eyes would snap out and he'd be swinging at me." He gives a short laugh, "Well, at least he could try."

He's not that far off. If I could've gotten my body to work I would've. Dickhead.

"But hope is for the weak—I have faith," Mark tacks on.

"Each time you and I talk, I realize I don't know him. We happened so fast, but everything was intense and felt right."

She's wrong. She knows me more than anyone. Catherine sees the things I don't show anyone else. I let her in where it matters. Yet she thinks she knows nothing?

Shimmering lights all around, twinkling and growing brighter as the music plays. The sound of the bass reverberates through me as the drum solo plays in. My entire body vibrates with it.

Bam ... bam ... boom.

Standing at the beach with the sun shining upon my face. No one is here, just me as I wait for her. I close my eyes and breathe in the salt air. Allowing it to calm me, reminding me how I feel at home with the sea.

Slowly my eyes lift and I start to take her in as she walks toward me.

No shoes.

White dress.

As my eyes travel up to her face, I stand rooted in shock. Again she's here.

"Jackson," she whispers. "Come back to me."

My heart stops beating as I gape at her. Six years she was my life and then she was gone. Taking all my hope, my love, and part of my heart when she left. I was empty and dead inside, but now she's here again. Why? Why does she have to take from me over and over? Can't she let me be?

I open my mouth to tell her … fuck, I don't know what I want to say. Each part of me wants to say something different. To yell, beg, scream, and punch my way through this fucking nightmare. Tell her how she destroyed me, made me give up everything for her, only to have her take more.

"Why?" is the only word I'm capable of saying.

She stands unmoving letting my question hang in the air while my heart beats erratically.

"Why?" I ask again more forcefully. She needs to answer me. I step toward her and a smile crosses her perfect lips. "Goddammit, why?"

Her features soften, and as I get closer she finally says, "It wasn't supposed to be."

I stop moving and my eyes close in pain. Ice shoots through my veins leaving me frozen and void.

When I open them she's gone.

All over again.

"Fox, what's your view look like?" I ask trying to get the other half of the guys to give me a status update.

Nothing.

I try a different one. "Razor, do you copy?"

Silence.

"Bronzer, come in. What's your status?" I look around trying to remain still since it's daylight and I have no idea what the fuck is going on.

I turn to Mark and signal him to try. "Fox, Razor, Bronzer, do you copy?"

"We copy. We need to move. Out."

Their location must be compromised. There's no other reason they'd move in daylight. I signal to Aaron and Mark that we need to move.

"If they're on the move, something's wrong. Let's take to the other side and we'll meet them when it's safe," I say as we prepare to head out.

Everything feels rushed. Every moment feels like it's on fast forward. We make it to the edge of the village and try to find a place to wait it out. We're out of range to talk to the other three now, but Razor's in charge. We've done enough missions together to know each other's moves. If I were him, I would wait until the time we selected. We have our extract in three hours. It gives us about two hours to get what we need and get the fuck out of here.

I turn to Aaron, and before I can get a word out, the percussion of gunfire explodes in the air. We drop to the ground, ready to shoot back.

Pop. Pop. Pop.

Fast and steady, but it's not close to us. We hear screaming and the continuous shooting on the other side of the village. Mark starts calling on the radio to the other half of our team, but we're still out of range.

"Fuck this. We're going in." I grab my gun, and Mark and Aaron are on my heel.

"Muff, the left." I take the guy out before he gets a shot off.

We fall out to the side of the building and start to creep in. I see them. They're shooting, but they're outnumbered. Everything happens in slow motion. I watch the bullet perforate Brian's neck when he stands to take a shot. The stream of blood and the strangled scream he makes echo as he falls. Either Mark or Aaron shoots and kills another three men. We're moving as fast as we can, but it's too late. I eliminate another four by the time I reach Brian.

"Fuck. Hold on." I squeeze his neck trying to stop the bleeding, but his eyes are fading. "Fuck. Call and get the extract in here *now*!" I scream as Aaron's already radioing in our location. "Where is the rest of the team?"

"Jackson! Can you hear me?" Catherine is frantic. Why is she here? What is she doing here? *No!*

She has to get the fuck out of here. She'll die.

Please God don't take her too! I can't.

"I have to leave soon, I need you to wake up before I go," she whispers and I snap out of it.

Leave? What? No!

"Fight for me, baby."

I'm trying. If only I knew how ...

chapter

three

Catherine

DAYS PASS BY and nothing changes. He doesn't move or speak. I sit here wondering when or if he'll wake. Will he be the same man he was?

Jackson's mother arrived early this morning and she's everything he described her as. Her warmth is evident even in the situation we're currently facing. After she and Mark embraced, she took me into her arms and held me close. I hadn't been sure what to expect, but it certainly wasn't that.

"Mrs. Cole, do you need anything?" I ask timidly.

She smiles and places her hand on mine. "No, sweetheart. I'm okay, and please, call me Nina. I'm just waiting for him to stop being a stubborn ass and wake up." Her sweet voice reassures me that she has all the faith we need.

I smile at her as she sits in the chair next to Jackson. I take the seat on the other side of his bed with the man we love in between us. I grab his hand and hold it, feeling the heat that reminds me he's alive. The constant beeping of the machine gives me something steady to hold on to.

Beep.

Two seconds pass.

Beep.

One. Two.

Beep.

Nina clears her throat drawing my attention. "So tell me, how did you two meet? I wish I knew these things, but Jackson has been distant. His father and I are lucky to hear from him once every six months lately."

She smiles, but even I can hear the undercurrent of disapproval at his lack of contact.

"I didn't know he was being so ..." I struggle to find the right word, because really, I wouldn't know. We never had a meet-the-parents discussion. Not that my family would even require that.

"Oh, honey, it's not your fault. I raised him better than this. Once he wakes up, I'll give him hell, don't you worry. Now, tell me about you and Jackson." Her eyes are alight at the prospect of learning about us. Not that our story has a very happy ending at this point.

"Well, it's kind of embarrassing ... but I fell on him." I giggle remembering that night at the restaurant. "I was out to dinner with my friends, and I tripped and literally fell into his lap. He asked me to have a drink, but I turned him down."

"You did?" Nina smirks, and I blush.

"Yes, I wasn't really ready to ... I don't know, date or contemplate dating anyone. I was hurt pretty badly by my ex. So the last thing I was looking for was a relationship," I try to explain. Too bad I didn't stick to that—it would've saved me some heartache.

Nina shakes her head in understanding. "Ahh, we all have one of those men, don't we? Mine was right before Brendan. I swear I thought we had it all. There was always something keeping me back from going forward. However, as fools in love, we usually push forward against our better judgment. But then Brendan came along and showed me what true love was.

So how did you and Jackson end up together?"

My voice softens as I tell our story. "Well, I'm a publicist and my company was bidding for Raven. I won the account and Jackson was thrown back in my life."

"Sounds like fate intervened," Nina says with the voice of wisdom.

Fate or Jackson Cole.

"Yes, it did. We both tried to fight our feelings but I fell all over again. He's patient and understanding. He's everything I need. It was like no matter how hard I tried, I somehow found myself unable to resist him." I bite my lip and sniffle thinking about how much he owns me. "Sorry, I get a little emotional."

"You love him," Nina says as a statement.

"I do." I don't hesitate because it's true. "But I don't know how he feels anymore. He pushed me away when Aaron died. He told me we were done. I just ... I couldn't."

"You don't have to explain to me, Catherine. I understand these stupid, stubborn Cole men better than anyone. Jackson has a lot of issues from losing a lot of people he's loved. You have to give him time. He's one of those who feels the weight of the world on their shoulders. He's always been that way. Even as a child. You'll work it out—I have faith."

That word again. Everyone is always saying to have faith. To trust in each other and our faith that things will work out. I've learned on more than one occasion it's not always reality. Life has a way of slapping you in the face and then kicking you a few times just for good measure.

"Our relationship happened extremely fast," I pause trying to figure out how to explain what's in my heart. "It's been a whirlwind, but I thought we were finally on the same page."

Fate intervened again by rearing her ugly face. Reminding me what a cruel bitch she is and that I shouldn't get too comfortable.

"When it's meant to be, things have a way of working themselves out. Brendan and I separated once," Nina says holding my gaze.

"Jackson never mentioned."

"Jackson and Reagan were still young and they probably don't know or don't remember," she explains. "I couldn't take the deployments anymore. The nights of being alone, waiting and wondering. Then there was the fact that he was following his passions while I was stuck at home. I felt trapped."

I'm stunned.

"Wow. What made you guys work it out?"

"I loved him. He was gone, but it wasn't because he didn't love me and the kids. It was quite the opposite. He hated being away. Loathed the times he missed, but he was willing to walk away from his dream for me. But I never wanted to be the reason he gave up the Air Force. I knew he would resent me at some point, if I forced his hand. Imagine knowing you were the reason he gave up his dreams. Give him time, honey. He'll come around."

"God, I hope so."

I have to leave tomorrow. Despite my intention to stay, there's talk about Raven and problems within the company that need to be dealt with. I got an email from my boss asking when I'd return, and I'm running out of excuses as to why I need to be here. Yes, he's my client, but I don't need to sit vigil by his bedside to manage the story. Nina and Mark are out talking to the nurses trying to get answers on the recent spikes in heart rate.

"Jackson," I whisper, softly brushing his hair back. "Baby, I can't do this. I don't know what to think anymore. I need you. Please. Please, I'm so alone." My heart is aching as I beg him. "I l-love you, Jackson. I love you. D-Do you remember the zoo? Remember how you held my hand and we walked through the park?" I pause as the memories of our time together start flooding back. "I remember every moment. I remember how it was when you left me too, and I can't have it end like this. I can't have the last memory I have of you being you walking away from me. I need you to love me. To choose me." The steel in my voice hardens as I become more resolved. This has to work out. "I need you to wake up and be the man who watches movies with me, who holds me when I cry. I need more of that, Jackson. But I'm so scared. I'm so scared you're going to wake up and push me away again—or not wake up at all. I'm terrified that this is it for us. I'm begging you—I ..."

"Catherine, honey," Nina says softly behind me.

I swipe my hand across my cheeks and take a calming breath. "Sorry. I'm just ..."

There's really nothing I can say at this point. It's unclear when he'll wake, and each day that passes, my hope dwindles.

"He'll come through. You have to be strong."

"I'm trying. It's been so long. And I d-don't want t-to ..."

"Do you still have to leave?" his mother asks.

"Tomorrow morning. I have to go back." The words taste bitter as they roll off my tongue. "There are things I can't do from here. God, it's ripping my heart out to leave him when he's still ..."

"I know. But you have to keep fighting."

"I hoped he'd be awake by now. I don't want him to think I wasn't here."

"Oh, Catherine, we would never let him think that," Nina pauses. "Why don't I come back later?" She gently pats my hand and grabs her bag.

"Are you sure?"

"Yes, I have some things I need to get done, and I think you need to talk to him. Now, don't you leave without saying goodbye, okay?"

"Of course, thank you so much," I say as she strolls out of the room.

I curl up on his bed careful not to touch any of the wires. I need to touch him, feel his body and warmth. Even if he's not really here with me, it comforts me. All of the anger I held on to is gone. The fact that I could potentially lose him again erases the previous fight. He was so lost in the shock of that phone call and all I wanted to do was be there for him. Yet, he pushed me away.

My hand rests on his chest as I feel his heart beneath me. "I never got to tell you what happened while we were apart." I use this time to tell him about the things we missed during our separation after the fight we had at my apartment. "I read the letter my father wrote me. The night I pushed you away after the fight with Neil, I figured, why not? And I opened it. I sat there on the floor and read everything I always needed to hear from him. He basically apologized for everything. After I got through the entire letter, do you know what I hated most?" I pause, letting the question remain unanswered by him. "That I was more upset about pushing you away. I hated myself for being so weak. For being so scared." Jackson consumed me. He took a part of me I wasn't sure I could give and it made me push against him. "How is that? This man who I've longed for since I was a kid gave me answers, yet all I wanted was you."

And then he left me.

"I never believed in fate, but then I met you. Who falls on someone's lap? I mean, that's just crazy. But it happened." I grab his hand and pull it to my chest, weaving our fingers together.

"Life has managed to slap us around a bit though. We keep fighting this current pushing us the wrong way. Yet here I sit, waiting, hoping, praying you'll wake up and we'll get back on course." Leaning over gently, I press my lips against his cheek and then his lips. I wait, hoping in some ridiculous way I can break the spell. "I hope you know how much you own my heart. And I hate you for it. I hate that you've stripped me of my defenses and made me feel, when all I want to do is be numb. Then this wouldn't hurt so damn much. I would be able to grab my bag and walk away. Let you fight your demons on your own." I take a deep breath. "But instead I'd rather watch you breathe."

Lying here with him, I relish in his touch. I focus on the man who showed me I was enough, who gave me the strength to love again. With Jackson, I can be me without fear. We both have a lot to overcome, but our love can endure it. He would never cheat or deceive me. Closing my eyes, I let the sound of his monitor lull me to sleep against his shoulder.

I hear the door open and someone moving around. My eyes open and I realize I fell asleep in his bed. Glancing at the sliding door I see the charge nurse enter smiling. Carefully, I climb out of his bed and instantly feel his loss. Being close to him gave me a small amount of solace.

"Sorry, honey, we need to take him for testing."

"Is he okay?"

"They want to run some precautionary tests to make sure there isn't something we're missing," she explains as she moves around the side of his bed.

"Should I be concerned?" I ask as my voice breaks.

She gives me a small smile. "The doctor will be in to talk to you and the rest of his family soon."

I look back at Jackson and bite my fingernail hoping nothing's wrong. It's been eight long days that we've been waiting. The doctors thought he would've woken by now and had been worried about some irregularity in his heart. Suddenly, I see Jackson's hand move.

"Did you see that?" I ask excitedly. "He moved," I say to her, but she smiles and looks away.

"It was probably just a muscle spasm."

The nurse moves his IV, dismissing what I swear I saw. As she moves over to check the paper on his heart monitor, I stare, waiting for something to happen again.

Suddenly, a noise jolts through the room.

Beeeeeeeeeeeep.

The sound echoes and time stops. Then everyone is in motion.

"He's crashing!"

"Jackson!" I cry out.

Nurses are running.

"Code blue!"

"What's going on?" I push against the nurse who's lowering his bed.

I can't breathe. Doctors are barking orders, running into the room, but no one will answer me.

"What's happening?" I cry again, trying to get to him. He can't die. "Do something!" I scream and the nurse holds me back.

I fight against her. This can't be happening. "Calm down, Catherine."

"Get the paddles," the doctor orders the people around him.

My stomach falls and I want to die with him.

Please God ... I'll do anything. Please don't take him from me. I can't lose him too.

I sob and clutch my stomach as she pulls me back further. "Jackson, please! Fight!" I call out to him. Begging. Pleading.

"Get her out of here!"

"No!" I try to reach him. "Jackson!"

They push me out of the room and my hands find the cold, glass door. The curtain closes, blocking my view, and my world fades to black.

CHAPTER

FOUR

JACKSON

WHITE LIGHT.

All I see is the bright glow above me.

The haze of death. This is it.

I inhale and exhale. Fresh air. It's clean and pristine like the radiant light above me. It calls to me, begging me to come.

The luminosity is beautiful and calming.

Am I ready to go?

I know what it feels like to be left behind. The pain of agonizing over the loss of a loved one. Watching them cry and fall apart because they wish it wasn't happening. What will this do to everyone? To Catherine?

I draw a deep breath and wait for something. Hell, anything. Death is pretty anticlimactic. Where's God? Where are the angels and shit? I figured I'd hear some horns or trumpets. "Taps" maybe? I've been gypped.

There are no sounds in heaven.

It's eerie and tranquil.

"Fight, Cole!" I hear someone call out.

Fight for what? For the pain I feel?

No, thanks.

My heart stops and I feel the tension in my body. I try to draw in air but it lodges and I begin to gasp and choke.

Here comes the end.

"Charge to seventy," another voice speaks, and my mind tries to grasp what's happening.

"Clear!" he yells, and a current tears through me.

There are no sounds. No one says anything as the beep registers on the monitor before I let go. I have no fight left.

"Push another round of epi!"

It hurts to breathe, so I stop trying.

The darkness returns and then the light takes over, my vision blurs. I keep my eyes closed.

I'm not ready to go … to lose everything and everyone. As much as I'd like to live with no guilt and no remorse anymore, I can't leave them all.

So once again, I find the fight I have inside of me. The part of me I rely on when I have to find a way. I'm about to use everything I have left—if I can't get through this black there'll be no going back.

"Charge to eighty."

"Clear."

The electric voltage travels through my body shocking each nerve alive.

"Pulse is eighty," a female voice says.

My chest heaves as I struggle to gain control of my body.

The bright ray returns and it's blinding. Taking all of the warmth I felt before. Now, I'm cold. There's pain everywhere, each bone feels like it's shattering. The fucking agony is unbearable. Maybe death is the better choice if this is the shit I'm going to go through. Although, if this is death shouldn't there not be any goddamn pain?

I'm going to miss her. Maybe I can still hear her, touch her, and see her from heaven. She's my heaven on Earth. She gave me the will to love again, even if it nearly broke us both. She's my downfall too, but it was worth the pain to have the time we had. I never told her though. I never really explained how much she gave me. I'll never have that chance now.

No.

Fuck this.

Regret is a motherfucker.

"Pulse is rising," another voice says.

My eyes open and I see someone in my face. "Cole. Can you hear me? Get the family in here." I struggle to figure out what's going on as my eyes close. "He's waking up."

Time passes and I hear a lot of movement, but I can't focus on anything.

"Jackson, if you can hear us, open your eyes." I feel something press against my arm and tighten.

Drawing a deep breath I smell vanilla. She's here. I will my eyes to open as I feel the pain again. The muscles lock in my body as I will them to obey. The light grows brighter and brighter. Fucking hell, this shit hurts.

"Jackson?" I hear Catherine's voice crack.

I try to move my hand and I feel her soft hand grasp mine. I felt that. All of it. I can feel her skin.

Closing my eyes again, I try to adjust to the light. I'm awake—alive. Tilting my head to the side, I open my eyes and look at her for the first time.

Breathtaking.

That's the only word I can think of. She's beautiful. Even with her puffy eyes and quivering lips—she takes my breath away.

chapter

five

Catherine

"Hi," I SAY softly with tears blurring my vision. He's awake. He's alive. A week of wonder and fear, somehow he fought through it all.

Jackson looks around confused as his heart rate starts to accelerate on the monitor. I wipe the happy tears and try to reassure him by placing my hand against his cheek.

My throat croaks as I try to get my emotions under control. "Shhh ... don't try to talk." His brow furrows as I speak. "You're okay, baby. You're in Germany at the hospital." I reach out and smooth his brow, the desire to touch him is too great. His eyes close as my fingers float across his skin.

When his blue-green eyes open again, they latch on to mine and the emotion shines through. Fear, love, and regret all mashed up. I've missed those eyes.

"Catherine ..." Jackson tries to speak but it's strained.

I lean close and press my lips against his rough cheek. The feel of his skin against mine causes my heart to race. He's really awake and he said my name. "I'm here. Just relax," I try to reassure him. "It's going to be—"

Before I can finish, the doctor draws our attention to him. "Mr. Cole, I'm Dr. Allison. Welcome back. You gave us quite a scare. I'm going to look you over real quick, okay?"

Jackson nods but doesn't try to speak again.

Dr. Allison starts assessing him. "Okay, Jackson. Your heart rate is steady and stable. Blood pressure is a little low, but it's expected. How do you feel?" he asks.

Jackson's strong hand wraps around mine and he gives me a small squeeze. He swallows and winces. "Water?"

"Sure, you can have a little water. I need you to tell me what you last remember," Dr. Allison states in a no-nonsense way.

After he takes a sip, he finally speaks. "I d-don't." He looks around and lets out a huff. "How l-long?"

"You've been unconscious for eight days. Do you have any recollection of how you arrived here?"

Jackson closes his eyes and shakes his head. "I remember the HELO and the sniper." His eyes open as he grips the blanket looking around. "Mark?"

I grasp his hand and he relaxes a little. "He's fine. He'll be here soon. I can call him now," I say looking for my phone.

"No." Jackson tightens his grip. "Am I o-okay?" He asks the doctor apprehensively.

"Your injuries were quite severe and you had a few complications during surgery. And extreme blood loss. Your body has endured an intense trauma and I want to keep a close eye on your heart."

Jackson's eyes close and his grip loosens a bit.

"Is he going to be okay?" I ask

"He's young, strong, and he's out of the coma now. He's not out of the woods, but we'll watch him closely," Dr. Allison explains and looks over the monitors.

I glance at Jackson and his eyes open again. "What about my leg?" he asks with fear in his voice.

Dr. Allison turns and pats his shoulder before speaking.

"The injury to your leg was a through and through, which should heal in a few weeks. The bullet that entered your abdomen caused some damage to your spleen. We were able to repair the injury and stop the bleeding. As for your shoulder, there's some muscle damage, but we can address all that later." He takes a break and allows Jackson a few seconds to gather his thoughts.

"Jackson, do you remember anything else?" I ask softly.

His eyes are pensive as he shakes his head. "Not much." He clears his throat and grabs the cup to drink again.

"That's normal," Dr. Allison states.

Jackson's eyes dart to me and he squints. It seems like he's trying to remember. His fingers release mine as he rubs his face. "You shouldn't be ..." he trails off.

My heart sinks. Maybe I should've left a few days ago. We're not together, things didn't end well, and then I'm here when he wakes up. I look at the clock and realize my flight leaves in three hours. I can still make it if I leave now.

"My flight is in a few hours, I need to call the airlines." I reach for my phone. "I'll call everyone and give you a few minutes with the doctor." He grabs my arm before I can turn completely.

"Don't." He coughs and winces. "Please," he says, still holding my arm.

I nod while returning to his bedside. "Okay." I'll stay for now. It feels like it's been so long since the fight happened. In reality it has been, but Jackson wasn't really here and we have a lot to talk about. I don't know where I stand, what he's feeling, so many questions, and I'm not sure I want the answers.

Jackson returns his gaze to the doctor but doesn't relinquish his hold on me.

Dr. Allison checks his shoulder wound and then his leg. "You need to take things easy. Rest as much as you can. You still have a long road ahead of you. I'll be back in a little while to check on you again. Do you have any questions?"

"How long ... here?" Jackson says while grimacing.

"You'll be here at least another week. I'll give you something for the pain. For now, we need to make sure there aren't any further complications. If you need anything just buzz me," Dr. Allison explains and leaves the room.

Jackson closes his eyes as the nurse inserts medicine into his IV. I try to extract my hand, but he tightens his fingers and looks at me.

Our eyes lock. "It's going to be okay," I say softly, trying to absorb the fact that he's alive and okay. We gaze at each other, neither of us saying a word, yet it's as if we're having an entire conversation. I give him everything through this moment. Opening myself wide open so he can see all the feelings I've held the last two weeks. The tears stream like raging rivers down my face, but I don't care enough to stop them. It's grief, anger, elation, and so much more. My emotions stack up like bricks around me one by one until I feel buried. I want to breathe again. I want him to be my air.

Jackson lifts his hand and presses it against my cheek. "S-sorry," he stutters and I lean into him. Needing to have the closeness of skin on skin. His eight-day-old beard scratches against my face, but I want to feel—remember how eight days ago his life hung in the balance and today we almost lost him.

How is it possible to love someone this much but hurt so much more? He's taken my heart and I don't know that I'll ever get it back. "Do you want me to call everyone?" I ask, trying to break the silence.

"No," he says with an air of finality. "Just you." His eyes close and he fights to open them again.

My throat goes dry as I try to breathe. "Okay, but—"

"Don't leave me," he says as his lids fall.

I need to be close to him—this could be my last chance. I climb and sit on the bed facing him. My hands brush his hair back as my heart races. He steals my breath, and all the strength I have is gone. I allow the tears to fall as I'm overcome with emotion. I continue to touch his face, his hair, and he settles as his hand rests on my leg.

"Sleep. I'm not going anywhere," I say as he tries to relax, but I can sense his unease.

"Promise?" he asks hesitantly.

"Yes, I'll be here when you wake up." I smile and press my lips against his cheek.

His eyes close as he drifts off to sleep.

Watching him stirs all of my fears. What if he doesn't wake up again? What if he wakes up different than this time? The trepidation gnaws at me and embeds deep inside. I grab my phone and call Mark and his mother to let them know they should head here. Neither one answers, so I send them both messages.

"Hey," I hear Mark come in the room behind me.

"Hi, I sent you a text message." I place Jackson's hand down and he stirs.

"He moved!" Mark's loud voice booms through the room.

"Yes, shhh ... he just woke up for about five minutes," I say and push him out the door so we can talk in the hall. "It was really brief but he woke up. I tried to call you earlier. God, Mark. He crashed. I almost died. *He* almost died. Then they came back and brought me in there and I thought he was dead." I take a deep breath and shake while Mark wraps his arms around me.

"But he's okay, right?" Mark asks, trying to sound strong, but I hear the undercurrent of fear.

"I think so. I mean, he fucking died! I was there and they pushed me out of the room. Where were you? I called. I-I was so scared!" I start to sob as Mark rubs my back.

"I'm sorry. It's okay though. He'll be fine?" he asks again.

"The doctors checked him over. He said a few things and then fell back asleep."

"He'll wake back up, right?" Mark asks both excited and a little nervous.

"Yes, the doctors said he'll be tired and needs to rest," I

reassure him.

I start to pace a little, trying to work through my thoughts. My heart is so full it could beat right out of my chest, but at the same time I'm terrified. There's a long road ahead for Jackson. He will most likely need physical therapy, his company is going through a lot of changes, and he's yet to deal with Aaron's death. The status of our relationship isn't my first priority, but I can't pretend that it doesn't lie heavily on my mind.

Mark grabs my shoulders, stopping me from walking past him again. "Hey, Kitty, calm down and stand still. What happened when he woke up?"

We stand in the hallway as I replay the few minutes he was awake. Mark looks a hundred years younger just from knowing he was able to talk and move. I bite my lip when I think about how intense his eyes were asking me to stay. I'm so damn confused.

"All of this is good—hell, it's fucking great! Did you cancel your flight?" Mark asks as he pulls me into a hug. His deep voice sounds lighter and more carefree.

I push back and start creating a plan. He's awake now but I need to handle the things I've neglected. "I need to reschedule it. I'm not sure what I should do now." I run my hands through my hair and try to think.

His arms cross his chest as he puffs his chest out making himself seem scary. "Well, you better not fucking leave now. You know he'll flip his shit. All the business crap can wait. He needs you. Whether you two can get your heads out of your asses long enough to see it or not ... you both need each other," Mark says with one brow raised, clearly not budging.

"Let me make some calls to the office and see if we can release a statement on his condition tomorrow. It should help both Raven and Cole Security. In regards to the rest of our shit, we'll work it out. But today is definitely not the day, so give me a chance to think."

"I'm letting you know now ... I won't watch you two fuck

this up," Mark states standing there as the anger rolls off of him.

Great.

Now I have a big brother—or the male version of Ashton. This should make things fun.

"You can't fix this," I reply with my arms crossed.

"I didn't say I could. I'm just saying you two are going to fix this before I leave. I don't know what the hell happened, but when he got on that plane, his head wasn't right. Then you've been spouting off shit about how you shouldn't be here since day one. So, here's my thinking, which I'm usually right—you two got in a fight before he got on the plane. Now, my first inclination would say Jackson was his normal jackass self. But then again I know what a jackass you were a few days before that." He states and pauses.

"He left me," I say as I ball my fists. He's got me so angry. I don't want to talk about any of this. I was stupid when I pushed him away and then Jackson did the same thing.

"I'm not going to lecture you on the reasonings of Jackson Cole. He acts like he was the only one in Iraq. You'll never meet someone more loyal than him. At the same time, you'll never meet someone who thinks he's more at fault for the bad shit in the world. Like I said: fucking jackass." Mark smiles trying to lighten the mood a little and pulls me into his side. "I've seen him up and I've seen him in the lowest place you can ever imagine. But when he was with you, he was different. Happy."

I look at him with my mouth gaping open at his statement. He squeezes my shoulders and lets that sink in around me.

"Enough of this shit. Tell me, have you talked to Ashton?"

I laugh and slap his chest. "She'd chew you up and spit you out."

His booming laugh reverberates through the halls and we get a few looks from the nurses. "You tell her any time she wants to chew me up, she's more than welcome." He smirks and walks away.

I stand there thinking about all he said and decide to call Ashton to fill her in.

"Hey, Biffle," her cute voice comes through.

"Hi." I let out a sigh wishing she was here.

"You at the airport?" she asks probably thinking that's what has me sounding forlorn.

"No. I missed my flight. Jackson woke up." The smile spreads across my face as I think about how many days we waited on bated breath for this to happen.

"Cat!" Ashton screams into the phone. "That's fantastic! I'm so happy. Is he okay?" she asks excitedly.

"He died, Ash. Literally. They brought him back and he's okay now, but he died. I thought I lost him."

"Wow, are you okay? Is he okay?" she asks with concern prevalent in her voice.

"I'm okay. I think. Yes, he seems okay," I sigh and shake my head. "It was a short amount of time he was up, but he has a long road ahead of him. The doctor told him to rest as much as he can. But I can't leave now."

She snorts at the last statement. "Like I thought you would. Gimme a break, you weren't going to make the flight regardless. You've stood by his bedside waiting, and I get it. He's your guy, babe."

"He is, but am I his girl?" The words slip out like poison in my blood. I don't know the answer to that question and it eats at me.

Ash let's me stew before she finally speaks again. "He'll let you know that in one way or another. You both push against each other, for whatever reason. I've said my peace to you more times than I care to think about. Don't fuck this up, Catherine. Do you hear me?" She's stern bordering on hostile.

"Yes, Mom."

We both start laughing at my acquiescence. I miss her so much. Being around her and having her to lean on makes things easier. Mark's been great, but he's no Ashton. Although my friendship with him has grown stronger, she's the rock in my life. I fill her in on the entire few minutes I had with him along with the worries I have.

"They're all normal feelings," Ashton reassures me.

"I'm ready for some damn happy times."

"I think you both need a come-to-Jesus moment and it'll all work out. Until then, be patient and remember guys like it when you push them around a little bit. So be the bitch for once."

I wish I could. It's never been that way for me other than in business. When I'm dealing with a client or the press, I don't back down.

I exhale loudly. "I need to get back in there. I should make sure Mark isn't poking him in the face," I explain.

"How is that dipshit?" Ashton asks at the mention of Mark.

During the few days Ash stayed in Germany, they flirted a bit. I don't think anything actually happened, but they seemed to get along well. Mark needed her strength when I wasn't able to keep it together. After his surgery, Jackson was touch and go for a while. There was no holding each other up because we were both crumbling. I've never seen someone so desolate. But Ashton was there, propping us both up, holding his hand and making sure he remained strong, while also keeping me from falling apart. She's really a remarkable woman.

"He's fine. Have you two spoken at all since you left?" I wonder.

She lets out a deep breath and I picture her sinking in a chair. "No, it wasn't like that for me. He lives in Virginia, number one, and number two, I think we'd kill each other. It's like who can be the biggest smart ass."

I laugh because it's completely true. They would either fuck constantly or beat the shit out of each other. Between her strength and his sarcasm, it's like setting a match to a piece of wood soaked in gasoline.

"It would be so much fun to watch though. I don't know

when I'll be back. Is everything going okay?" I ask.

"Yeah, everything is fine. Look, you need to be there. He's going to need you, Cat. In so many ways, that man needs you," Ashton says as her strength resonates through the phone.

"I need him too. I just need him to not dick me around. I want him to want me, not push me away again," I explain with my heart breaking all over again.

"If I remember correctly, you did quite a bit of pushing as well."

I huff at her not-so-gentle reminder. "Yes, I know. I got this lecture from Mark already."

"Good. Maybe you'll realize that you have to fight for what you want. Nothing in this life is guaranteed. So fight for him! Fight with every ounce of your being."

"I plan to. He's worth it. I can't make him love me though," I say effectively shutting her up.

"No, you can't. Nor do you want to. But I don't think that's a fight you'll have."

I peek my head in to see him still sleeping. "Okay, I need coffee, so I'm going to run. I love you and I'll try to call you in a few days. Miss you, Biffle."

"Miss you more. Kiss Jackson for me and maybe Mark too."

"I will," I reply with a smile.

I put my phone in my pocket and walk to the family waiting area and grab a cup of coffee. I should've been getting on a plane in a few minutes, instead I'm here, because he asked me to stay. So many questions float in my head. Sinking into the chair, I rest my head back and try to get a grip. I've never had a moment as scary as watching him flat line. My heart starts to race when I replay them pushing me away as he was dying. Needing a few minutes of peace, I close my eyes.

This trip I've only slept in bits and pieces, never more than two hours at a time. And never in a bed, most of it was in a chair at his bedside. I think over the conversations with Jackson's mother, Ashton, and Mark through the past week. Some of their words really strike a chord in me. I'm not the same girl I was a few months ago and I'm definitely not the same one who pined over Neil. The girl who thought she wasn't good enough for any man and deserved to be treated like shit. I won't be neglected or cheated on again because I deserve more. I won't stand for someone who will sleep with my friend, or walk away and not look back. Jackson gave me more. He allowed me to open my heart again, but at the same time I'm not sure if he's ready to give me the same ...

I sit there and let it all sink in. I look at the clock and realize two hours have passed. I must've fallen asleep. Scrambling up, I grab my now-cold coffee and head back.

Entering the room, my breath hitches as I look up and I catch a glimpse of his smile as he sees me. He's awake again. Looking at him, I know what I have to do. I'll stay for as long as he wants me to be here, but at some point we're going to talk about everything, because I can't go through him walking out like that again. Neither of us deserves to go through any more pain, and I won't be the one to inflict it upon him.

chapter

six

"I THOUGHT YOU left." Jackson's voice cracks at the end.

I step forward to his bed and give a tiny shake of my head. "No. I was on the phone and then I fell asleep in the chair. I told you I wasn't going to leave."

"Oh," is all he says before looking over at Mark.

Mark scoffs, "Dude, I fucking told you she'd be back. Pussy."

Jackson gives him the finger and smiles. It's nice to see them together. I can still feel the weight of our worry about how this would play out.

I stand there awkwardly in the room, unsure of what to do. We survey each other with the questions and uncertainty stifling in the room. Each tick of the clock my anxiety builds.

Mark clears his throat, "Well, I can see I'm not needed here. And you two need to talk. I'm going to make some calls—including your mother again. She hasn't answered and I'm afraid she might kill someone. That woman scares the shit out of me." He gently clasps Jackson's shoulder. "Glad to see you decided to stop being an asshole and finally woke up. Maybe next time you won't be so dramatic about coming back to life." Mark smiles at me and looks back at Jackson. "We'll catch up later."

Jackson smirks and Mark walks by and kisses my cheek. "Be good and call me if you need anything. Talk to him."

"Catherine, please come here." Jackson puts his hand out

and waits.

Stepping forward until my leg hits the bed, I shudder from his proximity. He draws this from me. His presence and power elicits these reactions from my body without permission. Jackson grabs my hand and rubs slow circles against my skin. I close my eyes and savor his touch.

"Are you okay?" he asks.

My eyes open and I stand there shocked. "Shouldn't I be asking you that?"

"Mark told me. He said you were alone in the room," he explains.

"Yes ... no ... I don't know. I've never been more scared in my life. I wasn't sure if you were alive or dead. I just ..." I can't say anything else without losing it. I don't want to think about what happened. My heart pounds and my chest heaves.

"I'm sorry, baby."

"Jackson," I say softly.

"Forgive me. I was a complete tool." His eyes tell me it isn't about what happened hours ago.

"Please, I don't want to talk about this now." I struggle as I say the words. As much as I want answers, his health is far more important.

"I can't wait to make this right. I need to fix—"

"No." I put my hand up and soften my voice. "You can't fix everything any more than you can save everyone."

He pulls my hand and I sink on to the bed. "I can fix *this*. I was wrong." Jackson's eyes swim with unease.

I love this man. That's the bottom line. I don't want to spend any more time apart. We've already lost two weeks because of our insecurities and fears and misguided heroics. At what cost? We're both miserable and fighting for the same thing, but both scared.

"Yes, you were. But please, let's talk about all this later." He looks exhausted and he needs to rest. The last thing I want is to be the cause of any complications.

Jackson looks away uncomfortably. "All I can think about is that you won't be here if I go to sleep. When I opened my eyes and saw you I thought I'd died."

"What? Why would you think that?" I ask confused.

He turns to me with love and conviction as he grips my hand. "Catherine, you're my heaven. So I thought I was dead, because that's when I thought I'd see you again."

I'm speechless. Which never happens, but seriously? That's his answer? I lean forward and kiss him. With my lips pressed against him, everything feels right. It's like the world has righted itself in this single instant. Gently, my fingers touch his face as I memorize this moment. I hold all I need between my hands.

I lean back and meet his eyes still holding his face. "Every time you manage to do this to me."

"Do what?" His brow furrows.

"Disarm me. Make me forget everything. The thing is ..." I draw in a deep breath and let it out, staying locked in his eyes as I do. "You left me. You walked out the door. After you promised you wouldn't do that." Tears form in my eyes as I remember the heartache I felt at that moment.

Jackson reaches toward my face and winces. "I know. I fucked up. I wasn't able to think of anything other than I had to get away from you."

His words are like a knife through my heart. "You had to get away from me?"

"I needed to save you in that moment. Do you understand I killed a man?" Jackson asks.

"No, you didn't." He breaks my heart when he says these things. The turmoil and guilt he carries is unnecessary. The man who would do anything for anyone somehow has this warped view of himself. He's noble, kind, forgiving, and yet he thinks somehow he intentionally or even unintentionally causes these things.

Jackson grabs my chin forcing me to look at him. "I'm not

asking you to understand it. Fuck. I don't understand it. But I want us. I want this to work. Stay with me."

"I almost lost you. Not once but twice," I say, enunciating my words, trying to make him understand. "I don't know what I would've done if you had died. I couldn't breathe, I couldn't think. I had to stand there waiting for them to tell me I'd lost you forever."

He grabs on to his shoulder, grimacing in pain.

"I'm here now," he retorts.

The urge to touch him is so great I can't fight it. My hand tenderly tangles in his hair as his eyes close. "Yes, by a miracle. There are a lot of things we need to agree upon before we can just go back."

Settling a little, he opens one eye before saying, "You're still not answering me."

My smile spreads from his playfulness. "We can talk later," I assure him.

His breathing regulates as the muscles in his body relax. I'm hopeful his pain is subsiding. "Promise me," I hear him whisper.

"Promise you what?"

"You won't leave me. I'd be lost." Jackson's eyes lock on mine. I watch the fear roll through them like a storm.

"I'll always find you, Jackson," I say, reciting the words he spoke to me when I told him how I feel around him. Leaning down, I place my lips against his and a low hum comes from his chest. Pulling back, I see the satisfaction shining in his eyes.

Jackson sighs and cups my face with his good hand. "I love you, Catherine Pope. I'm a complete and total fucking idiot for leaving you that night. Please, forgive me. Be mine. Let me fix us."

My lips part at his admission. He's never said those three little words. Each nerve in my body tingles and my throat grows thick.

I lean forward and grip his face in my hands. "You just

did."

"I mean it. I love you. I should've told you that before I left. I don't want to lose you." His eyes bore into mine, showing the honesty of his words.

My heart is so full. Jackson looks at me waiting for me to say something. The words fall from my lips effortlessly, "I love you. But there are some things I need from you."

"Anything and it's yours."

"You might want to hear them first," I laugh.

"Name it."

I sigh not wanting to have this conversation so soon, but he's insistent. "Okay, you know I have ..." I pause struggling to find the right word. "Fears ... I've been hurt by a lot of men."

Jackson grips my hand. "I know and I'm sorry I'm one of them."

"Let me try to get this out." Jackson nods and I continue. "When you left me that night, I didn't think I would ever talk to you again. You hurt me much more than Neil ever did. I can't ever go through a breakup like that again. Cheating, lying, manipulating me ... these are non-negotiable—complete deal-breakers. I won't stand for it. I need honesty, respect, loyalty."

"I don't have a problem with loyalty, Catherine."

"You need to really understand. I've seen it all happen. I watched my worst nightmare unfold. My dad left, Neil broke me, and then you turned around and walked away—immediately after I'd faced my own fears. I know what I did was wrong. I know that I shut you out and let my fears push you aside. For that, I'm so sorry."

"I understand fear, baby."

"But you saved me. You gave me hope that I could be enough for you. Losing you would devastate me. If you want someone else, then please end it with me first. I'll promise you the same."

His hand grips the back of my neck and he pulls me to his

mouth. His kiss is rough and strong. It penetrates every inch of my body. It seals everything in that moment. We're going to be okay. We'll fight together and find a way. I break the kiss and the smile that forms across his face obliterates any remaining anger. "You'll never have to worry about me straying from you. I've got everything I need right here," he vows.

I sit there and watch him drift to sleep with hope soaring in my heart.

The next few days pass without any issues. Jackson's shoulder and leg are healed enough that they want him to start physical therapy. His abdomen is still where the primary concern is. Most of our days are spent talking and going over business issues. He's not happy with pushing back the launch of the new product. The press release was bumped back a few weeks, and I've now decided there needs to be a party after. I know he's against it, but in the long run it's better for him and for Raven.

"Your father is probably starving to death at this point. Plus Reagan is driving him insane," Jackson's mother says with a smile. Her flight is in a few hours. She was reluctant to leave but said he's in good hands. Plus she has to get back to the States with his sister getting married in a month.

"Probably, she's always been high maintenance."

"Oh, and you're not?"

"I'm a saint."

Nina and I burst out laughing as Jackson looks around as if he's serious.

Jackson clears his throat, "Whatever, I'm sure Dad is living on chips and beer."

"I'll never understand you men. You claim you're all big and bad, fought in wars and all, yet you can't manage to make anything more than a sandwich," Nina scoffs.

"I can also make pasta, so I'm better than Dad."

His mom rolls her eyes and then points her finger at him. "Now, you call me when you get back to New York. No more of this once-every-blue-moon phone calls. Do you understand me?" She straightens her back and grabs the handle of her bag.

"Yes, ma'am," Jackson says with a grin.

It's great watching them interact. He obviously loves her very much and she adores him. She leans in and kisses his cheek and then pats it.

Nina turns to me and smiles, "I want you to call me as well."

"Me?" I ask confused.

"Yes, you. If you ever need to talk, you have my number. Don't be a stranger and take good care of him, but don't baby him too much. He'll become even more of a pain in the ass than he is now." She laughs and kisses my cheek. "Okay, I expect to hear from you both soon and be good to each other."

"Bye, Mom," Jackson says as she throws her hand up but keeps moving out the door.

I watch as Nina heads into the elevator trying to subtly wipe her cheeks. The fear she must've felt having her son nearly die has to be overwhelming. I look back at the man I almost lost and my chest tightens. It was so close to that. Not wanting to be away from him, I climb on the bed and nestle into his chest.

"Hi," he says with a chuckle.

"Hi," I say back softly. I need to feel his warmth.

"You okay?" he asks clearly concerned with my sudden need to be with him.

I snuggle in closer and his hand gently grazes my arm as I relax into his embrace. "I'm fine. I just wanted to touch you," I explain.

His laugh is close to a bark. "I'll never deny you touching me." I feel his lips touch the top of my head and my eyes close of their own accord. "I can't wait until we can do much *more* touching."

My giggle escapes as I slap his chest. "Ass."

"I'm in a hospital bed. You shouldn't ask to see my ass."

I scoot closer so I can look at him. The smile spreads across my face at his teasing. "I don't recall asking to see anything. In fact, I have no desire to see anything at all." I quirk my brow challenging him.

"Really? Is that so?" he asks as his hand slides down my side.

"Yup, no desire." I try to control my breathing as his hand glides back up and gently rubs against the side of my breast.

"Interesting ..." He trails off as his hand makes its way around the front, outlining my bra.

My acting abilities are far from perfect and I'm sure he can tell the change in my breathing. I feel my nipples harden as he dips his finger inside my shirt. The warmth of his breath against my ear causes me to shiver. Damn him.

"Still no desires?" His voice is husky and low.

Turning my head toward him, I nod. The fire is coursing through my veins. I try to hold still, but his hand grips the back of my neck and he pulls me down, stopping right before I touch his lips. Somehow, I hold back a groan, but I don't want to always be so predictable. I need to hold my own with him or he'll swallow me up. Plus, I know it turns him on when I give it back to him.

His eyes practically glow as he's waiting for me to make the next move. It's only been a few seconds, but it feels like years as we keep our eyes locked. I grip his face and tenderly press my lips against his. We don't rush the kiss. Jackson's hand tangles in my hair as he holds me against him. I revel in his embrace. His love blankets me and in this moment it hits me like a bolt from the sky.

He loves me.

Warmth radiates through my body and I could cry with joy. This beautiful man who I love with my whole heart loves me back. A tear falls and slides between us.

Jackson breaks the kiss. "Hey," he says with concern. "You're crying. What's wrong? Did I do something?"

"No, no. I think it just hit me," I say earnestly.

"What hit you?"

"It's been a crazy few weeks. I've lived in a constant state of worry, but you're okay, I'm okay, we're okay. I feel like I can breathe again."

"I'm here, baby. I'm not going anywhere. I love you," he says as he cradles my head.

"I love you too, Jackson."

"Good, now feel free to kiss me again." He smiles and pulls me closer.

"You've got a lot of making up to do, Muffin." I bring my lips to his before he can say anything else.

chapter

seven

"I'M READY TO get home," Mark says leaning back in the chair while propping his leg up. "You fuckers are boring and I miss my bed."

Jackson sighs, "I need you to get back and make sure things are still running. Catherine won't give me any details." He's so focused on everyone else it's driving me nuts.

"You need to worry about yourself, not the companies or any other crap. I have Raven covered. Danielle is doing an excellent job. Mark has everything with Cole Security under control. Stop being a baby," I chastise him playfully.

There's a knock on the door as Dr. Allison enters. "Good afternoon." He approaches Jackson and shakes his hand. "How are you feeling?"

"Good. Ready to get out of here," Jackson replies.

"I bet you are," he says, examining the wound on his shoulder, and I see Jackson's hand clench. "Everything is really healing well. There are no infections and your leg looks a lot better. You need to start your therapy and we want you to start getting mobile. I could see you going home as soon as next week."

"Thank God. I need to get the hell out of this bed." Jackson's entire demeanor changes. He's animated and starts to throw the blankets off himself.

"Don't we want to take this slow?" I ask hesitantly. Taming him is going to be impossible.

Dr. Allison smiles. "Yes, this won't be an easy road, Jackson. You have injuries on both sides of your body. Your left shoulder will be the biggest issue. It has to remain immobile for another week or two. Our goal is for it to heal without further injury. Also, you can't bear any weight on your leg yet, and without use of your arm, you won't be able to use crutches. There will be a lot of things that will require someone to help you." The doctor looks at me.

He scoffs and says, "I'm sure I'll manage just fine." Jackson turns his head, clearly frustrated.

"I'm sure you could, but you'd also be right back in the hospital with another surgery," the doctor states matter-of-factly.

I lean in and grasp his hand before he looks up at me. "What did you think, babe? You were shot. Three times," I remind him gently. "You're going to have to take it easy so you don't end up back in here because you screwed up your leg again."

"I'll be fine, Catherine."

"Yes, you will, because you're not going to fight me on this." I smile and tilt my head letting him know I'm not playing around. He can be defiant all he wants, but he's not going to hurt himself because he has to be all macho. We see where that got him.

Mark laughs, "I see who wears the pants in this relationship."

Dr. Allison steps in before Jackson can reply to Mark. "Jackson, there are some things that will either be too painful or flat out impossible with your injuries. We can arrange a live-in nurse or you can stay with friends or family."

"No," is his only reply.

"Then we can arrange for you to be transported to a rehabilitation center," the doctor answers smoothly while writing something on his chart.

Jackson looks at me and his eyes say it all. He's extremely unhappy. This is a man who fights through pain. He has no desire to be laid up and babied. "Well?"

I laugh at his one-word question. "Well, what?"

"Well, am I going to stay with my parents or do you want to stay with me?" he asks and lifts his brow.

"Are you going to be an asshole?"

"Aren't I always, according to you?" Jackson says with a half-hearted laugh.

I giggle and kiss his cheek. "I guess I'll stay with you, but you're going to owe me."

"Like I don't already," he chuckles and squeezes my hand before turning toward the doctor. "Okay, when can we get back to the States?"

"Let's get you up a few times and then we'll start talking about release and ways you can move around safely." Dr. Allison closes his chart and heads out the door.

Mark walks over and puts his hand on my shoulder. "I'm going to book my flight back home. There are still issues we need to go over and things we need to take care of. Natalie needs some help too."

Jackson's face falls and his entire body tenses. "I need to call her. We need to do something."

Mark nods. "I already had them send his body Stateside. I transferred money over, but knowing you, you'll do more. She's probably ready to have the baby any day, so I'd like to at least be there. I know her family is there, I just feel like he'd want ..."

"Go," is all Jackson says and Mark once again nods.

"The private plane is here so you can get back home that way." Mark squeezes me to his side and kisses the side of my head. "Take care of him. Slap him if he's a dick, which I'm sure he will be."

"Hands off her if you want to keep them," Jackson warns.

Mark laughs at his threat. "Funny, dickface. You're so scary lying in bed wearing a pretty dress. I could haul her over my shoulder and you couldn't stop me."

"Try me."

Trying to diffuse the excess testosterone pulsing through the room I put myself between the two of them. "Okay, okay. Both of you are badasses and *ohhh* so scary."

They both burst out laughing and Jackson pulls me on the bed.

"Oh, Kitty. You're so cute," Mark says and ruffles my hair. "He isn't scary at all. Neither are you. But seriously slap him, and if he's really being a fucker you can poke his shoulder." Mark laughs and Jackson glares at him.

"Don't you have a plane to catch?" Jackson's question is harsher than I've heard him with Mark.

"Relax, he was a perfect gentleman when you were unconscious." I stand and give Mark a hug.

Mark pulls me close to which I can hear Jackson grumble behind me, but Mark was a great friend through this time. He was strong when I felt weak, and he gave me faith that when Jackson woke, we'd find our way. Sure, he gives me hell too, but that's par for the course.

"Don't fuck this up," Mark says as he pulls away.

I'm going to miss him. He's like the brother I never had. The one who picks on you, but if anyone else did he'd kill them. Which he's more than capable of doing.

"When I'm back to normal we're going to roll."

"I think you could use a good ass kicking," Mark says as he laces his fingers and cracks them.

"Dude, you've never beaten me when we wrestle. Ever," Jackson smirks.

Mark puts his arms up and flexes as I roll my eyes. These two are worse than a couple of kids. "I'm ready for you, Muffin. Now be good to her."

"I'm always good. Well ... that depends on your definition."

Mark laughs as he walks over to Jackson.

"Maybe, but I'm better."

"Be careful getting home, glitter boy."

Mark leans close and whispers something and Jackson's

eyes dart to me before closing and shutting me out.

My gut tightens as I try to calm the fears that that one single moment brought out of me. His eyes showed pure fear at whatever Mark said.

"Catherine?" Mark says snapping me out of my trance.

"Sorry," I say shaking my head to rid myself of the panic traveling through my body. What could've made him look so scared?

"I said I'll call in a few days. Check in on how we need to handle the press statement for both companies. Is that how you still want to proceed?" Mark asks studying my face.

I smile and nod. "Yeah, that sounds fine. The release is next month so I'd like to maybe push it all to happen at once. If I can control the story we can keep the shareholders happy and show that we're business as usual."

Jackson clears his throat drawing my attention back to him. "Are there any issues I should be concerned about?" he asks.

"Nope," I say turning to Mark so I don't betray my false statement.

There aren't huge issues per se, but there was a dip yesterday. The fact that Jackson hasn't personally addressed his company has spooked a few people. During the last few years, there has been a lot of change and this appears to be another moment of instability. While I've been able to handle a few small things, the bottom line is I need to make a formal statement and I need to be in New York City to stay on top of it. Being here is delaying the news. I'm putting out fires instead of preventing them.

"Okay." Mark looks over my shoulder to Jackson and then back to me. "I'll see you guys soon." Mark walks to Jackson and places his hand on his shoulder. "Glad you didn't die. I would've had to kill you."

Jackson laughs and playfully smacks him in the stomach. "Thanks for being here."

"No thanks needed. Just don't do it again." He winks and kisses my cheek before heading out the door. I'm going to miss him even though he gives me hell.

"Then there were two," I hear Jackson say, his voice heavy with emotion.

Not wanting to be away from him for even a second, I smile softly and snuggle into his side, careful not to touch his leg. We don't speak, we enjoy the solace of being in each other's arms. Together—in every sense of the word—we found our way back through the storm. Despite the rough seas, we discovered our calm waters.

I don't know how I'm going to handle pretty much living with him. Even when I was engaged to Neil, we never lived together. I'm determined to be more open with my feelings, give him everything, including my trust. While there is a large part of me unsure how I'll fight against every defense mechanism I've built, I know it's our only chance of survival.

chapter

eight

*H*IS BREATHING GROWS deeper and steadier after a few moments of lying silently. I hear the vibrating of my phone and extract myself carefully so as to not wake Jackson. Grabbing my phone, I see it's a New York number.

"Hello?" I say quietly as I exit the room.

"Hey, babe, it's Gretchen."

Immediately I smile hearing the sound of one of my best friend's voices. I miss them both so much. "Hey, stranger."

"How's Jackson doing?" she asks with concern.

I smile looking back into the room where he sleeps peacefully. "Really well. I'm hoping we'll be out of here soon. How are you?"

"Good. You know me, always busy. Anyway, I'm calling because I heard some rumors floating around about Neil from a few of my lawyer friends."

My good mood fades instantly at the sound of his name.

"Why would you hear that?"

"When the fight between Jackson and Neil happened I asked a few to listen for your name or Neil's."

My gut sinks. "What rumors?" I ask her, already knowing where this is going.

She sighs and I hear her shuffling some papers. "Right now he's looking for a lawyer to go after you pro bono for losses he's sustained. The engagement ring and the ring you purchased.

I heard a few things about assault but no one is grabbing his case at this point. Ashton told me about the fight before Jackson left. I know why you didn't want to tell me, but she knew I could help. I called in a few favors and had everyone keep an ear out. One of my friends called and I explained I have possession of evidence to show that Neil assaulted you."

"How?" I ask quickly. What evidence does she have?

"You had some pretty nasty bruises. Ashton took photos and sent them to me. Do you want to retain me as your legal counsel?" Gretchen asks.

"Of course. I wanted to tell you, but everything happened so fast and I-I just ..." I trail off not really knowing what else to say at this point.

"I know. I'm going to handle this. You don't need to worry yet. But you may want to forewarn Jackson. Also I think we have a good shot at getting Neil to back down if we can show him our proof. And it's civil at this point, but I'm concerned he'll go towards criminal for the assault if we can't get him to withdraw. Seriously, though," she pauses, "I'm very good at being scary." I can almost hear her smile at the last sentence.

I laugh, "I know all too well."

"I think you need a refresher."

"Have mercy on me. It's been a rough couple weeks."

"Fine, I'll give you this one. Go be with that sexy man of yours. I love you."

"Love you too, Gretch. We'll talk soon," I reply.

"You bet. Don't worry about a thing. I'll handle the garbage." She giggles and disconnects the call.

All of this over what? Money? A ring? When did he really become so shallow? Sure, the ring is not small, but he makes a good salary. We both do, which is why things were never difficult. It wasn't like one of us was coming into the marriage making a lot more than the other. I made a little more since my last promotion, but his company started him off higher than I did.

I shake my head and head back into the room.

"How's Gretchen?" Jackson asks, rubbing his eyes.

"Good. Sorry I woke you."

He smiles and holds his arm out, inviting me back to where I was before. "You didn't, I just noticed you weren't here," he says earnestly.

"Awww, you missed me, huh?" I tease him.

"I miss you even when you're here."

I smile and climb into his embrace again. "You really need to stop being so damn perfect."

Jackson chuckles as I turn to look at him. "I'm far from perfect." He leans down and presses a tender kiss on my lips.

The feel of his lips on mine causes my heart to flutter. I never want this to end. I could kiss him all day. His lips turn up in a smile, effectively breaking my small moment of happiness as the kiss breaks.

Looking into his turquoise eyes, the joy I see stops my breath. Unable to control my reactions, I grin.

"So what did Gretchen say?" Jackson asks.

The smile fades as I think about what she said and the thought of Neil does nothing to halt my mood change. My immediate thought is to keep this from him, to protect him while he's healing, or protect myself. However, I'm not going to do that again. He asked me to trust him, to give him my heart, and I have. I love him and need to have faith in our relationship.

I groan, "Neil is apparently trying to file a lawsuit. Gretchen is obviously well-known and her friends alerted her that he's calling around."

His entire body clenches and he lets out a snarl through gritted teeth. I shoot up looking at where he's in pain but his hand is in a fist and his eyes are closed.

"Jackson." My voice is small, but I know he hears me.

"I fucking hate him, Catherine." Jackson's eyes latch on to mine and you can see the anger rolling through him. "I'll call my legal team. I'm going to bury that piece of shit one way or another." His voice is cold as ice.

"He's not worth it. Gretchen has photos and doesn't think it'll come to that. She's pretty sure with the proof she has, it'll be dropped."

"What fucking proof do you have?" Jackson asks clearly still angry.

He doesn't know about the bruises. I threw him out that night, and well, we didn't really talk much about anything that happened in the few days we spent apart. Which reminds me about the conversation I had with Piper as well.

"I had bruises on my arms." I see his hand once again ball into a fist. "Before you hurt yourself getting worked up, let me get through this, okay?"

I pause staring at him waiting for some sign he's going to allow me to tell him the story without ripping his stitches or trying to get out of bed. We both glare at each other until he finally lets out the breath he's been holding and nods.

"Like I said, I had bruises on both my arms from where he grabbed me. I'm not completely surprised since I bruise fairly easy, but Ashton took pictures on her phone. Apparently, she sent them to Gretchen to hold on to. I explained Neil's threat to Ash as well."

Jackson goes from anger to hurt. "I should've been there. I shouldn't have left you when you asked me to."

"I needed you to go. You leaving me showed me everything I was trying to ignore. I shut you out because I was so afraid. So you don't get to play the martyr. We both fucked up," I say, sounding much stronger than I feel at the moment.

I'm not afraid he's going to leave since he can't move, but the last time we began this talk a lot of things happened. None of which I'd like to relive any time soon.

I look up at him before he can say anything else. "But that's not all."

"Go on," he says sharply.

I hate every single second of this conversation. Climbing out of the bed, I walk to the window. "Piper came by my office as well. What happened between you two?" I sigh already re-gretting asking.

Not one bone in my body thinks he's done any of the bull-shit she spewed, but I want to hear what happened from him.

Jackson looks confused for a second before he composes himself. "I fired her."

"I'm aware of that, but why?"

"Because she was no longer needed. I hired you and I don't need to keep her on my payroll when I have you there to help me make the same choices she would be advising," Jackson says without any hesitation. "Also, I was preparing for when you came back to me. I wanted to keep her the hell away from you."

Somehow I manage to mask my emotions. It was his way of protecting me, or at least showing me he cared. "Well, Piper tried to tell me it was because she wouldn't sleep with you."

"That's a fucking lie!" Jackson yells and tries to move too fast. He groans while gripping his leg, clearly in pain.

I rush over and place my hand on his cheek. "Babe," I say softly, "I never thought you did. I told her she was full of shit. I recorded the conversation, which I don't know why I thought I should, but it was good I did. I'll send it to Gretchen too in case she needs it. But I need to handle this and make sure this doesn't get out of control. With you in the hospital, we need your image to appear commanding."

"Catherine." His voice is warm and washes over me. He grasps my hand that's holding his face before speaking. "I nev-er touched her. We never even had a moment where it could've happened. I was so mad at you. You infuriated me that night. But never, not once, did I even think of going near anyone else. She walked in my office and I fired her before I even knew I wanted to. Just the sight of her, knowing she hurt you in any way ..." He takes a deep breath. "I never wanted to see her, so I fired her. I told her I no longer needed her advice and to leave immediately. I don't want you anywhere near either of them."

"I never thought you did. None of this is relevant to what's going on now. I'm telling you Neil is apparently after something. Gretchen has this under control and so do I." I'm not conceding to him. I ultimately don't care about Piper or Neil. They're non-issues. My focus is Jackson and getting home. The launch is coming soon and he refuses to push it back again, so we need to get him ready.

"You need to stay away from him. I'm not kidding."

"I'm not arguing," I say back quickly.

"Stay away from him." Jackson's voice is cold as ice.

I can keep going back and forth with him or I can end this how he wants it. I'm going to handle Neil once and for all. He's pushed me to the point of no return. When I get back to New York, he'll be dealt with. However, I'm not going to keep fighting with Jackson about it either.

Time passes slowly while we wait for the charge nurse to release Jackson. The last week he's improved and of course also overdid it. He's going to drive me up the wall with his defiance. No matter how many times he's been told to slow down and take it easy, that seemed to only spur him to go at it harder. The poor look on the physical therapist's face when he tried to put pressure on his leg.

"What are they doing? It's a simple damn form, not an act of Congress," Jackson says, aggravated and impatient.

Which is his new normal attitude.

"Relax, she said it would be a few minutes."

Jackson sighs heavily while rubbing his hand down his face, "I want to get home."

I smile and try to diffuse his irritation. "I know, baby. I'm sure they want you out of here just as much as you want to be gone." My last words slip out a little harsher than I mean, but he's been less than easygoing. I know men are babies when they're sick but I'm really ready to slap him.

"What does that mean?" he says clearly surprised at my little dig.

"You've been an ass, and that's me being nice. Yesterday, I think you made the nurse cry. I know it sucks being reliant on people, but I swear, if you talk to me like that I will poke you in your bad leg." I grin trying to soften my tone and sound playful while ensuring the message is delivered.

He looks taken aback as though he has no clue what I mean. "She wasn't listening to me."

"Jackson, you've snapped at every single person. You yelled at Mark on the phone yesterday because he did exactly what you asked for. Poor Danielle called me asking why she got an email with a list of things she already did." I pause and sink down to look him in the eyes. "I know this is hard for you. God, I get it."

His eyes harden and he purses his lips. "No. None of you get it. I can't fucking walk. I can't use a wheelchair, or crutches. I need you to help me take a piss." He throws his hands up before rubbing the back of his neck. "I fucking hate this. I can't sleep, I have one leg and one arm that work, but they don't work together."

I reach out and gently rub his cheek. "Hey," I wait for him to look at me. "I have two arms and two legs, and I'm here. Don't push me away. I love you."

Jackson draws a breath and leans his head against mine. "I love you and I'll try not to make you stab me in the leg."

I laugh and kiss him, "I hope you try hard because I've refrained a few times already and I can't promise I have much willpower left."

Before he can respond the nurse appears.

"Okay, Mr. Cole. You're all clear. You have all the medication for the ride home. Dr. Allison already spoke with the doctor in New York who's going to follow up. All I need is your signature on this form and you can head home." She smiles brightly.

Jackson signs the form and we exit the hospital that's kept him alive. The ride to the airport is quiet as we both enjoy the freedom of the outside world. It's been a rough few weeks and it's not over yet. Luckily, it's not a long ride and we get on the plane easily, thanks to two sailors who rode with us to help. I knew I couldn't lift him, so the SEAL team in Germany sent help.

We head to the bedroom in the back of the plane and Jackson sleeps holding my hand. They gave him a mixture of painkillers for the long journey, and thankfully, he didn't argue about taking them because he knew it would be rough. I lie here looking at him and allow myself this time to let out the emotions of the past few weeks. I let the tears fall and watch each one stain the pillow. They're not tears of weakness, they're tears of strength. There is no shame because this has been hell. I've never been more scared yet determined in my life.

I run my fingers through his hair as he dreams. I listen to his breathing and marvel at him. This strong but damaged man who loves me. Jackson came into my life like a force of nature. Pushing me to feel and refusing to give me a chance to run away anymore. I'm sure I'll run again, only this time I'll run to him.

chapter

nine

"JACKSON!" I SHAKE him as he's gasping and clutching his chest.

This is the fifth night in a row he's had a thrashing nightmare. Even with the sleeping pills the new doctor prescribed, he still wakes in a pool of sweat and doesn't remember what happened—or at least that's what he says.

"I'm fine. Go back to sleep." He pushes the hair out of my eyes and cups my cheek.

"What's wrong? Are you in pain?" I ask as I start to shuffle out of bed.

He reaches for the pills on the side of the bed but grabs his leg. "Fuck," Jackson groans as his hand wraps around his thigh.

"I'll get you some medicine." I scramble by the bed trying to find the pills. "I think we should call the doctor. It's getting worse." The nightmares and the pain seem to be getting more consistent. Partly because he refuses to listen to a damn word that anyone says. I catch him without the walker trying to maneuver to the bathroom.

"No doctor. I'm fine!" he lashes out through his clenched jaw.

The first week he was home everything was fine. He seemed to understand his limitations and accepted my help freely. Now though, because he feels better, the aggravation overrides any understanding he previously had.

"Right ... sorry, I forget you don't need anyone," I say with sarcasm. I'm over his crap. I grab the medication and put the pills in his hand.

Such a jackass.

He grabs my arm before I can walk away. I don't look at him. I'm so pissed and tired of his attitude. It hasn't quite been two weeks yet and I'm ready to call for a live-in nurse and go home. He gently rubs his thumb against my arm.

"Please look at me," he pleads.

I look up but I'm pissed off. This isn't easy for either of us, but there's only one of us being considerate—and it's not him.

"You don't get it. My head is all fucked up."

"I don't get it because you won't talk to me," I say quietly, trying not to let this escalate into another fight. "Tell me then, what are the dreams of?" I ask, already knowing the answer.

Jackson shakes his head.

He keeps telling me they're nothing or he can't explain. I hear him though. I hear his screams for Mark and Aaron. When he yells about the shooter or cries out in pain, it doesn't take a genius to figure out what they're about. I've kept that information to myself knowing he doesn't want to talk about it. He grows more and more frustrated with each dream. More sullen and pushes himself harder to get past this.

"You don't get to treat me like shit because you're hurting. I'm tired too. I'm busting my ass working, getting everything in line for the launch. Then I come here and you're moody and crabby. I *know* this isn't easy for you. I know you're tired and in pain. So don't tell me I don't get it. But you're taking it out on me, babe, and I'm on your side." I let it all out as I fight back the urge to cry.

"All I remember is the end with extreme pain in my leg or arm. So I'm going to assume it's the shooting," he says, surprising me that he even said that much.

"Jackson, you went through a lot in the last month. You

lost a friend, and you were shot ... It's a lot."

"I have you though." He looks away and swallows the pills.

Standing before him, I take a deep breath and focus on him weighing each word before I say them. "Yes, you do—but I'm getting close to calling Mark—or your mom. You've gone through two nurses in a week. That's not normal and it's not you," I say the last part softly.

"When you go to work, I'm stuck here with that annoying nurse hovering over me. Maybe you should stay home all day. Or quit your job and come work for me," Jackson says smirking.

I laugh while shaking my head at his ridiculousness. "That's not happening. The launch is in a week. I've been inundated with getting things ready."

Jackson sighs and runs his hand down his face. "This isn't the way I wanted it to be when we spent more than a night or two together. I didn't want it to be because you had to help me fucking get a glass of water. I sure as shit never saw you coming home to me because you had to."

"Jackson," I say softly. "That's not fair. I *want* to be here. I could've let the nurse live here, or had you go stay with your family. I need you just as much—"

"Let me finish. This isn't how I saw this going, Catherine. I'm the guy who takes care of you. Not the other way. Being at the mercy of someone else isn't something I enjoy. All I can do are conference calls, video chats, and email, but even that's hard with my one arm still not back to normal. I wanted to shower together for other reasons." He raises a brow and smirks.

Smiling at him and wishing for the same thing doesn't change the fact that it's not how it is. "First, I wouldn't be here if I didn't want to be. I love you, so get that through your thick head. I know you're going through stuff. I get it. I need you to let me in. I'm trying. You have to lean on me. I want to be here for you, but I don't know what else to do."

"It's on me, baby. All on me." He pulls me close so I'm standing between his legs.

"Do you need something else?"

"No, I just need you." He wraps his arm around my waist and places his head on my stomach. My hands tangle in his hair and I tenderly massage his scalp. I take in this moment and try to remember no matter how much of a jackass he can be, he's alive.

"I'm here, Jackson. I'm not going anywhere." My voice is soft and yet firm.

Jackson leans back looking into my eyes. "Lie with me." There's no request in his words.

I don't miss the meaning in his words. It's been weeks since we've been intimate, other than a few kisses here and there. "But your leg."

"I'm not made of glass."

"No, but you're in pain ..."

He slips his hand slowly up my shirt—well, his shirt. He insists on me wearing his t-shirts and button-downs since I've been staying here. I swear he's marking his territory. I'm not complaining though. Every time I walk around in his shirt, watching his pupils dilate or his breath catch is enough for me.

Jackson's hand caresses my breast and he rubs his thumb across my nipple. The small touch causes me to tremble.

"It's been too long," he groans as he lifts my shirt and presses his lips on my stomach.

He squeezes my nipple and my head falls back as I moan. It feels so good. His hands, his touch. "Jackson, we can't." My voice is weak and quivers with need.

"You let me worry about that, baby," Jackson says as he kisses lower.

The feeling of his breath against my skin causes goose bumps to form everywhere he touches. It's been so long. Far too long since I've had him and even this feels so good I could weep. "Please ..." I trail off, unsure of what I'm pleading for.

Suddenly, I'm pulled forward as his hands grip my hips. My fingers instantly thread into his hair as he travels lower and slides my panties down agonizingly slowly. I should stop this, but it feels so good.

"I've missed this. I've missed you. I need you, Catherine." Jackson's voice breaks at the end.

"You have me," I say as his finger suddenly enters me. The groan that escapes my throat is freeing. His thumb grazes my clit and I begin to shudder, his touch awakening every part of me.

"Always," he says and I look into his eyes.

That one word causes my heart to accelerate. My need for him to take me, claim me, show me that I'm his bubbles up and grabs hold. "Prove it," I say, surprising myself with my brazenness.

Jackson's eyes harden as he presses his thumb against my clit, provoking a moan. "Oh, I'll fucking prove it. Lie down. Now," he commands.

I remember he's still injured and I hesitate. "Your leg and ar—"

"Get on the bed," he cuts me off with his firm demand, leaving no room for discussion.

Trying to move carefully, I climb on the bed as apprehension fills me. I don't want him to get hurt and I don't want to tell him no. Jackson shifts on the bed so he's lying on his back. He grips my leg pulling me closer to him. I gasp at the movement while his eyes fill with determination and mirth. "Climb on top of me," he says gruffly.

I start to move slowly as worry fills me. This isn't a good idea. He could hurt himself and the work he's put in to get to this point would all be for naught. "I don't think we should do this." The words seep out as I sit on my knees debating this.

"I'm not going to break, baby," Jackson says as he cups my cheek. "But I'm going to have you tonight. I need this just as much as you do. We'll be careful," he reassures, pulling my neck close to his. "If it gets to be too much we'll stop. But I'm done talking now," he says, and draws my lips to his.

We kiss slowly and tenderly. His tongue entwines with mine in a sensual dance. I give and take from him, allowing my heart to fill with love. His hands drift against my body, gripping the hem of my shirt tugging it up and off as the kiss breaks.

"Now, straddle my face." Jackson's voice drops even lower as he hooks my leg over him. Heat sears my veins, warming me everywhere.

I look at him, as he adjusts my leg over his shoulder, setting me in a straddle over his head. "Jackson?" I ask confused.

Before I can say or even think, his mouth is against me. I feel his tongue move up and down. I grip the headboard as his hand makes it's way up my leg slowly and then back down while his eyes lock on mine. Watching him spurs me higher. It's the most erotic thing I've ever seen. Jackson licks and sucks, pushing my hips to give him better access. The pleasure builds with each swipe of his tongue and my head falls back in pure ecstasy. "Jackson," his name is a whisper but I know he hears it when his thumb rubs against my clit in small circles.

My hips start to move and I ride his face as the heat blazes through me as I climb.

He uses his arm to pull me back, and I whimper from the loss. "Get comfortable, baby. We're just getting started," Jackson says as he inserts two fingers and sucks on and around the nerves that are throbbing.

I need to release, but he brings me to the edge and then backs off. Torturing me in the best way. He stops and again I struggle to remain upright. "I've been patient. I've watched you get undressed unable to touch you. I've had to lie next to you, feel your heat. Feel you brush against me. I'm going to consume you tonight just like you do to me. You're mine."

Tears form as the pleasure builds. I need to come, but Jackson removes his fingers and waits. "Yours. Please. I need—" I beg him.

"What do you need?" he asks as he places kisses on my knee, then the inside of my thigh. Going slow and taking his time before climbing higher up my leg.

"You." His eyes lock on mine as his mouth returns to my pussy. He licks and sucks while watching me. I moan and my head falls forward while I hold on to the bed frame.

"Like that?" He stops and my eyes snap open. "Or do you want me to stop?" Jackson asks while he inserts a finger and I cry out.

I'm so close.

"Don't stop. Please, don't stop," I beg him as the heat of his mouth returns and I fall apart.

It takes a great effort to remember to hold myself up and not crush him. I pulse around him as he pulls every last ounce of pleasure from my body. Once my mind becomes coherent I ease myself to his side again.

"I love you," he says and I press my lips to his.

"I love you, too," I say leaning over him. Raining tender kisses on his chest. I look at the red circle marring his body from the bullet and gently kiss it. "I love every part of you. The bruises, the scars ..." I say as I place another kiss on the other bullet wound from his past. "The pain." My lips press against the tattoo to remember his fallen friends. "The hurt." Our eyes stay connected as I move lower and kiss the second scar on his stomach from where they had to operate. "The fear." I hover over him as I move to his leg and kiss the final injury he sustained. Hoping to take the pain away. "There isn't one part of you I don't love," I say and he shuts his eyes. Refusing to allow him to shut me out, I take this moment and shift a little higher, sucking his dick into my mouth.

"Fucking hell, Catherine." His hand threads in my hair as I surprise him by paying him back.

I glide up and down his hard length using only my mouth. Using my tongue, I lick around the tip and Jackson's grip in my hair tightens. It spurs me on and I take him deeper. When he hits the back of my throat, he groans and pulls me off him.

"Not like this. Not the first time since ..." He lets that statement hang out there, both of us knowing what he means.

I nod understanding. We need to connect and become one again. I reach over him carefully to his nightstand. This will be the first time I feel him since he walked out the door. I want to feel all of him again.

"Catherine? Do we need them?" he asks tentatively.

I look at him and smile. "No, I'm on the pill."

"I want to feel you, baby. All of you. No barriers. Nothing between us," Jackson says, nipping at my ear.

I moan and sit up, aligning myself to take him and not touch any of his injuries. I need him to fill me. Give me back that part of myself only he can give. I lock eyes with him as I slide myself down his length. Jackson's eyes shut as we savor this moment. I stay still being mindful of his leg and abdomen wishing I could lie across his chest. Feel him against my skin, but even this is pushing it. I take him further into my body and adjust to him filling me to the brink.

"Feels so good, baby," Jackson says through gritted teeth. He laces his fingers with mine and I grind down.

I rotate my hips as I ride him slowly and carefully. "Jackson," his name a sigh as I feel him everywhere. I surrender myself to him. His body fits mine perfectly. I glide up and down as we hold on to each other's hands. I start to build again as my clit rubs against him. "I'm gonna come again."

"Come with me," he says as I rock back and forth creating the friction I need. "Tell me. I'm close," Jackson demands.

I allow my mind to focus on the feeling of Jackson. How he makes me feel. The way his body feels inside mine and I start to tremble. "Now!" I moan as I bear down and fall apart. My head falls back as he erupts.

"Catherine ..." he grunts and comes apart.

chapter

ten

"LET'S GO, YOU big baby," I call out to Jackson who's groaning in pain.

"I think we should call you 'Nurse Ratchett.' You're becoming sadistic."

I try to suppress a smile and stow my attitude. "We're already late, babe. To get across town we needed to leave ten minutes ago. You're supposed to be at physical therapy in fifteen and your orthopedic surgeon appointment is right after."

Jackson's been able to put small amounts of pressure on his leg with the use of his walker and his arm is out of the sling now. However, since he's found his sexual appetite again—not that he ever really lost it—I worry he's doing too much. I took off work today to go with him and make sure he's not causing more damage.

"If you weren't so damn sexy I would've been ready earlier," he smirks and rolls the walker over. "I get distracted."

Laughing and rolling my eyes, I grab my bag. "Let's go, no more distractions for you."

We arrive at the appointment late. They get him started on a few exercises while I stand there and watch him. He pushes himself hard and they're constantly telling him to take it easy. At least I'm not the only one he gives a hard time about what he's capable of. Typical man.

"Jackson, you did well, but I really need you to dial it down a notch," the physical therapist, Christy, chides him.

"I am so dialed down."

"Look, I know this is difficult and you're doing exceptionally well considering you're only a few weeks in, but you will set yourself back," she explains.

"Nah, I'm good."

"You're exasperating."

"Welcome to my world," I say walking up behind him and he huffs.

Jackson wipes the sweat from his forehead. "Another woman to boss me around."

Christy stands there and fixes her ponytail. She's kind but very firm. When I first met her, I wasn't sure if she'd be able to handle him. She's only about four-foot-eleven but she's been doing this for at least twenty years. Her height is an illusion because her attitude is about six-foot-five. Jackson towers over her but I'm pretty sure she could make him cower.

"I won't put up with your crap. I'll call the doctor and let him know you're pushing too hard. Then he'll put you back in that sling and we'll say no weight bearing at all." She crosses her arms as I watch the impending duel unfold.

"You wouldn't." He pushes himself so he's taller.

Christy doesn't miss a beat, taking a step forward and glaring at him playfully. "Try me, soldier."

"Sailor."

"Semantics."

I laugh at the two of them fighting for the alpha dog position. "My money's on Christy."

She smiles and nods in solidarity. "I like this one."

"She's all right," Jackson jokes.

"Don't let him kid you, he loves me."

Jackson grabs me and kisses the side of my head. "I do."

"Enough mushy stuff." Christy turns to Jackson and sighs. "You're doing more than most of my patients are able to, but that's because of your physical condition prior to the injury.

You were in top form and you're much stronger on your worst day than others on their best day."

His smile and eyes brighten. "See?"

"Before you bask in your brilliance, it doesn't mean that you can push too hard. You're not allowed to put pressure on your arm. You need to keep your weight supported, so no walking. The muscles have to heal."

I turn and smirk. "See? I'll be sure to mention this to the surgeon."

"I'll see you next week." She raises a brow and gives him a pointed look.

He gives her a salute. "Don't worry, Christy." Jackson wraps his arm around my waist. "I always behave."

She walks away shaking her head.

We arrive at the surgeon's office and once we get settled in the examination room to wait, Jackson and I talk about the launch plans.

"So, do we have to have this stupid party after?"

I huff and put my hands over my face, "I can't make you, but I think it's a good thing for the shareholders to see you. Alive."

"I'm still going to be in this fucking walker. I really don't think that's showing such a clear picture," he complains.

We've been over this at least five times. He argues his side. I argue mine. In the end I usually win, but he keeps at it.

"I think this is the best thing for Raven. I feel it will show strength, that even though you were knocked down you were able to rise up."

Jackson grumbles but before he can really put up a big fight, Dr. Flores enters.

"Mr. Cole." He shakes Jackson's hand. "Ms. Pope, great to see you both."

"Doctor, can you please write me a note that it's against the best interests of my health to go to any work parties."

"Ass," I reply before the doctor can give him a chance.

"I don't know that it's against the best interests of your healing as much as it's against the best interests of aggravating her." They smile and look over at me.

I take a measured breath before releasing it. "I think you should tread careful there, darling," I say sarcastically.

"Let's take a look at your stitches and how everything's healing, shall we?" The doctor quickly intervenes and Jackson gives me a coy look.

Dr. Flores is happy with how his incisions are healing.

"Any questions?"

Jackson speaks first, "I want to know when I can start working out again?"

"Jackson, it's been a few weeks since the shooting. I know you're anxious, but it'll be up to your physical therapist."

"So that's never. What about *other* activity?" Jackson's smirk is evident and so is his meaning.

Dr. Flores chuckles, "You should be cleared for other activity as long as you don't get crazy."

I blush and look at Jackson as the grin spreads across his face. "Wasn't waiting for that all clear, Doc."

"Most patients never listen to that one." He grins and I want to die.

This is the most embarrassing conversation I've ever had. The rest of the appointment goes on without any further blushing. We'll return in another few weeks and at that point he should only have to go to physical therapy.

"Are you going in to work?" Jackson asks on our way back to the apartment.

"I should. I have a lot to take care of."

My phone rings and it's Ashton.

"Hey," I say answering the phone.

"Hey, I'm in the area of your office. Wanna grab lunch?" she asks.

I look at Jackson and he smiles apparently hearing her through the line.

"Maybe I can swing it. I was heading in to work anyway."

"Oh, did you actually take a day off?" her voice rises in surprise.

Why does everyone think all I do is work?

"No, Jackson had a few appointments and I wanted to talk to his physical therapist. According to Captain America over here, he was able to start walking without his cane." I look at Jackson with narrowed eyes. "It appears someone wasn't very forthcoming."

"You only heard what you wanted to hear," Jackson speaks up.

"Ahhh, well, just tell him you'll make him watch the awful dance movies you've forced me to watch."

"You liked them," I scoff.

"Uh huh, sure I did. Okay, so lunch?"

"I wish I could but I have to make up all the work I've missed."

I hate this. I miss my friends, but right now my life has taken a different turn and I need to focus on Jackson and my job.

"Taylor, do you have the files for the Raven account?" I call out while looking for the paperwork I had ten minutes ago.

"No, it was on your desk last I saw," she says as she approaches my desk. "Did you bring it downstairs when you saw the design team?"

I groan and my head thumps on my desk. "I swear I can't even think anymore. I'm losing my mind."

"Are you sleeping at all? You know I say this with all the love in the world, but the bags under your eyes are ready for vacation." Taylor smiles and plops in the chair while I glare at her.

Sleep. Well, there's a concept. Between Jackson's night terrors and the amount of work I'm trying to get done, I barely get three hours a night.

"Being out of the country has put me behind a little. I'm trying to catch up."

The sad part is as much as I get done at night when he's sleeping, I usually spend another three hours during the day fixing it because none of it makes sense. I feel awful because I don't see or spend any time with Jackson. I've been staying in the office till after seven and then I get home, eat, and he usually passes out early because of the medication.

"Well, you have to take care of yourself too," Taylor chides and stands. "Why don't you head home early? Maybe you can take some time with your sexy sailor man." She gives me a sideways glance and winks.

I lean back in my chair looking at the stacks of papers and orders. I have most of the big stuff done. It's little tasks, which I can give to Taylor to get done easily. The excitement builds at the idea of going and surprising Jackson. We could lay on the couch, watch a movie, I could grab lunch from Little Italy, or take a nap. I grab my bag without allowing myself to back out.

"I'm leaving. Don't call me unless the building is on fire—even then just grab the important stuff. There's a stack on my desk of orders I need you to check on. I'm taking a mental health day. We have a week until the launch, so ... bye!" I smile as she gives me a knowing look.

"Go. I'll get it all taken care of," Taylor responds as I'm practically running to the elevator. I feel free and weightless. Giddy with excitement to have some time to not worry about anything. When I exit the office doors onto the streets of New York I feel the wind whip my hair, and I smile. It's like one of those cheesy commercials where you want to stretch out your arms and spin around. I can breathe and allow the sun to warm my face instead of fighting over why he shouldn't be trying to hop around and use the damn walker.

I grab a cab and head home. Home? I'm now calling Jackson's apartment "home"? It stops me for a minute. My phone beeps with a text, breaking me from overthinking my mental blunder.

Gretchen: I've sent the files to Neil's lawyers.

Me: So he's going forward?

Gretchen: I've got this. I think he'll cower. This seems to be completely financial.

"Hey, take me to the train station instead, please?" I make a split-second decision and ask the cabbie to change directions. I'm taking care of this. I won't allow him to put any more turmoil in my life. This ends today, once and for all.

The train into Hoboken gives me some time to plot about how to handle him. This is out of the norm, even for him. Taylor mentioned in an email that Neil's name was floating around the office because he applied for a position there. Apparently, he lost a few clients in his firm and is now floundering. If he's after money, he knows Jackson is wealthy. The bottom line is I will not allow him to use me or Jackson for financial gain.

Not going to happen.

Knowing the ring seemed to be his big concern, I head to my apartment to grab it. I don't know what else he's after but I want this done. There's nothing of his I want or need. Everything he's touched or even came close to is toxic, so good fucking riddance.

Walking through my door, I'm taken back to the call that changed the course of the last few weeks. The wall Jackson held me against, screwed me relentlessly, then everything fell apart. The couch where I promised I wouldn't run anymore, told him how I felt, and the door where I stood watching him walk away. I still don't know how I endured the week after he left. I was a shell of a human. Terrified for him, of him, and knowing I would still have to be around him when he returned. The one thing I feared most in our relationship was always that if things went south, how I'd continue to be his publicist.

My room is still a disaster from the trip to Germany where

I literally threw anything I could grab into a bag and Ashton and I ran out of the house. Then coming back since and grabbing more clothes to stay with Jackson. This is going to be loads of fun to clean up.

The jewelry box holding the ring sits in the closet where I placed it months ago. I open it and remove the diamond engagement ring. I hate him and everything this represents. While my feelings toward my father may have shifted slightly, my feelings of disgust toward Neil have only amplified.

Time to end it.

Time to be done.

Time to handle Neil and ensure that my relationship with Jackson doesn't have issues because of him. I grab my "Fuck You" ring as well. I want no part of Neil. I want him gone and every memory to fade away with him. The princess cut diamond shimmers against the wall and one day I know I'll wear a ring again. I'll marry someone who loves me with his whole heart. He'll respect me and be honest, instead of filled with secrets and lies. I don't know if Jackson will be that man, but I can hope.

For a moment I allow myself to dream. I'm filled with a vision of Jackson on his knee, giving me his heart, his love, and promises of forever. I see in his eyes the love that I dream of. The ring he'll place on my left ring finger that I'll never take off because our love will be true.

I can see my long brown, hair in a low knot. I'm adorned in a gorgeous, white dress on the beach by our lighthouse, the place where our magic happened. I smile and walk to him as he waits for me. A single tear forms when I see the smile across his face with Mark beside him. Ashton is on the other side with tears streaming, but I can't turn my eyes away from him. I place my hand in his and we say our vows that speak of the promise to love one another, respect each other, and forsake all others. Before our friends and family, we promise to hold our love sacred. Jackson kisses me, sealing everything spoken through the day, and of course in true Jackson style he somehow manages to do something inappropriate.

The smile spreads across my face as I allow myself to go further into my fantasy. I see my stomach round with child. He's putting together a crib, cursing at the directions and the fact that he can put a gun together in under thirty seconds but it's been four hours and the crib is still strewn around the room. I laugh holding my belly. It's all so beautiful and perfect, but I stop myself before I get too far.

chapter

eleven

I RUSH OUT of my apartment before Ashton gets home or someone calls. I don't want anyone to know where I'm going. No one will think this is a great idea—maybe it's not—however it's what I truly think will stop this. It's time to be done with Neil and I know him better than most. He's a chickenshit. He'll give up because he's driven by money and I have the upper hand. Gretchen is a fantastic lawyer, but this can't go to court. People can't know that not only did the CEO of Raven Cosmetics beat up a man, but that man is also my ex. It'll destroy us both.

The drive over takes no time. His car is outside his house, which surprises me—I thought I'd have to wait for him. I take a deep breath and ready myself for whatever might happen. Hopefully, we'll both come out of this unscathed.

Ringing the doorbell, I suddenly start to consider this is a mistake. Shit.

The door opens and Neil holds on to the door with his eyes narrowed. "Catherine, this is a surprise."

I place my hands in my pockets and hold on to the rings. "We have some things to settle and discuss," I say sternly. Luckily my voice doesn't give any of my fear away.

"Do we?" he asks, curling his upper lip.

"Why are you doing this? Why would you want to continue this? You've moved on, why am I not allowed the same luxury?"

I say emotionless. I'm trying to keep myself in check and to not let my own anger take over.

He pushes the door open and leans against the frame. "I don't care if you move on. You have my things and I need them back. All of this could've been handled easily. I told you I needed to talk but you were being a bitch."

Shoving down the anger threatening to spill over, I remember I'm trying to get him to go away and getting into a fight with him will only make matters worse. "Listen, I'm here to talk and handle all of it, but if you'd rather act like an asshole then I'll go."

I start to turn but he speaks up. "Wait, how do you think we can settle this?"

"I have no idea. That's why I'm here. I want you to leave me alone. So what caused you to come to my apartment and assault me?" I raise my brow and step forward. I need him to see I'm not afraid. He left bruises and I can easily prove it, but I won't play that card until I have to.

He gives a short bark of a laugh. "You're confused, love. Your boyfriend broke my nose. I didn't assault anyone."

"Don't call me 'love.'" I say acidly. "Jackson only kicked your ass after you grabbed me," I remind him and smile. "I'm not here to debate with you. I want to know what I have to do to get rid of you completely. Why are you doing this shit? We broke up. You made it abundantly clear you didn't want me, so why all the theatrics?"

This is the part that keeps confusing me. Things ended, I moved on, I didn't continue to make his life miserable even though I wanted to. Did I destroy some of his things? Yes, and I'd do it again. But something doesn't add up.

Neil shifts forward with his hand in his pocket. "I need my ring back and I need the money you took from me."

"Money? This is what made you come after me?" I ask looking at him wondering how all of this is over money.

He sighs and runs his hands through his hair and grasps

his neck. "I need the ring and the money. If you give me that, I promise you'll never see me again."

"Don't make promises you can't keep," I clip, infuriated. "If you need money why didn't you ask your new girlfriend?" I ask and then cut him off before he can answer. "You know what? I don't care. I don't want your rings. I don't want your money or anything to do with you. I'll give you the rings back and you can sell them, wear them, or hell—give them to Piper. I don't give a shit. I want you gone. I never want you to call me, text me, show up at my job, or anything. You'll never have existed except in some horrific memory that I'll do my best to forget." I grab the rings in my hand. "Do we have a deal?"

Neil steps forward and drops his hands at his side. I can't read him but he seems calm. "You have them?"

"I asked if you'll go away if I give them to you. That means you drop this bullshit about coming after me or Jackson. It means you take them and you cease to exist in my life. No more calls, no lawyers, no more money ... nothing. I loved you once. You owe me this." I step toward him daring him to push me. I'll take the rings and walk the hell out of here.

"I just need the money, Cat. I don't care about anything else," he says and looks at his feet.

"What kind of trouble are you in?" I don't know why I care but my curiosity wins out.

He looks up at me and shakes his head. "Trust me, you don't want to know."

There's a small part of me that feels for him—an extremely small part.

"Fine, here." I hand him the rings and he grips them in his hand. "I mean it. We're done in every sense of the word." I turn without looking at him and get in my car.

I start the car and when I pull out, I give one last glance at the man who was my world for five years. The first person to ask me to be his wife. Of course he turned out to be the worst mistake, but for a while, I loved him. He's still standing on his stoop staring at me. I fight the urge to wave, so I drive away leaving my past behind me.

I look at my phone and see I have two missed calls from Jackson.

Great.

I grab my phone and quickly call him back.

"Hey, babe," I say trying to act nonchalant as a car honks past me while I try to silence my music.

"Hi," Jackson replies with a hint of confusion. "Are you driving?"

"Yeah, I'll tell you about it when I get back to your place. I'm stopping off at my apartment to grab a few things and I should be there in about an hour," I explain hoping it mollifies him for the time being.

"I can't wait to hear it. I called the office and Taylor said you left early and I should see you soon. I was getting worried since it's been two hours and not a word," Jackson's gruff voice radiates concern.

"I promise I'll explain everything when I get there. I love you," I say as sweetly as I can.

"I'll see you then. I love you, too," Jackson says and then disconnects the call.

No matter what I tell him, the fallout is going to be bad, so I might as well get it over with. He wanted me to stay away from Neil, but I simply needed to handle this. Part of my job is to protect him and Raven, and if he were to get pulled into some assault drama with his publicist's ex-boyfriend, it would get ugly real quick. I have to look at this like I was doing my job.

Now I need to convince Jackson of the same thing.

I get back to my apartment to drop off the car, and of course with my luck I turn and see Ashton is walking in the building at the same time. Seriously, my timing sucks.

"Cat?" Ashton asks with narrowed eyes.

"Hey," I say and walk over to her, wrapping my arms around her. I've missed her, no matter what tongue-lashing's about to come. I'm happy to see her.

She returns the hug and pulls back to look at me. "What are you doing here? I didn't expect to see you. Is Jackson okay?"

"Yeah, he's fine. I had something I needed to take care of," I explain with the hope that she'll let it drop.

Ashton cocks her head to the side weighing my words and somehow knowing I'm leaving something out. She's always been able to read through my bullshit. I don't know why I thought this time would be any different.

"Just ask me," I say, exasperated by her staring.

"Right, spill it." She crosses her arms and looks as if she has all the time in the world for me to explain.

"There's nothing to spill," I say and try to walk past her.

She grabs my wrist and stops me. "Cat, I'm not stupid. You have that look on your face. The one that says 'Ashton is going to have my ass so I'll pretend nothing's going on.' Plus, you wouldn't leave work early just because you missed me."

One day I'll be unreadable. "I went to see Neil," I say, waiting for the tirade. I know she's going to blow any second.

"Are you dumb?" she asks deadpanned.

"I don't think so, but I'm sure you and everyone else will disagree." I stand there ready to defend myself.

Ashton releases a deep breath and starts to walk toward the elevator. "Well, I can't wait to hear this argument then. Why did you go see the dickface?"

"I gave him the rings back and he agreed to leave us alone."

She laughs and enters the doors. "Cat, do you really believe a word he says? He's a fucking liar. I mean, come on! You can't possibly trust a word that comes out of his mouth. I'm waiting for you to sell me on how you're not stupid because what you just said sure as shit didn't do it."

Do I believe him? No, but then I do. There was gratitude in his eyes when he had the rings, and then there was the way he seemed almost ... apologetic.

"I think he's in trouble. He was home, on a random

Thursday in the middle of the afternoon. Either he lost his job or something else. The sense of relief on his face when I handed him the rings, even he can't fake. Maybe I'm dumb. Maybe I fucked up, but I can't have him starting shit up with Jackson right before the launch. Do you get that?" I say frustrated that I need to explain my decisions to her. She doesn't always make the best choices, but I don't berate her.

"I do get that, but do you think going there was the best idea?"

"I think it was the only option I had."

We make our way to the apartment without saying anything else. I think of how the hell I'm going to explain the same thing to Jackson without him blowing a gasket. If Jackson did it his way, who knows what would've happened. Neil was already looking at pressing charges if he couldn't get me civilly. If I didn't handle it, there would've been a press shitstorm. So I did what I thought would keep everything quiet and make it go away. Whether it was right or wrong ... only time will tell.

We enter the apartment and finally her silence breaks. "What do Gretchen and Jackson think?" she asks and that's where this brilliant plan of mine has the snag.

"I didn't tell them yet."

She stands there staring at me, opening and closing her mouth. Which I guess is better than hearing it. Although, the fact that I've rendered her speechless doesn't really make me feel any better.

"Okay, I don't really know what to say to that. Just ... wow. For someone so fucking smart, and, Cat, you are *so* smart ... you're also the dumbest person I know." She shakes her head in disbelief. "But, well, it's done. Gretchen is going to be way worse than I am right now. So if I were you, I would prepare yourself for her. She's going to kick your ass and I'm going to sit back and enjoy the show." Ashton spills her feelings, ranging from frustration to excitement talking about how she's going to enjoy my Gretchen-whipping.

"Well, I'm glad you'll get some amusement from all of this."

"The bigger question I have is do you think he'll actually leave you alone?" Ashton asks in a soft tone.

I shake my head unsure of what to think. "I don't know, but at this point I have nothing left of his. Plus, I didn't want the rings—or need them. I don't want anything he touched or that came from him. He's completely out of my life."

"I get that," Ashton finally says as she puts her keys down and heads into the living room. "Sit, let's talk. I feel like I haven't seen you in weeks. Well, I guess I haven't."

"Wait. That's all you're going to say?" My voice is high and I'm shocked. This is very un-Ashton like.

She laughs and tucks her feet under her butt. "I get it. I would want to be rid of anything that was my ex's. Was spending his money on the ring fun? Sure. But at the same rate, your job is to protect Jackson. You don't come into my lab and tell me how to do my job. I'm not going to tell you how to do yours. I wish you would've let me go with you. Or *told* someone what you were up to."

I smile and snuggle into her. "You're such a good friend. If I brought you, it would've made him feel threatened. Plus, I really don't think he's violent. I think he's in deep shit and is trying to find his way out. If he needs money, those two rings should effectively shut him up. Enough about Neil, what do you want to talk about? Mark?"

She slaps my leg and hops up, refusing to answer my question. After a minute, she returns with wine and two glasses. I open the bottle and Ashton launches into a long rant about her job. It's great sitting and talking like we did when I was still staying here. I tell her about what my days are like, trying to catch up on the missed work and how Elle and I are still front-runners for the new position at CJJ.

"How's Mark?" Ashton asks after a few minutes of silence.

The smile slowly forms across my face as Ashton pretends

to pick lint off her pants. "Mark? Do you mean the adorable ex-SEAL who lives in Virginia?" I question, deciding to play coy.

"Oh, don't be so stupid! And adorable isn't the adjective I'd use for that piece of meat."

I laugh so hard I'm clutching my stomach. "Meat? Oh my God, Ash. You're a hot mess."

"Bite me, twunt. Have you talked to him since you've been back?" Ashton's entire demeanor shifts to being interested.

"You and that stupid word." I giggle and take a sip of wine. "Jackson talks to him daily. Have you called him?"

She shifts around looking uncomfortable and grabs her glass. She wipes her finger around the rim while I wait for her to answer. "He's called me a few times but I haven't answered. He's really hot, and I don't know, like I said, he lives in Virginia and I'm not about to start chasing a long distance relationship." Ashton looks up. Her eyes are probing me to give her answers.

I grab her glass and put it on the table. "Ash, you don't know what the future holds any more than I do. Neither one of us is twenty-one anymore. Mark's a good guy. He was there for me in Germany and we became good friends. I think he is about the only man in this world that could handle you. Plus, he really is hot." I slap her arm and get up. It's been over a half hour and I told Jackson I'd be back in an hour. Which already isn't going to happen. "I gotta run."

Ashton stands and pulls me in for a bone crushing hug, "I miss you. Tell your boyfriend to get his ass better so I can have my Biffle. Although, I wonder if he'll return you."

I laugh and hug her back. "I'll be back. I don't think we're at that stage yet."

"You tend to be a little behind on these things, my friend," she says, throwing up a pillow so I can't hit her.

"Why would anyone want to come back to this abuse?" I chide.

She scoffs. "You love it!" she yells as I start to walk away. "Don't forget about me."

"Like you'd ever let me," I say as I close the door laughing. Now time to deal with another headache. Hopefully he won't be in too bad of a mood by the time I tell him this story.

"Jackson," I call as I open the door into the apartment already bracing myself for what I'm sure is going to be one hell of a fight. Good thing he can't really move around too much. At least I can run easily.

"In here!" he responds from the kitchen. *Great.* He's around sharp objects.

I smile as I see the mess before me. He has noodles all over the stove, parts of what look like red peppers on the floor, and every ingredient you can name strewn around the counters. "Well, this looks interesting," I say trying not to laugh.

"You try doing this with one arm and one leg. I have no idea if anything is edible, but it has to be better than the dog food that nurse you hired made for lunch."

My smile doesn't falter as I walk over and grip his cheeks and give him a kiss. He drops the item in his hand and grabs my neck refusing to let me end the kiss. Fine by me. I'll kiss him all night if it delays the inevitable battle coming. Jackson releases me and looks at me skeptically.

"So, where were you?" he wastes no time in asking as he picks up the knife to continue whatever cooking mission he's attempting.

I sigh and steel myself for his reaction. "I went to Neil's to return the rings."

The knife clangs against the counter and he lets out a deep menacing sound from his chest. "You're fucking kidding me, right? Because you wouldn't possibly go see the man who cheated on you, grabbed you, and basically stalked you for weeks."

This is going well already.

I stand toe-to-toe with Jackson. I did what I needed to do.

Whether he agrees with it or not, I don't give a shit. I protect him the same way he protects me.

"Yes, I did. I gave him back the only thing left. It's done. He's out of our lives, and I expect we'll hear from Gretchen soon that Neil's backing off from his bullshit lawsuit."

"I guess you're not kidding! Goddammit, Catherine, I told you to stay away."

"As your publicist, I needed to get rid of the threat to your company prior to your launch. If you think about all of this, he was playing a game he could win. He knows me, and my number one priority is Raven and you. So you can be an asshole or you can say thank you. Which by the way ... you're welcome," I say, refusing to let him get a word in.

He gives a sarcastic laugh. "That's not going to happen, babe. You shouldn't have gone there."

"Well, I did!" I throw my hands up in the air and they make a loud slap when they hit my leg. "You know you're not the only one who gets to make decisions around here. I'm an equal in this relationship. I could've lied to you but I'm here listening to the shit I knew I was going to have to hear. I promised not to keep secrets from you." My eyes narrow as I let him know how I'm not going to stand here idly and listen. "I'll take my lumps because I believe you're just an idiot who thinks he needs to keep me safe. But guess what, buddy?" I raise my brow. "I've been taking care of myself for twenty-nine years. I think I've done a damn good job so far. Have I screwed up? Sure." I throw my hands up again. "God, you infuriate me."

For a second he looks stunned and unsure of how to respond to my mini rant. He recovers quickly and wraps his arm around my waist pulling me close to him. I inhale his scent and gently place my hand on his chest. Looking up into his eyes I see him battling himself.

"I'm not happy," he finally states while glaring at me.

"I don't doubt that."

"You shouldn't have gone there."

"I don't agree," I retort.

Jackson takes a deep breath and breaks from our staring contest. "You drive me insane."

I shrug and kiss his chest. "You're not the first person to feel that way. I did what I felt was right. It needed to be done." I turn my head and listen to his heartbeat waiting for him respond.

"And what if something happened to you? What if he hurt you? I would've been here, not knowing where you were or what stupid plan you had. When you were hurt or God knows what, how would I deal with that?" he says as I hear his heart accelerate either in anger or fear.

Leaning out of his embrace, I look at him, willing him to look at me. I'm not weak, and while a part of me understands his apprehension, he can't deem me incapable of taking care of myself. When he finally looks over, I smile softly and try to explain more calmly. "You're in the middle of a rather large product launch. You were shot. You lost your best friend on top of a slew of other things. I understand your need to protect me ... most of the time it turns me on." I wink and try to ease the tension. Jackson smiles and I continue. "But ... and this is a big but ... you can't. I'm going to handle things the way I think is best. It might be wrong and I'm going to make mistakes, but I'm allowed to make them. Now, cook me dinner while I go shower."

"This is ridiculous. I asked you to stay away from him. You won't make me out to be the bad guy here."

He's pissed and to a point I understand that, but this isn't about him. "I won't let you make demands, and I'm also not the kind of girl who's going to be obedient. You should know this by now."

"I'm not asking you to obey me, Catherine. I'm asking you to fucking stay away from a piece of shit who bruised you. An asshole who I got in a fistfight with because he put his hands on you. The same bastard who then wanted to come after us."

Jackson runs his hand down his face and his chest is heaving. "I understand you're not happy. I'm not asking you to understand. I'm telling you it's done. He's out of our lives." He gives a cynical laugh. "I'm assuming *he* told you that? Because he's a real trustworthy guy, right? When he files charges now and we have no rings as a bargaining chip ... then what?"

I draw whatever strength I have left, between Ashton earlier and now Jackson. Besides the fact that I also dealt with Neil, I haven't slept in what feels like a year, and the launch is in a few days—I'm running on a limited supply of patience.

"I love you, but I'm done talking. I need a shower, a nap, and for you to trust me. Do you trust me, Jackson?"

"Of course I do." The exasperation in his voice is clear.

"Do you trust me as your publicist? Do you trust me to do my job?" I ask because I need him to see the two correlate.

"I wouldn't have hired you if I didn't think you were good at your job." Jackson hesitates, as he seems to see where I'm leading him.

"Good, then let me handle it. Now, I'm going to get naked." I smile and saunter out of the kitchen.

I glance over my shoulder and drop my shirt and bra on the floor while he stares at me.

"Not fair."

"You could always join me." I turn standing before him in a skirt, half naked as he drinks me in.

Jackson groans and slowly maneuvers his way to me. "You're going to be the death of me, woman."

My lips turn up. "I think you're stronger than that. Come on and show me just how far I can push you before you break."

chapter

twelve

JACKSON FOLLOWS ME into the bathroom and I pretend I don't notice. Standing practically naked I turn the water on and then I feel him against my back. He stands there unmoving as I face the glass enclosure.

I wait for him to say something, or touch me, but he doesn't. My breathing grows shallow as the anticipation builds. He's toying with me and I'm a moth to his flame.

Unsure of what to do, I slowly slide my underwear down and I feel his warm breath against my ear. I can feel the heat emanating from his body. His chest barely grazes against my back when he breathes. I close my eyes and inhale the mix of steam and Jackson's cologne. Every part of me aches for him. I want to move or speak, but I don't want to break the spell.

We stand like that for what feels like an eternity. The large glass door is fogging up and I lift my hand to open it, but Jackson's grabs my wrist.

"I'm still angry." His deep voice causes the hairs on the back of my neck to rise.

I slowly turn and my hand gingerly skates across his chest. Somewhere between the kitchen and the bathroom he lost his shirt. My hand falls to his waistband and our eyes remain glued to each other.

"Let me make it better," I rasp as I unhook his belt. "I think your anger is misplaced." I unzip his shorts and they fall.

Jackson grabs my breast and squeezes, his thumb rubs back and forth across my nipple. "Did he touch you?"

My breath catches at his question. "No," I say softly as I touch his face. "He didn't touch me."

His other hand rests on my hip since he can't move it higher but his fingers crush the skin as he tightens his grip. "I can't," Jackson drops his forehead to mine.

"Can't what?"

Jackson releases a measured breath, "I can't think of his hands touching you."

He rolls my nipple in his fingers and I moan. "I wouldn't let him," I croak as he repeats his movement.

His hand drops as he slides the glass door open and nudges me in.

Carefully, we enter the large marble two-person shower. The jets shoot out of the sides and the rainfall showerhead cascades down on us. Jackson seats himself on the bench that takes the back wall. His eyes beckon me forward.

I push my wet hair back and settle between his legs. His hands tug at the back of my thighs pulling me forward.

"No other man should touch you." His lips press against my stomach as his fingers indent my skin and dig in, thrusting me forward even more.

The hint of pain only heightens my senses.

"No other man's hands should feel what I feel beneath my palms right now." Jackson's hand slips between my legs as he pushes them apart. My hands slap the cold marble tiles as I try to stay upright. "You're my everything," his voice is laced with pain as he inserts a finger inside me. "I won't let anyone take you from me."

My head falls back as my legs shake while he plunges his fingers over and over. He twists his hand so his thumb presses against my clit. "Jackson," I whisper as my eyes roll back.

"Only me," he groans with a possessive tinge.

Everything about this time I can feel as if it's his mission to claim me. Each movement is him proving to either himself or me that I'm his. I belong to him. He belongs to me. In this moment we belong to each other. I look at him and his eyes pierce my soul. "Only you," I reply.

"I'm still pissed."

"Good. I like pissed off." I smirk and his eyes narrow as he weighs my words.

He continues to finger me as I climb toward my orgasm. Every part of me is alive. His hands awaken me and cherish me. Even though I know he's angry that I went against his wishes, right now he adores me. Protecting me even when he's being rough.

My legs begin to quake as I get closer to release, but the desire to be filled by him is too great. I drop my arms and grip his neck. Leaning in I kiss him with everything I have. Our tongues push against each other, swirling and volleying for power. I need him to take it all away. Take the doubt, the pain, and the weeks of dread I've held on to. And he does. Jackson takes it away with each twist of his tongue. Each thrust of his hand ... he takes it away.

"I need you inside me," I say breathlessly as his lips press against my neck.

Jackson groans before I feel his teeth graze the sensitive skin. "Do you now?" His hands don't relent as he grinds his thumb harder against my clit. My knees are weak and I have to hold on to his shoulders for support.

"Yes, now," I beg.

Shifting my leg over his I try to align myself, desperate for him. I close my eyes and try to fight off my release a little longer. I want him inside of me when I let go. I want to feel him fill me to the brink, where I can focus on nothing more than how we fit together.

He grabs my hips, halting me from being able to take what I want. "Not yet," his throaty voice breaks through the fog.

"Stand on the ledge," he instructs while I step on the bench. Jackson runs his hands on my leg and lifts my leg up over his shoulder. "I'm going you make you come in my mouth first." And I know he means it. Jackson licks and sucks while using his finger to torture me. I get closer and closer, but he stops right before I'm ready to burst. Each time is stronger than the last. Each build goes higher than the one before. I'm going to die from the onslaught of pleasure. But what a way to go.

"I need you," I groan as he continues. "To let me ..." I stop unable to say more. When he pushes his tongue inside of me, I lose it. I writhe and scream as he draws out the most powerful orgasm I've ever had. Stars paint the walls and my hearing is gone as I float in complete bliss. There's no strength left in my body as I sink to his lap. The water rains down, keeping me from being cold.

Opening my eyes, I see the desire burning in his eyes. I refuse to wait another second. I gently push him against the back wall allowing myself enough space to move.

"Don't ever let him near you again." Jackson's eyes flash with a hint of anger.

"Don't ever doubt me," I say as I sink onto his cock.

His eyes close as I allow myself a second to adjust. He smirks and it pisses me off. I lift myself up and slam against him. Jackson's head snaps up and he glares at me, but the love is evident beneath the anger we're both fighting through.

Anger at his doubt. Anger at his demands. Anger that he's angry at how I chose to handle it. I'm furious.

I ride him harder than I intend. I hear his grunts and groans, but when I start to let up, his fingers dig into my hips forcing me to keep my pace.

"Fuck me harder," Jackson demands.

I groan and hear the slapping skin as we force ourselves together with reckless abandon. We fight the war between our wills through our bodies. Each grunt reminds me we're still fighting for each other. The sweat that trickles down my back is evidence of the struggle we're ready to endure. The heat that surges through my cells proves how I'll give myself to him.

"I'm gonna come," Jackson says with his jaw clenched.

"I love you," I cry out as I fall back into the abyss again.

The tears form in my eyes as I'm overcome with emotion. I love him with all that I am.

Jackson seems to sense the shift as he brings his hands up to my neck. He cradles my head as I look into his eyes. Gently, he swipes under my eyes. "I love you."

I smile tenderly, "I know."

"I didn't mean to be a dick before. I fucking hate the idea that you could've been hurt." Jackson's hands push the hair out of my face as he waits for me to respond.

"You can't save me all the time."

"I can damn sure try."

We kiss briefly and take a shower after our non-shower.

Jackson washes my hair and body, and I in turn do the same for him. The intimacy established between us takes my breath away.

"Almost done?" Jackson asks.

"I'm going to take a few minutes to myself."

"Okay," Jackson says as he heads out of the shower.

I stand there alone and enjoy the solace. Replaying the last few hours in my head, I realize why he was so angry. Things could've gone differently, but they didn't, and I'm grateful for that. I finish up and decide next time I'll let someone in on my brilliant plans.

Once I'm dressed and comfortable I head out to the kitchen. He stands there assessing the damage. I hold back a laugh because it's going to take hours to clean this up.

"Okay, Chef Boyardee, how about you order take-out?" I smile and come around the counter.

"No, this is perfectly edible," Jackson scoffs and starts to stir the pot.

I cross my arms across my chest and at first I think he's

kidding but he continues stirring. "Jackson, I'm not eating that." I look in the pot and it's turning colors. "What the hell is *that*?" I ask incredulously.

He laughs and turns the burner off. "Fine, we don't have to eat it."

"Can you even name what it is?"

"It's a surprise." He smiles and pulls me against him.

I look up biting my lip to stop myself from busting out laughing. "Was the surprise whatever we taste at the first bite?"

"Smart ass," he retorts.

"You like my ass."

"That I do."

"Perv. I'll order Chinese. Maybe we can watch a movie?" I suggest as I call the restaurant.

Luckily they deliver quickly and before I know it, Jackson is in the doorway, leaning against his walker with one of his shit-eating grins.

After a minute of no reply I look up. "What?"

"Food's here."

"Good, I'm starving."

"How about we play a game?"

I don't like the looks of this. I can see the wheels turning in his head. This can't be good.

My eyes narrow as I try to figure out what game he could possibly want to play. "Why do I think this is a bad idea?"

Jackson pretends he's affronted and throws his hand over his heart. "Don't you trust me?"

I smile and shake my head.

"Come on, we can play a board game," he cajoles, clearly already having thought this through.

I hate board games. I always lose, but knowing my competitive boyfriend, he's clamoring for something to win at.

"Anything but Monopoly." I smile and grab the plates.

Jackson's lips turn up in a grin and we make our way to the table. Once we've dished the food and gotten settled, he pulls a box out from the chair beside him. When I see the game he's chosen, I burst out laughing.

"Battleship? For real? Are you twelve?" I say in between my giggles.

"Don't insult this game. It's a classic. Besides there's no way in hell you'll be able to win," Jackson says as he starts to pull the game pieces out.

"You know every time you say these things it makes me even more determined to kick your ass?"

"I know, and it turns me on when I see you get feisty." His eyes darken as his voice drops.

The blush spreads across my cheeks and I try to take a bite to stop my mind from going there.

Once I've gotten myself under better control, I start to set up my game board, placing the ships and wondering about the best positions to confuse him. "Okay, it's been a long time and I don't trust you not to cheat so where are the directions?"

Before I can grab the box, he swipes it and tosses it back behind him.

"What the hell?"

"The rules are simple. You put the pieces in and guess. But for every wrong answer you have to take off an item of clothing." He wiggles his brows and I roll my eyes.

"Right, I'm not sure we played this Battleship when I was ten."

"My Navy. My rules. I'm the admiral." Jackson crosses his arms and leans back in the chair.

"I don't think so."

"Fine, then for every correct answer, you take off an item of clothing."

"And for every wrong one you have to answer a question," I say and smirk.

He seems to consider my counteroffer. After a few seconds of mulling it over, he leans forward. "I'm fine with that. But if you don't want to answer, you can remove an item of clothing."

Now it's my turn to think it over. "You can only pass twice. I don't see you having issues getting naked."

"I also have no issues with you getting naked," his voice is full of humor.

After a few turns I'm left only in my tank top, underwear, socks, and bra. Jackson is almost fully dressed. I swear he's losing on purpose. *This* is why I hate board games. However, we're laughing and enjoying the time together.

"Okay, A-12."

"Miss," I hoot, smiling and batting my eyelashes. "Hmmm, first kiss?"

Jackson sighs before answering. "Reagan's best friend, Sharon, in a game of Truth or Dare. Fifth grade. You?"

"I didn't lose that turn. C-3," I say and he smiles.

"Miss. First kiss?" Jackson asks.

"Andy, under the stars in seventh grade. Honestly, my first kiss was what every girl dreams of."

"How so?" he asks.

"I liked him a lot. We went to the fireworks in town and he kissed me during the grand finale. It was perfect and memorable." I laugh remembering how sweet it was and how as soon as we finished kissing we both ran off to tell our friends.

"Kissing Sharon wasn't memorable in a good way. We had no idea what we were doing and when I shoved my tongue in her mouth she almost started crying," Jackson laughs and then his eyes begin to smolder. "Not like when I kiss you."

I fight off the lust that starts to churn. "I would hope you don't kiss me like an eleven-year-old boy. But, I do like it when you shove your tongue in my mouth."

"And other places."

"You're so gross," I laugh at his crassness.

"Deny it!" he challenges me.

"Nope," I wink and point at his game board. "Make your pick, Muffin."

"F-9."

It takes everything for me to not start dancing when he gets one right. "Hit." I smile and he has to remove another item of clothing. "Take the shirt off." I say for selfish reasons. If I have to sit here, I might as well get to ogle.

"Fine. Your turn."

"B-8." I smile knowing I had to have hit and possibly sunk a ship.

"Miss. You can't outsmart me, baby. I'm not sure I want to ask or get you naked."

"You don't get to decide. Ask," I state. No way, he doesn't get to choose—I do.

"Fine, where did you go to college?"

"Fairleigh Dickenson University for undergrad and then for my master's I went to Seton Hall. You?" I can't help but ask, even though I know it's not in the rules.

"I went to Oklahoma since my dad was stationed there at the time. Then, I enlisted."

Looking at my game, I realize I suck at this game since I haven't gotten one right in a while. Jackson smiles as if he's thinking the same thing. "Okay, A-1."

If I didn't know his competitive streak, I would think he's trying to get them wrong so I have a better chance of being naked. "Miss," I narrow my eyes and he leans back under my scrutiny. Staring at his glorious chest I look at the tattoos. I know what his frog means, but he has the tribal and the sun. "What does the sun tattoo mean?"

He looks confused for a second and looks down where my gaze is. "It was a cover up. Nothing really special."

"What was there before?" I ask curiously.

"That's two questions. You can save that for your next round. Now, pick your next move so I can get your shirt off and stare at something for a while."

I smile and of course guess correctly. Which means I'm now in my bra and underwear—and socks.

"C-1," Jackson guesses.

"Miss! Ha! Okay, now you answer about that tattoo," I challenge him.

"Nothing big, stupid things we get when we're young."

"A name?" I ask. Ashton and Gary went and got each other's names together in college. I thought they were ridiculous. Ashton had hers covered up with a butterfly. Luckily her tattoo was on her shoulder and they had room to play with.

"Yes, a name. Now, let's get back to getting you naked," Jackson wiggles his brow like a villain.

I laugh at the expression on his face and I make my next move.

We laugh and play the remainder of the game. By the end I'm completely topless and Jackson is completely naked. He of course won the game. Which infuriates me. However, I love the fact that he answered the questions so easily. We've gotten so many funny answers and I've learned a lot about him. What his first car was, why he'll never have an animal, what his favorite color is, and how old he was when he lost his virginity. But I wonder who was important enough for him to get a tattoo of their name across his heart.

I wake up early to another one of Jackson's nightmares. Unable to fall back asleep, I do some work from home. The press release for the upcoming product line is five days from now and then the launch party is that night. I have a few things to do to confirm everything is in order. Taylor has taken care of most things, but I need to make sure it's perfect.

"You're up early and on a weekend," Jackson's deep voice breaks the quiet.

I jump at the sound of his voice and clutch my chest trying to settle my heart. Even without being able to walk around he's still able to scare the crap out of me. "I swear ... I'm going to put a cow bell on that damn walker."

Jackson settles on the couch and pulls the papers out of my hand. "We need some fun. What do you say we do something today—just us?"

I link my fingers with his and grin. "I could do with a little us. Plus, I'm actually ahead of the game for once. I like fun and I happen to like you." The blush paints my face as I remember our shower three days ago and how much fun we had with each other.

His throaty laugh echoes in the room. "That kind of fun will be later. How about we go to the park and watch the boats, or we can head to a museum?"

I love the Met, which is only a block from his apartment, but I don't know how fun a museum would be for Jackson considering he can't walk. The boat pond would be relaxing and we could always lie out on the grass at the park. "I think the park would be a great way to spend our day."

Jackson leans in and presses his lips to mine. The look in his eyes when he pulls back stuns me. All I see is love and desire. "You know how I feel about you?"

"I do."

Jackson hesitates and then he cups my cheeks while his eyes pierce through me. "You're it for me. I love you."

My pulse spikes and I lose myself in this moment. "I love you, too."

Needing to feel him, I kiss him again. I feel his tongue against the seam of my lips and I open to him. Our tongues glide against each other's as the kiss deepens. Jackson's hand slowly drifts up my arm and around my back. He presses me flush against his chest as he holds me against him. Kissing me feverishly as if his life depended on it. It's a desperate kiss. One that I feel in every fiber of my being.

Lust spikes and I can't fight it. I need him. My hand cups his head as I push back into the kiss, giving myself over and taking everything. I'm ravenous for him. I devour his mouth, breathing him in. The kiss goes on and on. I lose myself completely and it could be minutes, hours, who knows—I couldn't care less.

Jackson breaks the kiss and presses his forehead against mine as I whimper from the loss. "If we keep this up, we'll never leave." His voice is husky and breathless, clearly affected by our intense make-out session.

"And that would be bad why?" I ask trying to catch my breath.

He laughs and kisses my forehead as I try to pull him back to my lips. "Let's go out first. Then I promise I'll be very bad."

I grin. "Oh, Muffin ... you couldn't be bad if you tried."

"Baby, you're going to pay for that."

"Maybe you can pay me in fun."

Jackson groans and I giggle, running into the bedroom.

"You can run, but you can't hide," I hear him yell from the other room.

I take a little extra time trying to delay coming out but know it won't help. He will take full retribution when I least expect it. I can only hope it's the naughty kind, since our last few times have been really ... interesting. Trying to maneuver without getting hurt has made it adventurous and Jackson's made sure I haven't suffered—at all. I grab my black shorts, a cute tank-top, and throw my hair into a messy bun.

When I get back into the living room, I don't see Jackson there. I start looking around, waiting for him to pop out and scare the crap out of me. "Jackson ... this isn't funny," I say trying to keep an eye out for him.

If anyone had a camera right now I'd kill them. I must look ridiculous walking around the apartment checking each corner waiting for him to suddenly appear. "Okay, babe. I'm going to the park for our date. Looks like you're stuck here." My voice gives away the slightest hint of fear. I turn around and he's standing right there.

"Ha!" he screams and I can't help the squeal that comes from my throat.

Damn him.

"Jerk," I say and start to stomp away, furious that once again he got me.

I hear him behind me as he wheels faster. "Oh, don't be like that. You had to know I always win. I've told you this numerous times. I never lose." His arrogance is shining through.

Spinning on my heels, I turn to face him. "I wouldn't say never, darling."

"When have I ever lost?" He cocks his eyebrow and it takes everything inside of me not to jump him.

For some inexplicable reason I find him sexiest when he's like this. Who am I kidding? I find him sexy all the time. Damn dimple and abs—I didn't stand a chance. I smile since this is the perfect time to finally get my time from that godforsaken obstacle course he made me run. "Show me yours and I'll show you mine." I give him my best seductive grin.

Jackson clears his throat as I slither up to him. "Show my what?"

"Time. I want to see your time."

His head tilts and he looks off to the side. "I'm going out on a limb here, but are you talking about the O-course?" A slow smile creeps across his face as he figures out what I'm talking about.

"Yup," I smirk and start to slide my finger down his chest. "You know, that photo you have of my time." My brow rises as his breath hitches while my hand goes lower. "The one where you owe me a whole lot of shopping and a massage."

Jackson grips my wrist before my hands reach his pants. "What about when you see how much I schooled you?" He leans forward dropping his voice into a low seductive whisper. "What do I get then, baby?"

The heat against my ear causes me to shiver and I hear him chuckle at my reaction. "What do you want?" I try to play it cool and not give away the way he's making my body react, even though it's blatantly obvious.

"What do you want to give me?" His deep voice travels from my head to my toes, igniting the low flame of lust into a raging inferno.

My breaths are shallow and my pulse is beating so loud I'm positive he can hear it. "Well, why don't you show me and find out."

"Nah, this is more fun," Jackson says and stands up opening the door.

"You're not going to think this is so fun in a few hours." With my arms crossed I lean against the door so he can't get through.

Jackson smiles and waits for me to move. He's in no rush and it makes me want to stomp and scream at him. It seems he's back to his playful, jackass self. The walker he uses to get around has a seat and he perches himself on it while I stand there. The smug smile on his face causes my irritation to claw its way up.

"I've got all day," he sighs dramatically and starts to look around.

"I'll make another deal with you," I say. "Even though I don't know why I bother since you don't keep up your end anyway," I tack on just for good measure.

"I'm all ears."

He infuriates me when he's like this. I don't know whether to slap him or kiss him—maybe both. "We'll go to the park and settle in for our beautiful date. Since you're feeling better, you'll tell me my time and I'll tell you yours."

"I'm waiting for the concession here," Jackson cuts me off and taps his fingers on the chair.

I huff, "I'm getting there, Muffin. But you so rudely interrupted." I smile and cock my head to the side. "As I was saying, you give up the goods and if I won then you take me to a Broadway play. Then, you'll treat me to a spa day. If you win, then I won't call you Muffin for at least two weeks, and I'll run that stupid obstacle course again."

"One month," he says quickly, counteroffering my two weeks.

"Two weeks."

"Not good enough, and you'll do a lot more than the obstacle course. As soon as my leg is back to normal and I get the green light from the doc, you'll start running with me every day."

I laugh and roll my eyes. "I think you have a better chance of me becoming a nun before that ever happens."

"Take it or leave it, Kitty," Jackson says, cocky and so sure he has it made.

"My final offer is three weeks." I smile and place both hands on the walker, backing him into the wall. He's completely trapped and his eyes narrow as he looks at the position he's in. "And unless you want to become celibate, you'll retract the running clause."

His lips quirk up into a lazy smile. "You see, baby, I win. I have the time. I have the upper hand. I already know I smoked your beautiful ass. There's no way in hell you beat me, so really this deal has to work in my favor. So you ..." Jackson's fingers wrap around my neck as he pulls me down, "... Are really the one who has to suffer." His lips graze mine and I feel the heat of his breath against my mouth. "Take it. Or leave it."

I can almost feel his smile against my lips. Unable to resist him and hoping this diversion tactic works, I press my mouth to his. My hands thread in his hair and my tongue plunges into his mouth. Controlling every aspect of the kiss, I push further. When he finally let's go and starts to give back, I give him a moment. I need him to get lost in it so I can hopefully have him distracted. Plus, I know he's already excited from our previous kiss. As soon as I hear the moan escape him, I push back and take an extra step out of his grasp. My lips tingle from the kiss and Jackson's eyes are wide as he admires me. The bulge in his pants makes it obvious he was wanting much more.

With his defenses lowered, I move back another step

letting him see who really has the power. "You better slow me down before I head out the door." I pause for dramatic effect.

"What game are you playing?"

I start to lift my shirt but stop as I see his pupils dilate, "Jackson?"

He doesn't answer, just watches as I hike it a little higher.

"Do we have a deal?" I ask softly.

"Whatever the fuck you want," Jackson doesn't hesitate in answering.

"I thought you'd say that." I smile and take a step in his direction. He licks his lips and uses his index finger to try to call me over. "Now, come here and finish what you started and then somehow managed to bully me into giving you your way."

Another small step in his direction, but I stop, grab the basket and blanket, and turn on my heels. "Nah, I'm in the mood for the park."

"You're killing me, Catherine. Absolutely fucking killing me," Jackson groans but I hear him moving behind me.

When we're out the door, I turn to him feeling victorious and a little devious. "Guess you don't always win, now do you?"

We quickly reach the boat pond area of Central Park, which is only about a block from his high rise. To say he lives in the most desired area of New York City would be an understatement. It's perfect. I'm glad he pulled me away from work and the launch. We both need this time together.

"I think we should steer clear of any more competitions for today. My balls can't handle it," Jackson says while laughing.

"Awww, my little sore loser."

"When I show you the photo of your time, we'll see who's sore."

I wave my hand dismissively. Even though I added a good four minutes on to his time, the reality is—I have no idea what my damage was. I didn't really fall or struggle too much, but Super SEAL over there didn't even break a sweat. "Want to sit at the end of the hill?" I point to the grassy section that has a small incline. That way he can sit easily and use the height to get up without too much effort. I know how much he hates the limitations his leg injury is causing. At least this is a way to minimize it. Also, he's heavy and difficult for me to maneuver on my own.

"Sounds great. What do you have in that basket?" he asks curiously trying to peek the lid open.

"Just snacks, a few books, and some drinks." I smile as we slowly make our way to the tiny piece of tranquility we'll have in the middle of this metropolis.

"You thought of all that in an hour?" Jackson asks with disbelief in his voice.

"I didn't make a gourmet meal. Also I didn't make a disaster of the kitchen while grabbing things."

He smirks. "I think that night worked out for the both of us."

The blush spreads across my face as I hear the double meaning. Yes, it most definitely did work out for both of us.

Laying out the blanket, I help Jackson get comfortable and I settle in.

"Hey, get over here," he calls and pats his good leg. "Do you want to read for a little while?"

"We have all day, babe. We can do whatever."

It's beautiful out. There's a small breeze and the sun is overhead but we have some shade thanks to the trees. I lie on his leg and look up at him. His strong jaw, beautiful eyes, and short stubble take my breath away. I start to remember the first time we met, how much he affected me. Then, when I realized he was my new client, the electrical charge I fought so hard against was undeniable. But nothing like the first time I saw him without a shirt on—which reminds me of the course.

He leans back on his side and smiles. "You wanna know, don't you?"

I sit up practically bouncing up and down. "Yes!" I'm so excited. Here comes a play, no running daily crap, and a whole lot of taunting. Well, I hope at least. As quickly as I can, I grab my phone and scroll to the photo with his time and clutch it to my chest. "Okay, you ready, Muffin?" I smirk and ready myself for the moment of truth.

"Oh, baby, I'm more than ready. I hope you get yourself a new pair of running shoes."

"I hope you're ready to lose to a girl."

"If you beat me, I might cry," Jackson jokes.

"Now that I want to see."

Jackson's loud laugh cuts through the quiet as he grabs his phone.

"Ready?" he asks.

"As I'll ever be. Time to pay up, Muff."

"Better get it all out of your system, sweetheart, because that's the last time you'll be saying my call sign for a while."

I shake my head and try to get my excitement in check. "Okay, let's both put the phones face down and then on the count of three we'll flip them over."

Jackson rolls his eyes and hands his phone over. "I'm not worried."

"Neither am I." Tentatively, I hand mine over, controlling my shaking.

We count it down, and then slowly flip the phones over and look at our times.

Game.

Set.

Match.

CHAPTER

THIRTEEN

JACKSON

S HE'S FUCKING KIDDING me.
There's no way in hell.

I look up at her and her smile says it all. "What's the matter, Muffin?" Her brown eyes are big and she knows she's got me.

"No! No fucking way. No way. How?" I ask, knowing somehow she fixed these times. She did something because I've run that course over a thousand times. I swear I could do it in my sleep. Hell, I could do it now in this stupid walker and still beat her.

She looks up, playing coy, "I have no idea what you mean. I started the timer when you told me to and then you ran it. You must've had an off day."

Off day my ass.

"Catherine, if you don't 'fess up, I promise you'll be running daily and it won't be because of a bet." My brow rises as I try to imply what she'll be running from.

I gotta hand it to her though. She got me—and good.

"A lady never reveals her secrets."

"I'll figure out what you did."

"You can try, Muffin."

"Okay, that's fine. You know you never specified what play, when I had to take you, or what kind of spa treatments." I tap her nose knowing it drives her nuts. Let that sink in ...

Her eyes light up when she realizes the hole in her plan. Like I was ever going to let that happen. "Oh, no. You're not going to loophole your way out of this. I won! I beat your ass. I mean, you are at over twelve minutes. I'm under. I win. You lose." She's talking so fast I have to try to keep up. I love getting her riled up. It's so easy.

I shrug and grab the book, not knowing what the hell it even is but anything to keep pissing her off. "I didn't make the bet. I'm just adhering to the rules."

Catherine scoffs and looks away, "I swear."

"A lady never swears."

She grabs her phone and starts fumbling through it.

"What are you doing?" I ask.

"Looking up what plays have tickets for tomorrow." She gives me a snarky smile.

I cough and grab her phone out of her hand. "Not happening since you cheated."

"We're going to see a play tomorrow."

"The hell we are."

I'll take her anywhere she wants to go, but this is almost too much fun. Her eyes glow as she gets more and more frustrated.

"I hate you."

I laugh because she's so cute when she's petulant. "There's a very fine line between love and hate. I'm pretty sure you love me. I'm pretty loveable."

"You're also a giant pain in my ass. But ..." Her eyes light up and I see it all right there. "I do love you. Even though you feel the need to drive me insane. However, tomorrow there are seats available for *The Lion King* or we can see *The Vagina Monologues*."

My mouth drops slightly and I wait for the punch line.

"Are there vaginas in the show?"

"None that you'll see." Catherine smirks and slides up

to my side. Her voice drops into a seductive whisper, "It's all about menopause. So are we going to see that or are you going to pay up and take me to see *The Lion King*?"

Leaning up, I grab her hand and hold it in mine. I love the way she feels against me. She links her fingers with mine and I pull her forward. "I love you, and I love driving you crazy ... in every way. There's no way in hell we're going to see a play about pussies."

Her grip tightens and she leans forward and kisses me.

I get lost in her. She makes it a little easier to breathe. Shit doesn't suck so bad and my head gets a break when she's in my arms.

"I can't lose you," I say out of nowhere.

She pulls back and her forehead wrinkles as she looks at me. "Why do you think you'd lose me?"

There's so much of my life that she doesn't understand. The constant fear that when she walks out the door in the morning she won't return.

It keeps me up at night.

Haunts me in my dreams. I see her walking away. Asking me for things I'm not capable of giving her and deciding she's had enough. Each night they're the same dreams only different ways of losing her.

chapter

fourteen

Catherine

"JACKSON?" I ASK him again. He's staring off and seems lost. Leaning up I touch his face. "You okay?" The concern is evident in my tone.

"Just remembering something that bothered me. I'm fine," he says, trying to dismiss my worry.

"You know you can talk to me, right?"

Jackson nods and closes his eyes, "Natalie called yesterday."

And there it is.

"She said you guys talked the other day too, right?"

Since Aaron's passing I've grown close to his wife, Natalie. We spoke once while Jackson was in the hospital and since then I speak to her every few days. At first, she didn't want to speak to Jackson or Mark. I understood, considering they were his closest friends, but she said they used the same phrases and it hurt too much. So we talk about life, her pregnancy, and how she wants to go back to work. My heart breaks the most when she tells me about what life is like as a widow and how much she prays this baby will be a boy.

Jackson pulls me onto his leg and attempts to get comfortable. "I sent a large check and arranged the plane to pick up her parents to bring them in. I don't want her to have to worry about anything. She's due this week. Mark has been keeping in touch, but he said she doesn't want to see any of us."

I can't even begin to imagine the pain she's in. Plus, I remember when Neil's sister was pregnant, she was a mess. Crying over toilet paper commercials and then the next minute she was screaming over the way you buttered toast. I wish there was more that we could do for Natalie, but she refused to do a memorial or anything until after the baby is born. I sit and listen to him as he finally starts to open up about Aaron and his death.

"It should've never happened. I want to do more for her. She shouldn't have to go through this alone. I know some of the military wives down there have brought food and things over. But he should be there with her."

"I know. It was senseless and tragic, but you can't make Natalie want your help." It's unfortunate but true. She needs to be ready, and if being near Mark or talking to Jackson is too hard on her then they need to respect that. "She really does seem to be doing better. At least she's talking to you guys now."

Jackson rubs the side of my face and closes his eyes. "I just know if Aaron were here, he'd want his brothers to step up. He'd want us to take care of them. She asked us to arrange everything for him, do a memorial and then a burial. He has a plot in Pennsylvania. Will you be there?"

Without hesitation I respond, "Jackson, you don't even have to ask. I promise I'll be there. No matter what."

"Thank you."

"You don't have to ask if I'll stand by you. If you need me, I'm here."

He lies on the blanket and I scoot up so I can curl into his arm. Jackson grabs our books and hands them to me, letting me know he's done and needs to stop talking. The struggle is evident and I don't want to push him too far.

We both get lost in other worlds, mine of course is about love, while he reads some suspense novel. But we enjoy the solace and the fact that we're here—together.

After about an hour, Jackson starts to get restless and starts shifting and grunting.

"You ready?" I ask, knowing either his pain meds are wearing off or he's asleep.

Jackson lifts his head and looks around. "I'm awake," he says, clearly caught napping.

I giggle and start to get up and put our things in the basket.

"Since you somehow cheated and won the other bet, how about we just let you take what's left of my balls and go to the boats?" Jackson half-laughs and half-snorts.

"There's a lot of truth in that statement, but I'll let you decide which part I mean."

I'm enjoying this winning thing.

"When I first moved to this part of the city I used to come here with Garrett and race him."

"Garrett?" I don't remember anyone by that name.

"You met him. He was at dinner the night we met. Not that you stuck around long enough to really meet anyone, but he's Mark's older brother," Jackson explains while he tries to get up, but he winces and stops.

I put all the stuff down and get behind him. "Let me help you," I say gently, knowing how quickly his mood can shift when he needs help.

"You just want to touch my body."

"You know it," I reply, hoping he'll play along.

We get up pretty easily and he grips the walker and puts his leg on the seat. Only one more week and he will be able to start walking with crutches. His arm is almost fully mobile, and he's growing stronger and moving much more easily.

Jackson and I play for about an hour at the boat pond. I can't for the life of me understand how the man has the drive to make anything a competition. The pond is filled with other boats but there he is trying to maneuver a tiny battery operated boat that doesn't go more than two miles per hour. I let him win since I had no idea what in the world the rules were.

"At least I win this round," Jackson boasts and pulls me against him, kissing the top of my head.

"Yeah," I say without any enthusiasm. "You sure showed me. I'm buying the tickets to the play for tomorrow."

"We're going to pretend this isn't happening. Since you cheated." Jackson places a kiss against my temple and then grabs my hand. "Let's go home. I have some plans for you."

Home. Even he's calling it home when we talk about it. As much as it thrills me that he's so comfortable with me in his home, there's a small part of me terrified we're moving too fast. So much has happened and yet we've skipped the whole getting to know each other stage and fell into the living together stage. I don't doubt my feelings or his, I only want to make sure we don't screw this up.

We walk the block to his apartment with my arm draped around his waist. "I hope those plans include food and maybe ice cream," I say as my stomach growls.

Jackson's eyes dance with mischief. "I fully intend on eating."

It takes me a second to understand the look on his face. "Oh my God! Jackson!" I laugh and he joins me.

"What? I ordered take-out."

"Sure, that's what you were insinuating."

"I'm a gentleman," he says as we enter the lobby of his building.

"Right, and I'm an angel," I say and board the elevator.

He maneuvers us into the corner and spins his walker so I'm in between his arms, making it impossible for me to move. "Did you have something else in mind?"

My tongue swipes across my lips and Jackson's eyes track the movement. "I could be open for suggestions."

His arm slides a little lower and it amazes me that even injured he can find a way to seduce me. "Hmmm," he says as the distance between us closes.

It takes every ounce of restraint to let him lead and not maul him. The rise and fall of my chest has his attention as my nipples pebble. His scent of crisp linen and cologne overwhelms me and I want nothing more than to be surrounded by him. I've never been more happy about the lack of that arm sling than in this moment when he snakes his other arm around my neck and one around my back and carefully pulls me flush against him. "I'm going to love you, and then I'm going to make you pay for toying with me all day." The sound of promise in his voice causes heat to pool in my core.

And he's back.

The doors open and he turns, leaving me in a puddle on the floor. I don't know what I look forward to ... the punishment or the love.

"You coming?" Jackson calls over his shoulder.

Oh, I hope so.

I smile and when I turn to close the door, I feel his heat against my back. "Games are over," Jackson says against my neck as his mouth finds purchase against my shoulder. His mouth moves slowly as he rains kisses against my exposed back.

Sensually, he moves the straps from one side down, giving him the access he wants, and my hands press against the door. "Stay like this," Jackson commands when I try to turn.

"I want to feel you," I reply in a whisper. It feels so good being cocooned by his warmth. His arms give me safety like they always do. With him, I'm stronger—we're stronger.

Jackson grips my wrist holding it above my head and his other hand wraps my arm around his neck giving him control. I could easily break from his hold. The hand that holds me is his bad arm and I know he doesn't have much strength, but I know he needs this. The feeling of some kind of power when his life has been anything but in control. "I'm not asking. Stay put." His voice is steel wrapped in velvet.

His hands lower to my hips and his hand snakes up my shirt as he pulls it up over my head.

"God, you're beautiful."

"You're not so bad yourself," I reply over my shoulder.

He kisses his way from my shoulder to my neck. Moving slowly until he reaches my mouth. Jackson's hand grips my head and he pulls me into him. I turn as much as possible into the kiss. My brain ceases to exist as I spin and clutch myself to him and he winces.

"I'm sorry," I say as he grips his leg that's resting on the chair. "I just—"

"Shut up and kiss me," he says as he grabs me and slams his mouth on mine.

And I do. I kiss him relentlessly. Pouring myself into him and taking all he gives me. When our mouths collide, everything else fades away.

I feel his hands twine up my back as he unhooks my bra and my breasts fall free. His hands cup me and gently massage them while rolling my nipples in his fingers before pulling on them. I gasp as pleasure fills my body and I struggle to keep upright.

Jackson grips my hand and pulls me along while maneuvering himself through the apartment into his bedroom. "As much as I'd love to fuck you against the wall again," he smiles while tugging me to him, "I don't think I'm strong enough for it yet. So get on the bed."

I grin while unbuttoning my shorts and let them fall to the ground exposing myself to him. "I'm sure you'll find a way to make it up to me," I say as I hook my fingers in my purple thong and slowly slide it down. "Won't you?" I watch his pupils dilate and his eyes rake my body.

"Fuck yeah I will. Now, stop talking."

When he's like this I feel incredible. Every part of me lights up and I come to life. He elicits this power and raw sensuality from me. I feel bold, beautiful, and more than anything—enough. There's never a time I feel as though I'm lacking with him.

"Tonight, nothing else exists but us," Jackson says as he takes his shirt off.

Now it's my time to stare. Even with his scars, he's perfect. If anything, they make me want him more. Jackson wears his wounds and lives. It reminds me of all that he is and how I wouldn't change a thing. Does it scare me that he could return overseas? Of course. To know the man I love could go and possibly not return scares me more than I care to admit. But when I spoke to Natalie last week, she said something that spoke to my soul. She said, "Even if I could go back and tell Aaron not to go, I wouldn't. This is who he was. He was a soldier, a fighter, a hero, and he needed this. It fed his world. The fact that someone else didn't die and he had to bear that cross—it's what he would've wanted."

Jackson's deep voice breaks my thoughts, "Catherine, stay with me. Only me." He links our fingers and pulls me to the bed.

I climb up and settle on my side while he gets situated so he's facing me. His fingers glide up and down my ribs as we gaze at each other.

"What are you thinking?" I ask.

"About us, about how I wasn't sure I'd ever have you back again." Jackson's voice grows shaky at the end and I close my eyes.

"I think somehow we'd have found a way. But promise me you'll never walk away like that again."

"You don't ever have to worry about that. I'm not going anywhere," he says as our lips touch. Our tongues meet and my hands roam his glorious body.

My fingers trace the ridges on his arms then around to his back as we explore each other slowly and completely. There's no rushing. We savor each other as if this is our last time—or first.

The feel of his hands on my stomach causes the moisture to pool as I envision him going lower. "Jackson," I moan as his hand sinks lower and he rubs small circles on my clit.

I grip his cock in my hand and begin to stroke him, feeling him grow against my touch. "I want to feel your mouth wrapped around my dick," Jackson says against my neck as he thrusts a finger into my pussy.

The sound of my groan reverberates through the room as I imagine taking him. Giving him pleasure while he's merciless to my touch. Knowing I have the physical ability to do just that, I move and feel his loss inside, but I grow even wetter preparing for what I'm about to do. "You asked for it." I smile when he quirks his eyebrow and leans on his back.

Holding the base of his cock, I lick him from root to tip, enjoying the way the muscles tighten in his legs as I run my tongue around the top. His hands grip the sheet as I continue to torment him, refusing to take him into my mouth. I palm his balls and roll them in my hand and he thrusts upward. Once again I rim my tongue before taking him deep in my mouth.

"Yes ..." Jackson hisses when I hollow out my mouth. His hand threads in my hair as I sink back down taking him into my throat. "Fuck, you feel good."

I take my time and tease him, enjoying every sound or word that escapes him. It spurs me on, wanting to give him the pleasure he always makes me feel. I bob my head and his grip tightens letting me know he's starting to lose control. I pull up and release him from my mouth, needing to finish what we started together. "I want to feel you," I say breathlessly.

"Lie down."

"That's not a good—"

"Lie down, Catherine. I'm going to love you this time," Jackson says as he cradles my head in his hands. "Now, let me."

Against my better judgment, I lie on my back. He slowly

and carefully measures each movement, climbing on top of me. This is the most weight he will have put on his arm since the shooting. The fear is evident in my eyes and he smiles letting me know he's okay.

"If it becomes too much, do you promise you'll tell me?" I ask him, trying to quell my nerves. I don't want to see him back in the hospital because he needed to prove something to himself.

"It's always too much with you, baby." He lowers his lips to mine. "You make me lose control because I can't think of anything else but you." Jackson's tongue traces the shell of my ear as he continues to seduce me with his words. "When I'm inside you, all I feel is your heat, I feel your breaths, and I fucking love every second. Now," Jackson pauses as I feel him start to enter me, "I'm going to make you come so hard you see stars. Hang on, baby." He thrusts forward before I have a second to consider what he said and all I feel is him. I'm filled by him and it's heaven.

"God, I've missed you," I say. Even though we've been together a few times, there's been a part of him holding back. Not now, though. He's everywhere, the energy around us, not allowing me to see or feel anything but him.

Jackson moves slowly as he hovers and pushes deeper. "Look at me."

My eyes shift to his and it's suddenly hard to breathe. He rocks back and forth while staring into my eyes as we become one in every sense of the word. Our souls touch, and moisture builds in my eyes from the pure beauty of the moment. Before the tears can descend he kisses them away and I fight the urge to sob. I'm so overcome with emotion I feel as if my heart is going to beat right out of my chest.

His mouth lowers and he kisses me. I close my eyes and feel everything. The love, the anger, the hurt, and I give myself permission to feel it all. I know he has me and won't let me fall. Jackson will keep me safe even if it's from myself.

"You're fucking made for me. You feel so good, I can't think."

He moves sinuously, driving me higher and I fight the emotional high as well. The pleasure becomes overwhelming, but I don't want it to end. Every second with him feels incredible. Each thrust of his hips fills me with love.

After a few minutes, I can't fight the need to release any longer. I start to set the pace for him from the bottom. I grind my hips as he starts to moan and shake subtly. We're both so close to the edge.

"So close. I'm so c-close," I stutter as I rotate my hips cautiously.

"I'm not going to last much longer," Jackson says through clenched teeth as the sweat builds on his forehead.

Gliding my own hand lower, I start to circle my clit and Jackson groans when he realizes what I'm doing.

"Fuck, Catherine."

"I'm coming. Now," I cry out and fall over the edge as Jackson grunts and finishes with me. He lies on top of me panting and we're both covered in sweat, but I couldn't care less in this minute. I could stay like this forever with him.

"You ready, babe?" I call out to Jackson who is purposely taking his sweet ass time.

"No, I think we'll have to just skip it."

"Jackson Cole! You lost the bet. You agreed to the terms, now it's time to take me to see *The Lion King*." I saunter into his bedroom and he's lying on the bed.

I'm gonna beat him.

"Are you serious right now?" I ask staring at him fully dressed, incredibly sexy, and almost good enough to pass up on the musical. But not quite.

Jackson groans and rolls to his side, "I'm injured. I can't

go."

"You're going to be injured. The doorman said the cab is waiting."

His lip juts out and it's so cute, I lean forward and kiss him. He makes me smile even when I want to slap him.

"What was that for?" he asks with a grin. "Are you telling me you're going to admit you fixed this stupid game and now you're coercing me into this awful play with grown men dressed like animals?"

I laugh and shake my head. "We're going."

Jackson grunts and I suppress a laugh. He's so cute when he's not driving me insane. "You know, I was shot. Three times. I think this should score me some sympathy points."

I tap my forefinger on my chin. "Let's see. Since you're so injured, I think you're right."

His face beams but then he narrows his eyes. "I don't believe you."

"And here I thought you were dumb. Let's go." I grab my purse and straighten my dress.

Finally, he gets up and looks at me, smiling. There are times where just one look can melt me to my core—this is one. "What?"

"You're beautiful. Come kiss me, woman."

With a smile on my lips, I walk over and press them to his. Gingerly, Jackson's calloused thumb grazes my cheek and I shiver. His touch elicits so many emotions and I pray we never lose this. I want to get lost in him.

"Enough stalling. Come on, Muffin."

Jackson says something under his breath but I expect it. We exit the apartment and when we get to the street, there's a black town car waiting.

"I figured the cab wouldn't want to wait in case I was able to talk you out of this," Jackson explains with an easy tone.

I shrug and get in the car, "Too bad it didn't work."

We settle in the car and Jackson and I talk about the

musical a little. Apparently he has no clue what to expect. He's never been to Broadway before.

"I don't understand how you can live in Manhattan and never go to the theater."

"I work. A lot," he retorts and pulls me against his side. I mold to him and close my eyes feeling the way his rough hand rubs tiny circles on my arm. "Just think, we could be home. Possibly naked. But you wanted to see men in tights."

The giggle escapes my mouth before I can hold it back. "This isn't the ballet, although, if you're interested in seeing it, I'm sure I can get tickets."

"Not on your best day, sweetheart."

We pull up to the theater and Jackson grumbles play- fully. I've never considered myself a sadistic person, but I'm thoroughly enjoying his discomfort. It could be that if I lost he wouldn't have hesitated at all. I would have had to pay for it, and knowing Jackson, he would've found other ways than just no name calling.

"Muffin?" He looks up and his lip curls but then he smiles. "Time to find out about the circle of life."

"How long are these things?"

"A few hours."

"*Hours?*" Jackson asks disbelievingly. "As in more than one?"

I laugh and he pushes the walker forward. "Yes, babe. Like two or three."

Jackson and I find our seats and get comfortable. As much as I'm happy to be here, there's so much stuff I need to get done for the launch in a few days. I don't have much time and I've spent a lot dealing with personal things.

"Hey," Jackson pauses and tilts my chin toward him. "What's wrong?"

I smile and softly shake my head. "Nothing."

"If I have to be here, you're going to be happy." His lip curls and one eye closes.

Leaning into my seat, I give myself a mental break. Everything will be fine. Right now, I have the man I love sitting at my side and he took me on a date.

"I'm happy. How could I not be? I won."

He groans and takes my hand in his lap. "Do I get dinner after this?" I ask.

"No, but I did sign us up for the next 5k in town."

I gasp with my jaw hanging. "I'm not running."

"Oh, but you are. While I was paying for these lovely tickets, it popped up as an ad. I knew you'd want to support me the way I'm suffering—I mean, enjoying—what we're doing now." He rubs his hand on the stubble on his chin.

"I didn't lose a bet."

"Neither did I, yet here I am." Jackson smiles and sits back in his chair.

As the first act begins, Jackson's arm slides around my back and he pulls me close. I nestle into his side and kiss his neck. "Thank you," I whisper.

"Don't thank me yet," Jackson jokes quietly.

The show carries on and I look over at Jackson who laughs at Rafiki's antics and I would swear I saw a tear in his eyes when Mufasa dies. Of course I'll never be able to get him to admit it, but I will sure as hell taunt him with it.

The second act is being called and Jackson spent all of intermission explaining why it would be so much fun if we left early.

"That three-mile run is going to be so much fun."

"You can't make me run."

Jackson leans forward and his warm breath blows across my neck. "I can make you want to run."

"You'd have to do something pretty bad to make me run. Like lie or cheat," I smile waiting for a witty response.

Jackson's eyes flash with fear but he recovers quickly enough that I'm not sure that I saw it. Goosebumps form and my stomach tightens. I don't know what to call the sudden wash of emotion. But I can't help but worry there's something lurking.

The lights go out and the stage lights up. I shake off the ominous feeling and I'm lost in the beauty of the colors, the way they brought the African grasslands to life in New York. Jackson and I hold hands through the show and I feel peace. Everything in my life feels right. I have a man I love desperately and he loves me back. I have a job I love more and more each day. And I have amazing friends and Neil is out of my life.

Things are good, and I'm truly and blissfully happy. There's a small part nagging at me telling me not to get too comfortable, but I've been guilty of overreacting before. I suppress it and focus on the good.

chapter

fifteen

*S*HIT.

Of all the days to be running late it had to be today. The press launch is in two hours and Taylor is making sure everything is in order before we have to leave. I'm running around the office like a madwoman and she's running out the door to get to Raven to set up.

I continue to check through emails and the seating charts so I know who's who and which companies will give Raven the boost they need.

"Knock, knock." I look up and see one of my bosses standing in the door.

"Mr. Cartright, please come in." This is the absolute last distraction I need this morning.

He smiles and enters, looking around at the controlled chaos that is my office. "The press release for Raven is today, correct?"

I nod and grab the file I had opened and place it in my briefcase. At least today he's seeing me at my best. I have a deep crimson, knee-length dress, my hair has large curls cascading down my back, and my makeup is camera ready. "Yes, sir. We're happy to get this off the ground, and then of course we have the party tonight. Will you be attending?" I ask already knowing he won't be. The partners go away for a sales meeting in Bermuda every year at this time. It's really a huge golf retreat that they write off as a business meeting. I made the mistake of going once and was subjected to driving their drunk asses around in a golf cart for three days. To guarantee that doesn't happen again, I try to book this month with anything I can.

"My flight is tomorrow, but when we return on Friday, the partners would like to meet with you. We've been highly impressed at how you've handled the Raven account. You were able to change the tone of the company in a short amount of time, even with Mr. Cole's near death experience," Mr. Cartright says.

"Thank you, I'm glad everyone is happy." I'm beaming at his praise, and also wondering what this means for the promotion that has been on the table for what seems like forever. Taylor mentioned that Elle's last account didn't renew their three-month contract and the rumors are she is out of the running.

"If all goes well today, Catherine, I think you'll find yourself sitting in a very lucrative new position." He winks and strides out of the office.

As fantastic as his pep talk might be, I needed that distraction about as much as I need Jackson's ten phone calls reminding me of what he wants done. We agreed it is best that in front of the camera, he is commanding and doesn't appear injured. Tonight at the party, he'll be able to blend and it will be much easier for him to remain sitting without anyone noticing.

My phone dings again.

Jackson: Are you avoiding me?

Me: No, I'm working. I will call you in the cab so you can micromanage a little more.

Jackson: I'm not micromanaging. I'm supervising. From home.

Me: Whatever you need to tell yourself to help you sleep at night.

He's driving me nuts.

Jackson: I'd rather help you at night.

I laugh and throw my purse in my bag. Grabbing the files and my speech, I head to Raven for part one of my very long day. Once in the cab, I give him that promised call and allow him to say what he needs so he can relax.

"Hey, baby." Jackson's voice sounds strained.

"What are you doing? You sound out of breath."

Jackson grunts, "I was just moving something."

"Seriously?" I ask incredulously. Does he think he has some kind of magical healing powers? "You're supposed to be resting, and you have the event tonight."

"Look, I'm sitting here watching this on the damn computer. Cut me some slack."

I lean my head back trying to understand, yet wanting to crawl through the phone and smack some sense into him. "Please, I'm begging you. Relax, rest, and no moving furniture, cooking, or anything else that can risk any injury."

"I'll do my best."

"I'm almost there. If you have any questions, call Taylor. She will have her phone on her, but once I get on stage, you won't be able to change the outcome of anything. Trust me to do my job."

He gives a long sigh. "I will. I'll see you later. You're coming home to change, right?"

I smile thinking of the dress sitting in the guest room. It's a deep purple, one-shoulder, satin dress. It's tight in the body and then flows out but pulls up every so many inches, accentuating my curves. It took my breath away when I saw it. Paired with my silver, jeweled shoes, I can't wait to put it on. "Yes, I have to get my dress and pick up my hot date. Even though you can't really be my date."

The cab stops and I hear Jackson mumbling about firing me so he can have his girlfriend.

"I love you," I say, throwing some money and trying to exit the car.

"I love you too," he says and I smile at the petulant tone he has when he doesn't get his way.

I disconnect the call, and before I can step out of the cab, Taylor and Danielle are at my side firing off information.

"Everyone's ready. Everything's in order. You have the intro, then Danielle will present part of the slides. After she wraps up, you can do a Q&A and we're done." Taylor speaks so fast I have to really focus to hear everything.

"Breathe. It's all going to be great. Everyone is aware of what needs to be done. Start gathering the press into the large vestibule and we'll start in about ten." I smile, putting on my best everything-is-just-fine face.

Most of us call this our camera persona. I'm polite, witty, and always smiling. My cheeks usually hurt for a full day after any press or photo junkets. I'm ready to make Jackson and my bosses proud. This promotion is so close I can taste it, and my contract with Raven will be over soon, and then I won't have to worry about the morality of dating a client. Luckily, we've managed to keep things low profile and the people who do know have been extremely supportive.

"Ready?" Danielle says at my side as we both plaster on our smiles and open the door into the launch.

There's a small stage and a podium, with bright photos of the new products with a sheet over them for the actual unveil. My adrenaline spikes as the excitement grows. This is the part of the job I love. I command the press and all of my hard work shows in this moment.

"Good morning, thank you all for being here," I begin with my speech.

After a few minutes of introductions and going over the booklet they were given, I hand it over to Danielle for her portion of the presentation. I'm impressed with her. We spent hours going over camera posture and when to pause to allow maximum attention. Taylor and I prepped her for anything we could think of, ensuring she was comfortable.

She hands the microphone back over to me and I brace myself for any questions. This is the one part of the press conferences I despise. You can prepare all you want, but you can't predict the way the questions will go.

The first hand rises and I call on her.

"Ms. Pope, can you tell us a little about when the product will be available in stores?"

"We expect the rollout to begin in the next three months. The product has been tested and has been sent to mass production." I smile and call on the next hand that's raised.

A short woman with red hair asks, "How do you feel this product differs from the others in the market?"

"This product line is made with all natural ingredients. There are no fillers and Raven is able to keep the prices competitive with what some call over-the-counter makeup lines. You're getting high quality for a bargain price."

I field a few more questions regarding the price point.

Taylor signals it's time to close, since we want to keep this brief and exciting.

There's time for one more question. "Yes, Miss?" She's blond with beautiful features, her eyes are wide as she realizes I'm calling on her.

"Thank you for taking my question." I nod and she reads off an index card. "Can you tell us how Mr. Cole is handling the company considering his injuries?" I'm surprised it took so long for someone to ask.

"He's doing well. Mr. Cole has stayed in contact with his staff and ensured there has been very little disruption to the company during his recovery," I say as confidently as possible and begin to wrap up but she cuts me off.

"That's great, but the company has had a vast amount of change in the past year. What about the fact that the company's dealt with two new CEO's in eighteen months, with Mr. Cole's wife no longer controlling the company, and the last CEO resigning so suddenly? How is Raven coping with this revolving door of leadership?"

And the floor falls out from under me.

Did she just say "*wife*?"

"I'm sorry, can you repeat the question?" I say trying to catch my breath while appearing completely in control.

"With the company undergoing so many changes, with different CEOs, understandably first when Mrs. Elliott-Cole departed, but then another quick change of hands ... How are the staff handling yet another catastrophe?"

My heart falls to the pit of my stomach. I feel dizzy. Everything around me becomes hazy and I grip the podium, trying to stay upright. He wouldn't do this to me, would he? Would he hide a marriage? How? A wife? Is he still married? The questions bombard me one after another as I try to focus on the people in front of me.

I hear a throat clear from behind me and I realize I haven't answered the question. "This question would probably be best answered by Ms. Masters. She's been an employee through these transitions." I manage a half-mangled smile and the pity in Danielle's eyes says it all.

It's true and she knows I didn't know, which means he deliberately kept it from me.

Married.

I rush off the stage before Danielle finishes her answer. I'm going to be sick. Taylor rushes over with a glass of water and ushers me out the back. I slump in a chair, trying to get a grip on my thoughts.

What the fuck just happened?

"Cat? Are you okay?" Taylor asks, probably knowing I'm so far from all right.

"Married?" I ask no one.

She rubs my back as I try to hold back the bile building in my throat.

"There's no way he's still married, Catherine. You've been with him for how long now?" Taylor says as I push to my feet.

"No? I know nothing. No one ever mentioned a *wife*, Taylor!"

"Maybe because there isn't one. We researched and nothing ever mentioned a wife," she tries to rationalize.

My hand flies over my mouth as I try to stifle the scream threatening to escape. "The name. Elliott. Do you remember? All we found was the single name. There was nothing about a first name or a hyphenated name."

"The press would have different sources, but I don't know. No one ever mentioned a wife? Wouldn't Jackson have told you?" Taylor asks as she suddenly goes still.

She tries to reassure me but I can't be here. I can't think. I can't breathe. The walls are closing in and I look down the hall at his office. The place I sat with the purple furniture, it all starts to click. The vague answers, the photos in Virginia. So much information that he must have buried about his wife. How convenient. I'm a fool. A fucking idiot, who trusted him—and he's a liar. I warned him that I'd never take this road again. I guess he really didn't care or believe me.

After everything, how? I grip my hair and try to calm myself.

"Catherine?" I hear Danielle behind me. "I didn't know—" She stops when I look up at her with tears swimming in my eyes. "You should talk to him."

"No one thought I should know this? As his publicist? As his fucking girlfriend? How could everyone let me go into this blind? You know what ... I don't want to know. It wasn't your job to tell me."

Between my phone and Taylor's the ringing has been non-stop.

I've seen her silence it twice but as the screen lights up again, she puts the phone to her ear. I know it's him. He was watching the press conference on his computer. He got the show of his life—I hope he enjoyed it.

She responds in short answers and I hear him grow more

frustrated through the line. Taylor hunches down in front of me. "Cat, it's him," she puts her phone out for me to take. He must not know how to take a hint.

I grab the phone. Press the end button and hand it back.

"I'm already gone," I say and grab my bag heading out the door.

chapter

sixteen

I ARRIVE BACK at my office refusing the fifteen phone calls and unknown number of text messages from Jackson before finally shutting my phone off.

Fuck him.

There's nothing to say at this point. I'm way too angry, hurt, and disappointed to hear his voice. This isn't a conversation we should have over the phone anyway. This is a conversation we should've had months ago.

Taylor comes in and shuts the door. "I've lost count of how many times the line has rung, Catherine. You should at least—"

"No," I say with no room for discussion. "I'll deal with him when I'm ready. And I'm not ready. I have a party to go to tonight for a client. I need to make sure the caterers are on track." My voice begins to tremble as the emotions begin to surface. No. I won't do this. Not today. I need to be in my show mode dammit. "There's a lot I need to do."

Damn him.

Taylor nods and I look away as she exits my office. I will not break down until I've handled my job. It's all I have anymore.

Two hours fly by and I can't put off going to get my dress any longer. There's no way I can skip the party I've planned. I always knew this was a possibility. That's the part that kills me—I knew better. My mind is filled with a thousand questions and none of them I want the answers to. I hoped the time at the office would help me think straight. All it's done is make me more angry and upset.

I was honest. I told him everything. I explained how I couldn't live through this again, couldn't – wouldn't – put up with dishonesty. All this time he had, and not one word. We played that stupid game with all the questions, we spent hours in the park, the hospital ... all chances he had ... besides the obvious "Oh hey, I have a wife" gambit.

My nausea churns as I start to think over all the times we made love and he could still be married. There are so many questions about where she is. Are they separated? Divorced? I can't get my head to stop spinning. I hate the amount of self-doubt he's managed to cause with one question.

I can't delay this anymore. I have to get my dress. Maybe I'll pick up a date along the way and let him see how it feels— maybe Ashton knows someone. This shouldn't be like this. I shouldn't be sitting here thinking this. The plan for tonight was not *this*.

"I'll see you later?" I ask Taylor knowing she and her boyfriend are both attending tonight.

She looks up with wide eyes. "Cat, I-I think," she begins but looks away. "I think you should wear your hair down," Taylor says and I give the best smile I'm able to fake at this point. I know she wanted to say something about the Jackson situation, but being the friend she is, she stayed loyal—unlike some people.

"I'm going to get my dress and then I'll be at the hotel," I say as I stride toward the elevator.

Time to deal with my client.

All the strength and preparation on the subway has completely left me as I stand outside his apartment building shaking. Lies, a relationship built on lies.

I look at my phone and it flashes his face as he calls again. He'll talk to me soon enough.

Again it rings.

This time it's Ashton.

"Hi." I answer the phone but my voice sounds lifeless.

"What the fuck is going on? Jackson called me twice and then Mark called. Are you okay? They said they didn't know where you were." She sounds frantic. Bet they didn't tell her why.

"I'm not going to get into it now but expect me home tonight. So please don't taze me or hit me with a bat at two a.m. After the launch party is done I'll probably crash."

"What? I don't understand. All Jackson said was he needed to talk to you, but you wouldn't answer his calls. Why would you come home?"

I huff and shove away my disgust. "I need to handle this fucking party and tomorrow when I wake up, we'll talk. I love you, Ash. But I have to go to work."

She lets out a long breath. I know she needs more information, but right now, I don't have it. "This doesn't sound like you, but answer me this: On a scale of one to ring the alarm, what are we at?"

"Let's say the alarm is ringing and I'll need someone to break the fucking bell."

"Okay, great, so we're talking nuclear. And you're sure you don't want to talk to me now?" she asks carefully.

"If you want a preview of what our conversation will be, watch the press conference for Raven. Be sure to get some popcorn, because it's quite a show."

"Okay, but that doesn't explain where Jackson comes in."

"Oh, but it does. Ashton, I need to pretend my life didn't go from amazing to shit. Let's just say its broken and there isn't a way it can ever go back together. I have to go to this fucking party and smile, so please don't make me cry right now," I say, trying to control my emotions, but my voice slips when I explain how broken we are. There's no fixing this.

"So we're talking about calling in Gretchen and removing

all knives from the apartment. Got it. I love you, Cat. I'm always on your side. I know you don't want to hear it, but nothing is ever broken beyond repair." Ashton's voice is the only thing keeping me from falling to the ground right now.

I take a step into the building and hold on to the knowledge that this won't kill me. I'll survive this.

"I love you and I'll see you tomorrow."

Entering the elevator, I find a way to get myself under control. I slip into another role. The one where I'm on stage and need to perform. I can do this. I just need to breathe and remember I can fall apart later. This entire night will need to be an Oscar-worthy performance, only I won't be accepting any awards. Because in the end no one wins anything here.

I hesitate at the door as the turmoil rages like a war within. I've been living here for almost a month and this makes me question everything. Do I knock? Do I use my key? I'm not sure of anything since I no longer feel like I belong here.

Fuck it. He didn't really give a shit about boundaries, so why should I?

"Catherine?" Jackson calls out when the door closes behind me as he comes around the corner. "Catherine, please."

I put my hand up letting him know I can't listen to him. The sound of his voice is making me feel ill. "If you want me to remain civil at all, you'll shut up. You'll find a way to respect me in this moment and allow me to get through this. I'm getting my things and I have to work tonight, Mr. Cole."

He stops and I can see how much my words affect him. "You're not even going to let me talk, are you?"

"No. The time for talking was months ago. Today, I'm going to fucking work!" I skirt past him into the guest room and slam the door. My back rests against it and I slide down with tears streaming silently. Dammit, I wasn't going to cry.

He's hurt me so much more than I can ever explain. Seeing him standing there with the pain in his eyes just shattered anything left inside of me. He lied to me. Even if he's not married anymore, he never told me. All this time. The months, the countless nights I've been at his side, never once did he mention it. Not only that, his friends and family never said a word. I gave him my non-negotiables and he broke one anyway. I feel like a damn fool.

I hear his walker moving back and forth on the other side of the door. It stops and then moves again. He knocks twice but I don't answer. I need to get ready. Removing the dress from the bag, I wipe the tears from my face. No more crying. Show mode time. I put the beautiful dress on and pin my hair up allowing the low back to be seen. Trying to fix my make-up is more of a challenge. Each time I apply eyeliner, another tear falls without permission. After a few minutes and a lot of counting to ten, I manage to make myself look decent. It took a shit-ton of concealer and waterproof mascara.

Once my shoes are on, I open the door and he's leaning against the wall staring at me. His blue-green eyes are hollow as he takes me in. "You should get ready, Mr. Cole. You have an event in an hour."

"Stop it," Jackson says, taking a step toward me, but I retreat. His eyes go wide when he sees my reaction. "I tried to tell you a hundred times."

"Apparently, you didn't understand what I asked from you. I don't want to fucking hear it!" I scream and close my eyes releasing a breath through my nose. "I won't have this conversation with you tonight. I have a job to do and you've had plenty of chances to talk before. You need to let me go to this party and smile, telling everyone how wonderful you are. Even though right now I want to punch you in the face."

"Punch me, hit me, I don't care, but we need to work this out. You walk away tonight I know you're not coming back. I can't—" Jackson pleads but I cut him off as if he didn't speak.

"I have to look charming, happy, and not like my boyfriend just destroyed my entire world. Not like the man I spent weeks by his bedside praying he would live just single handedly killed me. Or like the hero I thought I had turned out to be a traitor. Does that sum up the emotions I'm feeling right now? Do I need to go on? No? Good. Go put your tuxedo on. If you could do it in this room so I can pack my things, I would appreciate it."

Jackson stands there staring at me while I shake with anger. My jaw trembles as I try to regain an ounce of control. I turn so he can't see my further breakdown. Just being close to him makes my heart break.

"So this is it then?" He pauses and I nod. "Fine. Once again you're shutting me out. I can explain it all, but you won't listen."

I turn with wide eyes and gawk at him disbelievingly. "I'm going to pretend you didn't just say that. I won't let you blame me for this! Fuck you! You will *not* make me the bad guy here. It was on me last time. This one, Jackson, is all you! Lies of omission are lies. I don't even know what the fuck is the truth. Was any of it real? Did you mean *any* of it? Or was I just a game?" My voice rises with each word. I'm seething. How dare he try to put this on *me*.

"Did it feel like a game, Catherine? Do you really believe any of the bullshit you're saying? You know me!" His voice drops into a gruff whisper. "You're the only one who knows me, dammit. Don't shut me out."

My eyes narrow into slits as the anger boils through my veins. "I don't know you at all! I thought I did. Guess the joke is on me. I warned you. I told you that day in the hospital what I needed from you. I guess your loyalty lies with your *wife*." I step forward wanting to slap him, hurt him like he's hurt me. "Go get ready before we say things we're going to regret." I turn and grab my bag to start filling it. Fuck it, at this point I couldn't give a shit if I have to buy everything new.

"Wow, okay, I see how it is. You've already made up your mind without hearing my side."

"What were the only things I asked from you?" I raise my

hand and tick them off one at a time. "Fidelity, well, that's shot to shit. Honesty, hmmm, we can cross that one off. Loyalty, yup, another winner. So not only did you break one, no, you got all three down in one fell swoop. Good job, Jackson, you sure came out on top." I'm seething. The anger rolls off of me in waves.

"I never—you know what, you're going to make your assumptions regardless of what I say. You'll never know how much I wish I could go back and change things. One day when you learn everything, then you'll feel different." He shakes his head and enters the spare room.

"Doubtful."

When the door shuts, I rush to the bedroom and start grabbing anything I see that's mine. I need out of here, his scent is everywhere. Everything is a memory. I can't look at anything without seeing us. The bed where we made love last night, the couch where we watched movies and read books, the shower, the kitchen, the memories are everywhere and I can't take it. My breathing is heavy and I feel dizzy. Everything is happening so fast. How much more can one heart break before it's past the point of repair?

As I approach the front door with my bag, I hear his voice. "You're going to leave after everything, without even talking?" His voice cracks at the last word.

"Did you miss the press conference?" I refuse to turn and look at him.

"No, I saw it all."

"I figured, since you called a few hundred times. I guess you missed the part where I didn't want to talk to you. You want to talk now, but the months we've been together you failed to mention it. Instead you lied to me."

"I never lied. I didn't know how to tell you," he admits and I still have no idea what part he means.

Is he married? Is he divorced? Is she going to show up one day and he'll run off with her? I spin and look at him with tears threatening, "Well, here is an idea ... hey, Catherine, I know we're getting serious, but I'm married, or I was married, or whatever the truth is. You didn't do that though." I step forward and my voice is laced with venom. I'm seething and my world is crumbling around me. "Instead you let me fall in love with you, care for you, and find out like that!" I hold on to my stomach as the pain slices through me. "I trusted you. I loved you with everything inside of me. I put my career on the line for you—for us. But you kept a marriage from me. Are you still married? Don't answer that. It's not my business anymore because we aren't anything." Jackson's eyes close as he stands there listening to me go on.

"I should've told you. I know this! Don't you think I wish I could go back and tell you about Madelyn?" he says with anger radiating off him.

I gasp and my hand flies over my mouth. God, she has a name.

"Why are you doing this? I don't want to know her fucking name! I don't want to know anything. I can't do this tonight. As your publicist, I advise that with your next PR company, you should be upfront so they don't stand before the press and look like a fucking idiot. Not only did your girlfriend—well, ex-girlfriend—have to find out in the most embarrassing and humiliating way possible, but your publicist was thrown for a loop on camera. Now I have to go to work. My client needs me. That's what you are. You lost me in any other capacity. I'll see you at the party, Mr. Cole."

I turn on my heels and walk out the door. My heart may have just been left in his apartment, but I'm going to work and I don't need it. He can have it, since it's dead anyway.

chapter

seventeen

THE HOTEL IN midtown Manhattan is arranged perfectly while everything else in my life is a mess. I look around and want to leave already. This is the worst possible place for me, being in this room, all dressed up but feeling naked and exposed. I was on camera when I found it all out, everyone saw. But more than that, he ripped me wide open when we spoke.

I hear people moving around me but I don't see faces. "Cat, there's a small problem in the bar area." Taylor's hand touches my shoulder and I jump.

"Sorry, Tay. What did you say?" I close my eyes and dispel all my issues for the moment, willing myself to focus.

When I finally look up, Taylor smiles and repeats her previous statement. "The rooftop bar is claiming we didn't reserve it exclusively. I handled it, but I figured you'd want to know," she says and looks at me, waiting.

Everything is in slow motion.

"Catherine? Can you handle this?" she questions me.

"I don't know," I say, looking up into her eyes, begging her to help me in some way. I feel lost. "I'm going to need you to stay by my side."

"Is he coming?"

"I couldn't tell you. I assume he is, but please," I grip her wrists and plead, "Keep him away from me. I can't."

She twists to hold my hands in hers. "I think one day you'll see the strength you actually have. You're going to get through this, but I'll be by your side the entire night."

I attempt to smile but fail. "Thank you."

"You look beautiful, by the way." She releases my hands and grabs her phone and answers. "Yes, I'm aware but the contract states differently." She pauses letting the other person speak. "Oh, that's fine, but then I want a full refund." Another pause. "You seem to have me confused with someone who cares what your problem is. I'll either be getting a full refund or you'll secure the roof. Figure it out." Taylor disconnects the phone and I'm impressed.

"Well, looks like my sweet, timid assistant has found her New York attitude."

"After spending enough time around you, it was bound to happen. Besides, when you get this new job, I'm hoping I'll be moved up as well." She smiles and I make a mental note to make sure that happens.

"*If* I get the promotion."

"You'll get it. I believe in you."

A few guests start to filter in and when I glance around the room, making sure everything is running smoothly—I see him. He's sitting at a table watching me. I want to look anywhere else, but my eyes don't move. We assess each other unsmiling and unwilling to break the only connection we have right now. His eyes don't waver even as someone approaches him. The hurt radiates through me remembering why we're like this. This morning, the sight of him made my heart race, but right now it makes me sick. Refusing to give him any more of my attention, I turn my head and walk to the bar.

"What can I get you?" the bartender asks, wiping the granite counter.

"A lemon drop."

"Martini or drink?"

"Shot."

He looks at me with a brow raised. *Yes, I said shot.* If I'm going to spend the next however many hours in the same room as my *client*, I need a little liquid courage.

"One lemon drop shot coming right up."

"You know what, fuck it. Just give me a shot of vodka." No need to pretty it up.

The bartender turns and places the shot in front of me, and before he can say anything, I throw the shot back and savor the burn. At least I can feel it. The alcohol flows through me and warms me.

"Another," I demand, and instead of any commentary, he refills my shot glass. "Thanks."

Without wasting any time I take that shot and place the glass down.

This is going to be a long night.

"So you're going to get drunk?" I turn and see Taylor looking at me with wide eyes.

"That was so I'd be able to be in the same room as him. Is it hot in here?"

Taylor shakes her head, "I think that's the shots. You need to introduce everyone in five."

I nod and head back into the staging area behind the curtain. The party is meant to be a fun way for everyone to see everything and get to meet the members of the company. We wanted to show that as much as Raven is a corporation, they're more of a family. *Ironic.* It seems that statement is true in more than one way.

The room quiets and I take my place back on stage. I wonder what fun information I'll learn this time.

"Good evening and welcome," I smile somehow and hope it's sincere enough. *This is your job, Catherine. Keep it together.* "On behalf of Raven Cosmetics, we want to thank you for all being here to celebrate the launch of the new line. I'd like to introduce the CEO, so please put your hands together for Jackson Cole." I clap and wait for him to stand as Taylor hands him a microphone.

I close my eyes and try to block out the sound of his voice. "Thank you, thank you." He pauses and waits for the applause to end. "I wanted to personally thank you all for being here, and I'm grateful to be able to spend this evening with you as well. This product line has been something that we've worked on for a few years and are extremely pleased it's ready to be launched. Sometimes the timing isn't right," Jackson pauses and looks directly at me. "I wanted to be sure everything was in order before going forward and ensuring success." His eyes don't move from mine. This is not the speech I wrote for him.

Son of a bitch.

"There are many things I planned to say tonight, but I'm having trouble remembering them all." He chuckles and the crowd joins him. "This was never a company I thought I'd have a hand in. As life happens, things change. We have to make choices and they aren't always the right ones, but we have to live with that." He pauses and looks around the room. "Today was a great day for Raven and I appreciate you all being here. Please enjoy yourselves and we look forward to many more celebrations together." He raises his glass and everyone claps.

I stand there dumbfounded at his words spoken directly to me. He's mingling with the guests but manages to look over and cement me to the ground.

Hate.

Love.

Anger.

Pain.

Lies.

Swirling around like a funnel cloud in my heart. Each twist tears another piece of me to shreds. He continues to hold my gaze until I hear someone behind me.

"Come on, Cat." She grasps my elbow and pulls me over to the side.

I draw a deep breath and when I let it out, a sob breaks

free. Standing where no one can see me, I lose it. I fall apart. The tears stream down my face and Taylor pulls me against her.

"Oh my God." My breathing is short and I begin to hyperventilate. "I can't be here," I say aloud while I struggle to catch my breath.

"Go. I can handle anything that might come up here. Everything's basically done."

"I'm so sorry, Taylor." I hold my torso hoping to keep myself together long enough to get out of here without falling apart again. "Just being in the same room as him right now ..." I trail off when I see him standing in front of me.

"You're leaving?" he asks calmly but the hurt is lingering under his question.

I look at him up close for the first time since the apartment. His eyes are bloodshot and he's barely holding it together. "Why do you care?" I ask acerbically.

"Really?" Jackson scoffs.

"I apologize, Mr. Cole, that was unprofessional. I've done my job. My staff is more than capable of handling any issues."

Jackson pushes forward and I step back. Seeing me retreat, he stops and looks down. "Taylor, can you give me a moment with my publicist please?" Jackson says softly and I look at her, pleading with my eyes not to leave me. Instead she places a hand on my shoulder and exits the room.

He turns to me, "I know you want space, but I'm asking you to give me five minutes. I don't deserve it. I know that. But please, I need to explain."

A tear falls and I straighten myself to stand tall. "If you would've trusted me, none of this would be happening. I'd be sitting at that table, holding your hand, whispering about what we could do when we leave. Instead, I have mascara down my face, a dress I want to burn, and a broken heart. I don't have five minutes to give you tonight."

I grab my clutch from the chair and start to leave, but he

clasps my arm, stopping me. "Don't you get it?" I ask.

"I deserve a chance to explain."

"You're right. You did. A month ago. Instead, you kept something from me. You did what every other man in my life has done. In one second, you managed to prove you're no different. My father, Neil, hell, throw in my mother if you want ... none of them hurt me as much as you managed to. But instead I was *humiliated.* I was thrown in front of cameras and left to find out something like *that*—publicly. So while I'd love to let you explain, Mr. Cole," I sneer while wriggling my arm from his grip, "You had your chance." I turn on my heel without another word.

Each step I take I feel pain—physical pain. How does it hurt so bad?

"I never lied about how I feel," he calls out and I pause. "I love you, Catherine. I would walk through fire for you," Jackson says and my heart stops.

I turn and look at him. "You wouldn't have had to. I would've put out the flames before they reached you. Instead you managed to burn me yourself."

Seeing the agony spread across his face at my words nearly kills me. I wanted to love him, protect him, not destroy him—too bad he didn't want the same things.

"Okay, I know it's only six a.m., but I need you to wake up," Ashton says, rubbing my back.

"Are you for real?" I ask groggily as I look over at my clock, hoping she was lying about the time. "Ashton! It's six in the morning." I roll back over trying to hide my face.

"Yeah, well. I saw the press conference and I need you to talk to me."

I open one eye exasperated at my best friend. "I don't need to talk. I'm done."

"Is he married?"

"I don't know," I say and start to sit up.

"What do you mean you don't know? How the hell don't you know? What did he say?" She fires off questions so fast I can't answer. She stands and puts her hands on her hips. "Answer me!"

"Don't yell at me!" I say as I get out of bed and head into the bathroom. What is with all the people in my life and their damn demands?

When I come out of my bathroom, she's sitting on the bed with an apologetic look. "I didn't mean to yell, Biffle. I'm worried about you."

I sigh and sit on the bed next to her. Funny how I feel the need to comfort her. "I'll be fine—at some point. He lied to me, Ash. I don't know if he's married because honestly I was afraid of the answer. We were together for months, I was basically living with him, and he never told me. To find out like that—in a press conference—was horrific. I felt like an idiot."

"He's the idiot, Catherine." Ashton places her hand on mine.

"I'm done. Those are the only words I can say. There's no fixing us, because there is no us. I can't go through another relationship where lies and cheating are even an option. If he is married, then I was his mistress. If he's not married and is divorced, how could he keep that from me—or why did he think it wouldn't matter?"

She sighs and gives me a few moments. "I'm in no way defending him, because honestly I hate him right now and I never thought that would happen. I've always been on your side. But I really thought Jackson was the one for you. Knowing all your issues with abandonment and trust, maybe he was afraid if he told you, you'd run. Instead he pretty much guaranteed that you'd be pushed to run."

"Right, and by keeping his marriage a secret he obliterated any trust I had in him." I clutch my pillow to my chest. It hurts so much talking about this. I can't believe we're back here again. "Unless there's something more behind all of this like he's still in love with her. It makes no sense."

Ashton shrugs. "I can tell you he was frantic. He was hysterical on the phone trying to find you. Mark called me too. He said Jackson is a fucking moron and fucked it up."

The half laugh escapes me at Mark's assessment. "Yeah, I'd agree with him on both. But, Ash, he didn't tell me either. You know that's the other part I feel sick over. I was in that hospital for how long with his mom and Mark and no one ever mentioned it. Which leads me to believe they knew he didn't want me to know."

She sighs and squeezes my hand. "I don't know. I really don't. He had to know at some point you'd find out. You going to work?"

"I'm up. I might as well. I gave Taylor the day off, but I'm going to have to figure out how the hell to handle this fucking account. We have less than a month left in this contract, but I'm not sure I can work side-by-side with him." I stand up and pull the dress from last night up off the floor.

"Don't you dare let him win. You go into work and you handle him. Are you going to be okay?"

I wish it were that simple. I wish I had the courage to go in there and pretend seeing him doesn't hurt. That hearing his voice doesn't make me ache ... but it does. He's a part of me— far more than Neil ever was. Jackson was everything to me. I wanted to stand beside him, love him, give myself to him, and in a way I did.

"I'll do what I always do—survive."

A small smile paints Ashton's face and she scoots closer. "I'm really sorry. I think we should buy an island and stick these fuckers on it and pick them off one by one."

"*Survivor* for men," I chuckle. "There are so many things I'm upset over, but the biggest is he knew. He knew, Ash. I told him what I could handle." I run my hands through my hair. "I was crystal fucking clear and we spent countless nights together."

"He never even brought anything up?"

"All I can think is there were these tiny moments I felt like he was keeping something. Small things that didn't really add up, but I have a tendency to overthink things, so I was giving him the benefit of the doubt."

She sighs and wraps her arm around my shoulder. "Are you going to hear him out?"

"He owes me answers, that's for sure, but right now I don't want to see his face."

"I get that. I think you're justified in a few punches to the junk."

We both snicker. "I have to get ready." I kiss her cheek and head into the bathroom.

"You'll always have me!" she calls out.

"Oh, how lucky I am."

"Damn right you are," I hear her say as the door closes to my bedroom.

I take my time getting ready and put on a pink shift dress and white sandals. When I head out to the living room, Ashton's keys are gone and there's a note letting me know she wasn't planning to come home, but if I need her, to call and she'll be here. I love that girl.

Once in my office, I sit in my chair and look out the window, thinking about the mess my life has become once again. It's a constant battle. And it's exhausting and I'm tired of treading water—I want to float for a while. I ponder if this is what I need. Time alone—again. I look out and my mind drifts to Jackson. My heart clenches as my mind allows me to see him again right before I left him. I see the way his eyes held sorrow and he was desperate for me to listen to him. The pain we both were suffering in that moment. I replay it all as a tear drifts down my cheek.

chapter

eighteen

"CATHERINE."

I spin in my chair as I turn to see my boss standing there. "Mr. Cartright. I thought you were away." I quickly swipe the tear and stand up as he enters the office.

"One day you'll remember to stop with the 'Mr.' bullshit." He slaps his hand on the doorframe and his face falls. "Meet us in the conference room in five."

"Yes, sir."

Without another word he strides out of the office.

Fuck my life.

Did he see me stumble on camera? Does he know I left the party early? Did Jackson call and complain? He sure as hell didn't look happy to call me into the conference room. I grab my compact and fix my face as best as I can and head down the hall.

"Good luck, Cat," I hear Elle's shrill voice say as I pass her desk.

"Thanks." I smile and keep walking. I don't have enough patience for a verbal chess match with her today.

The conference room hosts the three partners of CJJ, the head of human resources, and the director of client relations. Well, this doesn't feel promising. My stomach rolls as the fear starts to travel through my body. *Keep calm,* I try to tell myself, but no one is smiling. I clear my throat and enter as they look up.

"Good morning, Cat. Please have a seat," Mr. Jennings says and motions to the chair.

Mr. Jennings is the oldest of the three partners. He's barely in the office anymore and when he is, everyone walks around not speaking. I've only dealt with him a handful of times, but he's always been cordial.

"Thank you."

I smile looking around the room and everyone's emotions are well hidden. I can't get a feel on what exactly is going on.

"Let's get to it, Catherine," Mr. Cartright begins. "The board has been talking and we're very impressed with how you were able to secure the Raven account. More than that, when we reached out to Mr. Cole, he had a lot to say regarding your work with the company." Mr. Cartright pauses and my heart stops beating.

He wouldn't.

Would he? Would he really hurt me this way? Ruin my reputation regarding work?

"Anyway," he continues breaking me from my inner meltdown, "He told us how you nailed down every aspect of the campaign and made sure everything was taken care of. You were on top of the press and the stock regarding his company during his life threatening shooting. He was impressed, and so are we." When he stops speaking, the partners smile at each other.

"Thank you. I'm happy the client was pleased," I say softly wishing he was still more than my client.

"The company is taking a new direction, and we're opening several satellite offices in the coming year."

"Wow. That's wonderful for the company."

"We think so too," Mr. Jeffries speaks for the first time. "Catherine, we want you to head up one of the offices. You've been instrumental to our growth and we think you'd be the perfect candidate for the new office in California."

"Oh!" I say, completely thrown off guard. Run an office? In California? "I don't know what to say." I let out a nervous laugh and look around. Talk about a curve ball.

"Well, there's a first," Mr. Cartright jokes and it helps ease the tension.

We spend the next thirty minutes going over the details of the new position and the generous pay increase. Ultimately, I would run the entire office and be able to take any of the staff I want from New York for support personnel or I can start fresh out there. The perks are great, and they're willing to supply me with a furnished apartment for six months until I find somewhere else or take over the lease.

I start to think of all the reasons I should go and all the reasons not to. They look at me expectantly and I begin to panic. My heart and my head are at war and the reality is I don't know why. "Do you need an answer today or can I have a day or two?"

Mr. Cartright nods with a smile. "We'd like an answer by the beginning of next week. There are a lot of things that need to happen and we would like to get the ball rolling quickly. Do you think that'll be a problem?"

"No, not at all." They stand and I follow suit. "I want to thank you all for this opportunity. I'm honored and will have an answer to you by Tuesday."

Mr. Jeffries is the first to shake my hand. "Think about it, Cat."

"I will."

Mr. Jennings smiles and exits the room, followed by the rest of the team. I lean against the table and let out a long breath. Wow. My mind is spinning. Everything I've worked for just came through. All my dreams of being an executive and now here it is.

"I fought hard for you," Mr. Cartright says behind me, startling me a little.

When I started at CJJ, I was his intern. He guided me

through the first few years and has always been my biggest supporter. "You've always had favorites." I smile the first genuine smile in days.

"No, but I know quality. You were made for this position. You're not married, no kids, I thought I was going to have to look for flights leaving today, not hold off. What gives?" he questions.

I sigh and look away from him. "It's a big move."

He smiles letting me know he doesn't quite believe me, but he doesn't probe further. "Sure it is." He clears his throat and raises his brow. "You haven't been the same for a few months."

"Life has been crazy," I reply.

"What's his name?" he asks suddenly.

"Mr.— " I start but he cuts me off with a wave of the hand.

"I swear if you call me 'Mr. Cartright' I'm going to throw something at you," he jokes.

"Sorry. Sean, it's a fantastic opportunity. But it's clear across the country. I need a day or two to digest it," I explain.

"Liar. I know you better than that, Catherine. I saw you a few weeks ago. You were floating around the office. Not even Elle could get you upset. Now, some might think you were just in a good mood but I know better. I remember what that look in your eyes was like a few years ago. So I ask again ... what's his name?"

Sean has been more of a friend than a boss most of the time, but again I broke company rules by dating Jackson. If I tell him, I could lose this promotion, but if I don't and they find out, I run the risk of the same fate.

"It's over now, so it doesn't matter."

"I've known you for a long time. I've mentored you, watched you grow and become a remarkable publicist. You're able to predict and plan for things that are unexpected, which is a rarity. I, however, am able to see through bullshit. You, my friend, are full of it right now."

I gape at him. I've been trying to keep myself in control.

My tears are only in private and I've been doing a damn good job at pretending. "I'm surviving."

"There's a saying I know you've heard about when things are over, but the bottom line is: it's never over until you decide it is. The question I guess I should be asking is is he worth giving up on this job?" Sean gives me a pointed look and turns, leaving the room.

I have three days to make a choice and right now the sun and the sand are looking really good. This is the job of a lifetime and here I stand conflicted. He would've been worth it, but he's a liar.

I head to my office and close my eyes but the nausea rolls through. This stress is going to kill me. My phone rings and I ignore it. There's too much going on in my head to talk to anyone. A few seconds later the text alert beeps.

Gretchen: I'm going to beat you. I hope you understand me. You went and saw Neil? Against my advice. Lucky for you I was informed the suit has been dropped.

Me: I love you.

Gretchen: Yeah, yeah ... you're an idiot but I love you too. Let Jackson know we're all clear.

Seeing his name causes my heart to squeeze and stutter. How can I be so upset with him and yet miss him?

Me: Sure thing.

The office phone rings and I grab it on the first ring. "Catherine Pope."

"I thought I'd get Taylor again." I hear his deep voice vibrate through the line and I gasp. "Don't hang up, please. You don't have to say anything, just listen to me."

My eyes prick at the sound of his plea. "I can't. Please, let me go."

"I'm not ready to lose you. There's no one else in my heart but you."

"It's not that simple."

"It *is* that simple, Catherine. I love you. I'm not married anymore. I wouldn't do that to you," Jackson says and my heart beats for a second and then it falters.

A brief sense of relief washes over me as I realize I'm not the other woman, but it doesn't erase the fact that he never told me. There were more chances than I can even name, and somehow it slipped his mind? No, he purposely kept this from me.

"I'm not angry anymore—I'm resigned. You broke my heart. You should've trusted me. I loved you with my whole being and should've heard this from you before anyone else. You had friends and family keep your secrets. What else have you kept from me?"

"Let's talk. Come home and we'll talk."

"It's not my home. There are some things going on here. I need to go," I say and hang up the line.

"Ashton," I call out as I enter the apartment. I sent her a text after the call with Jackson that I needed her to come home. If I do take this new position, it will affect her. She's a huge deciding factor for me. Honestly, she's the only thing holding me here at this point.

"In here!" she calls out from the kitchen. "I have pizza."

My stomach growls and I realize I haven't eaten all day. I've been sick to my stomach over everything. The new job, him, and now the idea of moving. It's a lot to process.

"Yes! My favorite." I smile and grab a slice. "I could eat pizza every day. This is the best pizza in Jersey." I groan and take another bite.

"Okay, so I knew pizza would butter you up, keep eating and remember how much you love me," she says and I immediately stop eating. This can't be good.

"What did you do?"

"Nothing. Mark called me," she says apprehensively.

I look at her wondering where she's going with this. "Okay? Point?"

"He said Jackson is a mess."

"His company is doing well. That was my focus."

"Catherine, we know that's not what he's a mess over," she admonishes.

I sigh and roll my eyes. "What do you want from me? I spoke with him today, there's nothing left for us. I can't trust him. Words are just words, Ash. He says he loved me ... but then he kept something pretty serious from me. He says he would've walked through fire for me, but he threw me in it instead. My heart can't take anymore. I need a fresh start. I need a new beginning, because all of this," I wave my hand trying to make my point, "Is too much."

She puts her hands up defensively. "Okay, I just didn't want to not tell you we spoke. So what's the emergency that I needed to be home to talk?"

"I got the promotion."

Ashton squeals and starts dancing around the kitchen. "That's amazing! What's the position?"

Here it goes.

"They want me to head up a new satellite office," I pause making sure she's listening, "In California."

Her face falls before she recovers. "Like the state ... across the country? Three thousand miles away?"

"The very one."

"Okay, that's a big move. Head the office though?"

"Yes, I would run the CJJ Public Relations office in California. I'd hire the staff, get things set up. It would obviously mean a huge raise and title. It's my dream job, Ashton," I say, chewing on my fingernail.

"It sounds fantastic. Are you going to take it?"

That's the million-dollar question. I want this so bad I can taste it. The idea of moving away becomes more and more appealing. A fresh start in L.A. It means leaving behind all my old baggage and allowing myself to breathe again. I can let go of the ghosts that haunt me here. The company obviously trusts that I can do this, and I can. I know I can.

"I think so. I mean, there's only one thing holding me back."

"What?" she asks, clueless that she's the one thing.

"You, you jackass!" I laugh.

Ashton looks at me and you can see the moisture building in her eyes. "I love you, Biffle, but seriously I'm not a factor. You need to take this."

"But I need to know you'll be okay." She's my best friend and I don't want to leave her high and dry. This is our home and I would never put her in a position that would hurt her.

"Hello! You're an ass! I'll be fine and you'll be hanging out with all the famous people. Oh! Maybe you'll become friends with Vin Diesel and you can hook me up. If that does happen, be warned—I'll be visiting monthly. Maybe they need an embryologist out there?" she smiles and pulls me into a hug.

I start laughing and rocking back and forth with her. "Only you would think somehow I'm going to be your matchmaker."

"I'm so proud of you. You're going to be amazing and you'll miss me, but that's normal." Ashton giggles and grabs the pizza, trying to hide the tears I saw in her eyes.

I come up behind her and nudge her hips. "I'm going to miss you."

"When do you think you'll leave?"

"Not sure, but they need my answer by Tuesday. But I think I'm going to take it. I have a shitty relationship with my mother, my father is dead, and you're all I have here. I think this'll be good for me. I mean, running an office. It's huge!" I say and try to reassure Ashton and myself.

"It *is* huge, but seriously you deserve it. I think they've been priming you for this position."

We move to the table and talk through all the pros and

cons. The only con we can come up with is her. I'll be making more money, in a gorgeous area, my apartment is paid for, and I'll be running an office. It's a no-brainer.

"I need to ask you this: if you and Jackson were still together—would you go?"

Chewing the inside of my cheek, I try to be honest because my gut reaction is yes, I would. That's the anger though. "I don't know. It would've been a hard choice, but if he didn't want me to go, I probably would've thought more on it. How sad is that, Ash? I would possibly give up my dream job for him." I feel stupid for even admitting it, but I loved him that much. He would've probably been my choice.

"It's not sad. What's sad is that this is where you're both sitting. He's miserable, you're miserable, he's going to Virginia and you're going to California."

That news causes my head to snap up. "What?"

She looks over and shoves food in her mouth. "Hmmm?"

"What do you mean he's going to Virginia?"

"Why do you care? You're over it, I thought."

"Don't be cute," I say, growing annoyed with her.

Ashton gets up and grabs the plate from the table. "That's not possible. I'm always cute."

"Right now I'd use another word," I grouse, wanting to know what she knows.

She leans in so we're eye to eye. "You shouldn't care if he moves to Siberia if you're so over it." She kisses my cheek and walks out of the room.

She's right though ... I shouldn't care—but I do.

chapter

nineteen

THE FOLLOWING WEEKS fly by. I inform Sean and the other partners I am definitely taking the job. We go over the timeline and they want me in California within the month. Which leaves me three weeks to get everything accomplished.

I was able to give Taylor two options since she was one of my big concerns. She could accompany me and become a publicist in the office with me, or she could stay in New York and take a smaller promotion. She and her boyfriend, well, now fiancé, decided to stay in New York where his job is. I keep catching her crying or refusing to pack up any of the things that are in my office. We're in the process of moving all my accounts over to her until they expire. The clients are already familiar with her, and I'm positive she can handle them.

"There's another delivery here," Taylor says and she brings in a huge bouquet of Stargazer lilies. I don't need to look at the card to know who it's from. I've gotten something to remind me of our time together every few days. "Should I throw these out?" she asks being the ever-supportive friend.

"No, I'll torment myself for a day or two." I smile and return to the emails I have to handle.

"Can I read the card?"

"Sure, I don't plan to," I say turning my chair around.

I hear her taking short breaths and spin around to see tears starting to form in her eyes.

"Cat, please read this."

My eyes close as the frustration starts to build. He won't stop. It's almost every day I get an email, text, card, or gift. "I can't read it. I leave in two weeks. Please take it," I plead and fight the urge to rip the card from her fingers.

I miss him so much it hurts.

Some days I want to cry, scream, fight, and run back to him. But I've allowed myself to be happy about where my life is going. I got the promotion I wanted and it's better than I originally thought.

I was an open book. I told him about Neil, my father, Piper ... hell, everything I could, but he kept his secrets. That's not the love I want. The love I want is kind, honest, patient ... not deceitful and hurtful. I know in my heart Jackson is nothing like Neil, but I can't help but draw the comparisons here.

"People make mistakes, mistakes don't make the people." Taylor pauses at my desk putting the card in her pocket. "If he didn't love you, or still think of you, none of these would be here." She looks around the room at the various flowers, the game of Battleship, the lighthouse statue, and the letters that sit on my desk.

My heart accelerates as I look at each item silently taunting me, reminding me of the good times we shared. Why can't he just go away? Why can't he let me go? He did this. He severed all the trust I had. Ripped me to shreds and now I've had enough.

Taylor waits expectantly and I grow angry. "So I go back to him and say what? 'Oh, by the way, I'm moving to California.'" I pause trying to rein in the sudden burst of emotion. "No, I'm leaving. I'm getting a fresh start, a second chance. I'm happy about this job and the move," I stubbornly insist and turn in my chair.

"Yeah, you're probably right. Let some other girl have a shot with a guy like him," she rebukes and sits in the chair with her arms crossed over her chest. "I mean, hell, if things don't work out with Quinn, maybe I'll give him a call." Taylor's brow raises and my mouth falls slack.

I look at this sweet girl with a heart of gold whose horns are now showing. I don't know whether to be proud or scared. "This is beneath you."

"What?" she scoffs. "Truth hurts, sister. I never saw you as happy as you were with him."

"Lies!" I burst out suddenly. "God! This is the part none of you are grasping. He *lied* to me! For months I sat by him, slept in his bed—a bed he probably shared with his *wife*." I close my eyes trying to shut out the memories flooding in. "Wife. Say that out loud and let me know how it goes down, because I want to vomit every single time. She has a name. Worse than that, he had other people keep his secrets."

"I'm not saying he was right."

"Then what are you saying? Because all anyone wants me to do is let him explain. But here's the thing, Tay, he can explain all day and it doesn't change the fact that I got this amazing job. I'm moving to California and if I was still with him, I probably wouldn't be. So in the end this is better for me!" I say exasperated.

Taylor stands looking at me with a weary expression. "I'm just worried. I don't want you to run away to California."

"I'm not running. I'm starting over—which I deserve. There's nothing here for me other than you and Ashton. I need to finish up here and then I have some conference calls tonight. Can you make sure the new files are in the box to go to California please?"

She nods and exits the room. I swear I've had this same discussion every day with either her or Ashton.

I look at the stack of letters from the gifts he sent, all unopened by me. Taylor read them when I refused and I can only imagine what they say. He has no problem melting my heart—he never has. It's easy to get swept up in his charms. I don't know if any of it was real. My heart says yes, but my head says it's time to let go. The last time I didn't listen to my head, look where it got me.

Glancing at the clock, I realize I'm going to be late meeting the realtor in Scotch Plains.

"Taylor," I yell out. "Can you text me the agent's number who's handling my father's house please?"

Grabbing my belongings, I rush out the door.

"Sure thing, good luck." Taylor calls out as I head to the elevator.

Thankfully, I drove in to work today, so I can head straight there instead of going home first. I haven't been back to the house since I first was there, but I spoke with an agent as soon as I took the job in California. It'll help financially to sell it, and I don't need anything holding me back here. I want no loose ends. It'll be a clean break.

During the hour drive, I talk to my mother and let her know about the promotion. It's been weeks since we've spoken, but she sounds genuinely happy for me. Which is surprising, but I'm grateful to be leaving on good terms.

Pulling up to the quaint house it looks different. Even though I haven't been back here, I've had some things done to it. The landscapers took care of the overgrown bushes and I had painters do the outside. There are a few minor things I need to have replaced inside, but otherwise it's going to be an "as-is" sale.

I smile as I see Mary peering out at the driveway. I give her a short wave and the curtain closes.

"Catherine?" she calls out and heads over.

"Hi, Mary."

"I thought that was you." Her warm smile shines bright. "I saw the workers here this week."

Her honest concern for the house and for me is heartwarming. I'm sure if I lived here it would seem as if she's nosey, but not having the ability to look after the house myself, it comforts me.

"I hope they behaved."

"Oh, they were very nice to look at." She winks and giggles a little.

I chuckle, "I'm glad."

"Yes, they did beautiful work clearing the shrubbery," Mary notes as she looks at the house. "Hunter would be very happy."

I smile at the idea that he would be pleased, "I'm glad."

"I'm sorry, dear, how are you?"

"I'm doing well. I'm moving to California in a few weeks," I explain and her brow lifts.

"Oh, but you just got here. Why would you move all the way out there?" Mary asks.

We spend the next few minutes talking about the new job and about her grandson who came back from the west coast.

"I'm glad you're happy, dear," Mary says and puts her arm on my shoulder.

Happy? I'm excited about the job. I'm ready to take my career to the next level ... but happy? In one aspect of my life, yes. In another ... no.

Before I can say anything else, the realtor pulls up and hops out of the car. "Catherine Pope?"

Stepping forward, I extend my hand. "Yes, you must be Mindi."

"Mindi Erickson." She returns the handshake and nods. "Nice to meet you."

I explained the urgency of my move and how the house has to be sold quickly. Not having a mortgage or any debt on the house weighs in my favor. She seems very optimistic and already has a few couples she would like to show the house to.

"How about we go inside?" she asks and I bid farewell to Mary.

After a few minutes of going through each room, we make a checklist of things that would make it easier to sell and what can be the new owner's decisions.

"Do you think it's doable?"

"Yes, absolutely. How quickly can you have everything removed from the house? I think it'll show better."

For a second my breath catches. I didn't think about what I would do with all that's left of my father. While we didn't have any relationship, the last thing I want is to lose any ties I have to him. I don't know why this never occurred to me but suddenly it's as if a boulder is sitting on my chest.

"Oh, ummm, I didn't—" I stop trying to think of how to explain that I never realized I'd need to get rid of everything.

"If you'd rather leave it, we can, but I think if selling quickly is the goal then we should have the house staged. It's well worth the money. You'd need to have anything from here removed quickly. I can have this listed in a day if you tell me you're ready." She explains with a no-nonsense look, waiting for my answer.

"Okay, I just need to make a few calls," I say looking away.

"I'll put the sign up now, and then call me when you're good to go. Here's the number for the company I've worked with. They're fair and efficient." Mindi hands me a card and smiles. "I'm going to take a few pictures of the outside."

I head into the bedroom and look around. There's not much that's salvageable, but these are his things. I grab a few shirts and photos, then enter the office. The box that sits under the desk is empty. Taking a few minutes, I pack anything I might want at some point.

Opening the drawer to the desk I see a VHS tape sitting in the back that says: Catherine Grace.

The office has an old television and VCR. Curiosity gets the best of me and I put the video in and press play. I hear his voice for the first time in almost twenty years.

"Catherine, what does Santa say?" my father says from behind the camera.

I smile at the sight of myself at two years old. I have a pink romper on with pigtails.

"Ho, ho, ho." My mouth forms a tiny 'O' as I walk around saying it repeatedly.

"That's right! And what does Daddy say?"

"No, no, no." Everyone laughs and then my mother appears in front of the camera. "Hunter, put that down and come out here."

The camera is placed on something and I see him. He has dark brown eyes that mirror mine and scruff along his cheek that gives him an almost Mediterranean look. My father looks at me like I'm the sun. His eyes beam and glow when he scoops me into his arms and holds me close.

"My beautiful girl ..." he trails off and the camera flashes to another scene.

I'm maybe four years old lying on his chest asleep. My father turns the camera toward me and him as he rocks in the recliner.

"Hi, baby girl. Today's your birthday and you're sick. Each year since you were born you run a crazy fever and this year is no different. Your Mommy's sleeping so I got up with you this time. I decided I had some things to say while you're lying in my arms," he pauses and presses a kiss to my head and my younger self snuggles deeper.

I sit here and see the man who held me in his arms when I was sick, yet I have no memory other than him walking away. There's a part of me that finds peace, seeing it firsthand, knowing he loved me, and another part breaks because we missed out on so much.

"First, boys are stupid. Remember that. No boy will ever love you as much as I do. When I have to give you away, I'll never really let go. You'll always be Daddy's little girl. Okay, we got that out of the way ... The first time you said 'I love you, Daddy' was a day I'll never forget. To see so much honesty took my breath away. You're so beautiful, sweet, and perfect." My father's eyes shine with unshed tears. "One day, you'll hate me, like every teenager does. I want you to know, even at your worst—you'll always be the best thing I've ever done. You'll be a part of my heart no matter how much you despise me. Nothing in this world will ever take that away. You're a piece of me and I'll always be here for you—even if something happens to me." A tear falls from his eyes and he pulls me closer.

The best thing he's ever done ...

"The next thing is you should know how to change a tire. It's very important you learn this because you shouldn't need a man to fix things. Although ... it's how I met your mother," he ponders that and smiles. "Again, I reiterate the first rule about boys being stupid."

I laugh and watch as he rubs my back and rocks a few moments. It's a glimpse into the man I never knew. I look around at the room that I've packed up. It looks bare and empty, which is how I feel. Clearing out his belongings makes his absence that much more apparent. I've been avoiding this house, his things, because I was focused on Jackson. Now, I'm faced with it head on. The letter was one thing, but hearing him, seeing him, is completely different.

"Tomorrow isn't guaranteed. That may seem like a stupid thing to say, but you should remember it. If your life isn't what you wanted—you can change it. You have the power to make a change. Live the life you want to live. If someone doesn't treat you well ... cut them loose. If you want something bad enough ... go after it. There's nothing in this world that comes easy. Take your life by the horns and don't let go." He stops speaking as I begin to wake.

"Daddy?"

"Shhh, it's okay, Sunshine. Go back to sleep," he murmurs in my ear.

The screen goes black and it turns back on when I'm eight. It's the time my parents took me to the Jersey shore. I remember this. I watch my father hand the camera off to my mom. They smile at each other but it seems strained. The video plays as my childhood unfolds before me. There are good memories here, where I was safe, secure, and held tight. The last scene ends and I allow myself a moment to reflect.

My entire life I've felt as if I was fighting to be good enough for someone. Watching man after man disappoint and desert me. And my father was the first, but being in his space and seeing the life he lived—is sad. Am I any better? I push against the walls that surround my heart. I keep people at a distance and at what cost? I want to be loved but I don't want to grab life by the horns. Somehow, I always managed to get poked by them.

If only my father had made different choices ... if only he had had the courage to come to me before he died. We may have had a fighting chance. I probably would've been angry, but at least there was a shot. My mind drifts to Jackson. Am I doing the same thing?

Not wanting to waste the little time I have, I get up and get back to work. Mulling over all I've learned today. Trying to focus on the task of keeping my walls erect, but catching myself getting teary a few times.

This is much harder than I imagined but I've gone through all of the rooms and made a few piles of things to keep, but most will be donated. I sit on the sofa, exhausted and feeling run down. My phone beeps, but I'm too tired to even look.

I start to doze off and the phone rings. I let it go and try to nap. However, the caller doesn't get the point and calls again. I silence the call and close my eyes. My exhaustion is overwhelming. I could sleep for ten hours. Moving sucks.

My ring tone wakes me from a sound sleep.

"Hello," I ask groggily, turning over, looking at the clock, and seeing it's now nighttime.

"Well, well. If it isn't, Kitty." Mark's voice breaks through my haze and I'm instantly awake.

"Hello, Mark."

My defenses rise since I'm unsure of why he would be calling.

"You don't call, write, or smoke signal. I was beginning to

think you didn't find me attractive anymore."

"I'm sure you understand why I haven't be in touch."

He laughs the way only he would, "I know. I told you he was an idiot. I'm not calling about Muffin. Natalie had the baby."

"That's wonderful. How is she? I wanted to call her, but I wasn't sure if I should." My voice is shaky. I became close with her, and we haven't spoken since the break-up. A rush of irritation at myself washes over me. I should've called her. She didn't deserve to be left out because Jackson is a dick.

"She asked me to reach out to you. Nat scheduled Aaron's memorial for next week and asked for you to be there. She said she could use all the support she can get."

"Of course. I'll be there. Where is it?"

"Pennsylvania. In his home town."

"Okay."

Mark takes a second and lets out a long breath. "Fuck it. I'm going to say this to you because I sure as hell won't say it next time I see you. I'm not going to tell you what to do. I'm not going to ask you to do anything. Just know this ... he loves you. In all the years I've known the son of a bitch, he's never looked at anyone like he looks at you."

I start to cut him off, "Mar—"

"You both fucked this up and you're both miserable. Unless you're not?" he questions.

"I'm surviving," I reply, unwilling to lie to him but I don't want to give him any more.

"Isn't that great?" he answers sarcastically. "You're surviving, he's losing his fucking mind, and I'm ready to punch the both of you. This is your life, and far be it from me to give advice because I sure as shit don't do relationships. But I'll tell you this ... if I ever felt the way you both did about someone, I'd be breaking every goddamn door to get back to them. I wouldn't be waiting around for shit to magically fix itself, because it won't."

"That's the thing," I pause. "He already broke the damn doors around my heart. I never broke his. He never let me in." My lip begins to quiver as the emotions start to bubble up. "I loved him. He wants to keep secrets. Fine. But I can't have that kind of relationship. You lied for him, his mother lied, he lied. I don't know what's real anymore."

Mark doesn't respond right away. "I didn't lie to you. It wasn't my story to tell and from what I understand—you still don't know it." Mark pauses allowing his words to settle in. "You owe it to each other to talk and at least learn everything. Then you both can go back to being fucking stupid. I'll let Nat know you'll be there and I'll text you the info."

"I'll be there. I promise."

He hangs up without another word.

Next week I'll have to see him. Next week I'll have no choice. And then I can put this all behind me.

chapter

twenty

"I'M GOING TO go over the remaining accounts you're taking over and make sure you're all set. The movers come tomorrow to pack, so it's today or never."

"Why do you keep reminding me? Are you part sadist?" Taylor jokes, throwing her arms over her face.

"You know it," I laugh and toss a balled up paper at her. "Oh, please. You're not going to miss me that much. You just got a big, fat raise and a pretty sweet promotion."

"But I'm losing my friend and the only person I like in this office." Taylor's bottom lip juts out.

This is the part that keeps me crying every day. I'm an emotional wreck. I love Taylor like a sister. She's been a part of my daily life for years. On top of that she's a wonderful person—I'm going to miss her desperately. A very selfish part of me hoped she'd come to California with me, and then the other part is happy she chose to stay. She'll shine here and I think if she came with me, she'd have a hard time coming out of the shadows. I want her to succeed and she's ready to take this leap.

"You'll never lose me." I smile and tilt my head. "Here's what I think. When I call you a week after I'm gone, and you're in your new position, you'll have forgotten all about me. You'll be putting Elle's snarky ass in her place, and blowing people's minds."

Taylor turns, wiping at her face, trying to hide the tear I

saw falling. "Before I forget, your realtor called. She said every-thing checks out and the papers will be drawn up. The buyer's ready to close on Wednesday."

"Shit. The memorial is Tuesday. I guess I can go right there after."

"Or you can cancel moving."

"Not likely," I chide.

She throws her hands up and huffs. "Fine. Whatever. Ruin my life. Let's go over the Raven account."

My good mood plummets as I think about having to talk about him. I've been avoiding dealing with Raven up until the last moment. The way we've been handling the account trans-fers is through conference calls with each client where Taylor and I explain that she'll be their point of contact. Luckily, we haven't had any issues. Most of the clients already know Taylor and trust her. With Jackson though, I know he isn't going to allow it at all.

But the real issue is that I don't want to speak to him. Be-sides the fact that I don't want him to know I'm leaving.

"I'm going to see him in a few days. I'll go over everything with him then. You know pretty much everything, and at this point we've wrapped most of the account up. Now they should only need us if something catastrophic happens," I say, looking over the file hoping to mask my emotions.

"Right," Taylor says slowly. "I'd like an opportunity to talk to him before you leave. Jackson needs to be comfortable with me as well. You know, in case something catastrophic happens and all. Not like the man has been shot, had his best friend die, or anything major since we've had the account." She gives me a pointed look. "I'm not asking you to share your secrets with him, Cat, I'm just saying he needs to know that I'm his rep. Hell, I don't care if you tell him you quit or were fired."

She's absolutely correct, and I'm being unfair and a bit unprofessional, but these last few days I've been a mess. My emotions are all over the place, from getting excited when I picked out the apartment in California to sobbing when I had to sell my car. Everything feels so much stronger because of all the stress. Ashton keeps looking at me like I'm losing my mind.

"I'll be right back," I say getting up to head to the bathroom.

I'm becoming a chickenshit. This is my damn job and I shouldn't begrudge Taylor. If it were me in her position, I would call the client and handle it. But because she knows everything, she's trying to walk the line of our friendship. Maybe if I tell him I quit and took another job he'd let it go?

Yeah, right.

This is Jackson, the man who runs a security company. He'd track me down before I could even leave the city. I keep my head lowered thinking about what the right way to handle this is and I crash into someone.

"I'm so sorry!" I exclaim and look up to see familiar green eyes and platinum blond hair.

Sure, I can do this now. I mean, it's not like dealing with Piper on a good day isn't bad enough.

"You should be," Piper sneers.

I clench my teeth while balling my fist, ready to punch this bitch in the face. It's as if she's incapable of being a decent human being. "Why are you in my office?"

She gives her classic smile and I fight the urge to wipe it off her.

"Do you mean *my* new office?" She looks around and waves at Sean who's watching the two of us.

My eyes close and I choke the bile clawing it's way up my throat. I've never been happier about my move than I am in this moment. "You were hired?"

"Yup," she sharply enunciates the single syllable. "Isn't that great? We're going to work together every single day."

I give a half laugh and roll my eyes. "Didn't they tell you?" I lean in conspiratorially, "I don't work here anymore."

Her eyes widen briefly, letting me know I caught her off

guard. "You were fired?"

"Fired? No, don't be silly." I pause and smirk. "I was given the California office. I'll be running it. So in a way ..." I tap my chin and trail off.

"Isn't that nice for you," Piper says sarcastically.

"Yeah, it is. Hey, come to think of it, I guess you work for me." I smile when I realize there's a fraction of truth to that statement.

"The hell I do." Piper shifts so she's standing taller.

I've never been an evil person, however at this moment I'm enjoying every moment of her discomfort. She's caused her fair share in my life and I'm all too happy to return the favor.

I let out a dramatic sigh. "Yeah, you kinda do. It's okay though. You probably won't last long here anyway. Our company doesn't take well to lying, vicious sluts who don't know how to be professional."

"Really? Do they take well to sleeping with the clients?"

I rein in my reaction because that's exactly what she'd want. I stand there unwilling to break eye contact. There's no way in hell I'm going to back away from her.

After a few seconds, she sighs and puts her hands on her hips. "Oh, Cat, let's not fight. It doesn't matter anyway because I'll have your job just like I had your man—or should I say men," she goads me but I couldn't care less about the only man she actually has had.

Laughing at her bullshit, I smile and walk away. She's not worth the time.

"Oh, Catherine?" she calls out, stopping me.

Unwilling to make a scene in my office I turn and walk closer to keep my voice quiet. "What?" I ask acerbically.

"I saw your press conference online, I meant to call you but I knew I'd be seeing you soon."

My palms begin to sweat and I feel dizzy.

Piper begins before I can say a word. "You looked great, but I wish I recorded it so I could've seen your face again when you found out about Mr. Cole's wife. That must've been a huge blow. I was really happy to talk to Linda that morning. She's a great journalist and was eager to learn more about his story. How is his wife by the way?"

My stomach plummets and my fingernails are piercing the skin of my palm. "You don't know anything."

She smirks and walks towards me slowly with a gleam in her eyes, knowing she's got me. "Well, it appears you don't either. Such a shame. Another man, another betrayal." She sighs and puts her arm around my shoulder as if we're great friends having a friendly conversation. "I can't believe he never mentioned her to you. It was one of the first things we talked about. You would think considering your high-ranking position, you'd know enough to ask the basic questions. The horror. Just think, you're as bad as me." She laughs and I shrug out of her grasp.

"I'm not anything like you. I don't sleep with men who are knowingly involved with other people. I don't take pleasure in hurting others. And I sure as hell don't get fired from every job I've been at. No, you and I have nothing in common." I turn and walk away.

Fucking Piper. One day, karma is going to throat punch her and I'm going to laugh.

I forego the bathroom and head into my office and shut the door. Taylor jumps at the sound but I don't say a word. I'm sure all the color is drained from my face.

"What's wrong?" she asks concerned.

Is "everything" a good answer? Right now it feels like the floor is falling out from under me. It was bad enough losing him, but to know Piper knew about his wife when I didn't guts me. When are the surprises going to stop hurting? I don't understand how everyone around me seemed to know, but I was left in the dark. Every time I get close to being anywhere near feeling okay, something else slams me in the face about Jackson. The only saving grace is I'm leaving in a week and a half. Thank God I won't have to work with her.

"Piper apparently was hired."

Her mouth falls open. "Here?" she practically screams. "As in this office?"

"Yes, she waved to Mr. Cartright and walked over letting me know she and I would be working together." I groan and flop in my chair. "What in the world could the partners be thinking?"

"She looks good on paper, and in front of a camera."

"She's ugly everywhere else."

"*That* I agree with," Taylor says and laughs. "But you won't be working with her. Only I get that pleasure."

"Are you sure you don't want to come to California with me?" I ask her one last time, hoping I can sway her.

"Unless you want to hire my very sexy fiancé, I would say that's a no. But know I'll be sitting here plotting ways to push her in front of a bus. Accidentally of course," Taylor jokes and we both crack up.

"Yes, because all pushing of evil bitches in front of moving vehicles is accidental."

"I think we'd be forgiven for that one." Taylor smiles and I nod.

Yes, if there's anyone I think a panel of our peers would forgive, it's us for having Piper run over by a truck. She's the devil incarnate.

Taylor straightens up and picks up her notebook. "Okay, what else do we have to get through? I got me a hot date," she drawls, her Midwestern accent peeking through.

"You're a mess," I tease, dispelling the anxiety Piper caused.

"But you love me."

"I do. I do."

We spend the next hour going over what else her new job will require her to do. Since she could've easily done my job, there's not much we have to iron out. Most of the time we laugh or reminisce about accounts we'd forgotten about. There are a lot of memories in this office. Some good, some bad, but Taylor was a part of all of it.

"Okay, tomorrow is packing day. I won't be back in the office until Friday and then next Thursday is my last day actually here."

"I didn't think you'd work at all next week."

"I didn't either, but I need to make sure everything is done. There's a lot to do at home so I'll take some time this week and try to get that stuff straight. This weekend is girls' night out and then Tuesday is the memorial and then my flight is four days after that. You're coming out with us before I leave, right?"

Taylor sighs and stands up to leave. "I'm not sure, Quinn has a work function this weekend and I need to be there for support. Plus, I'll see you at work before you leave. You need this time with the girls."

"I wish you'd reconsider. Ashton and Gretchen won't mind."

"I know." She pauses and looks back at me. "You'll never know how much you mean to me." She smiles and heads out the door.

"Tay?" I call and she peeks her head back in. "Trust me I do know."

She nods and closes the door.

The sun is setting as I look out the window. As the minutes tick by, the exhaustion takes over. I'm run down, overtired, and this is only the beginning of what's to come. Tomorrow, my life will be packed up and sent to California. There are a few things left to do here and then I'll be on my own.

Ashton's already told me I can kiss her ass if I think she'll be home to watch them pack me. We've spent pretty much every night together since I accepted the job. I'm glad we've made time on Saturday for a final night out. I'm going to miss my girls, but they promise to come visit and Sean told me I'd have to travel back to New York for meetings.

I pack up and take the box with all my personal belongings

out of my office. I stand there looking at the nearly empty office and my stomach clenches. I've spent my entire career in this building. It's going to break my heart to leave all of this behind, even if it is to follow my dream.

"Ever feel like we're living déjà vu?" Ashton asks, standing in my now empty room. The movers took everything a few days ago. And now it's time for us to spend the night with Gretchen.

"How so?" I ask wondering where she's going with this.

She looks around the room and her eyes harden. "Come talk to me in the living room or something. I can't stare at this shit."

Ashton may seem tough, but this is difficult for her. We've discussed not living together at some point, but I don't think either of us thought it would include a move across the country as well.

I follow her out of the room fighting the urge to laugh because of her face. "Okay, I'm here."

"I hate this, Cat!" She flops on the couch while throwing her hands over her face.

Unsure of what to do, I sit on the table and put my hand on her arm. "I know you do. I hate this too, but I need to go."

She moves her hand and I see the tears threatening to spill over. "No, you're my family. I've never been alone. And Gretchen is saving the world, so I'll never see her. I don't have any other friends. I mean, I'd friend me," Ashton says as she leans back, meaning what she said.

I bust out laughing. "I have no words."

"What? I'm serious."

"That's the sad part."

"People don't understand me." She sits up and wipes the tear from her face.

Moving to the couch I pull her against me. "You're a bit

much to handle sometimes, but they just haven't had the privilege of getting to know you. Fortunately, I've been putting up with your shit long enough to know it's how you protect yourself."

Ashton uses her attitude as a shield. I've watched her do it since we were kids. She pushes people away before they ever get close to her. How we ever became friends I'll never know. Sometimes two people who don't look like a good match on paper, work perfectly in real life.

"I'll be fine. I'm just being dramatic."

"As usual," I chide.

"Bite me."

"You'd like it."

"You know it." Ashton laughs and then lets out a long, wavery sigh.

"I've spent most of my life listening to you tell me how I need to do things. Now it's your turn." I pause and when I see her blue eyes soften, I begin, "You have one of the kindest hearts I know, but it's got a steel wall around it. I know you don't let people in because it's safer. But you, my friend, deserve love."

Ashton wraps her arms around me. "Hello, pot ... meet kettle. Your walls are thicker than mine." Her brow raises and she tightens her hold.

"I don't think so. If I had walls, then I wouldn't be crumbling right now."

When the movers packed up my belongings, they found the note from the night Jackson left after the fight with Neil. I held that tiny scrap of paper in my hands for hours and cried. Tears ran continuously as I stared at the words that were my lifeline when he left. I held on to that promise he made during his absence and brush with death. He was everything for me. I wanted a life with him, but in the end, I'm left battered and bruised—again.

"Sometimes you have to crumble because you had cracks

and now you'll be crackless."

I laugh and so does Ashton. "You're an ass."

"A crackless ass?" Ash smiles and tries to look at her own ass.

"I think there's a crack in a few places," I giggle and hug her tightly. "I'm serious, Ash, you need to let people in. Let them see the sweet, warm, and caring person you are. You don't always have to be such a bitch."

She pulls back from my embrace and looks at me. "I know. And you ... I've watched you spend weeks pulling yourself together and pretending you're fine. I've seen you get up, get dressed, get promoted, all with a broken heart. You don't have to hide behind your armor but you choose to. I'm not half as strong as you. When Gary left me after college to go live his passions, I lost mine. I don't want to feel that again."

Gary and Ashton were perfect for each other. They met in college and had a whirlwind love. He promised her the world and left her destroyed. Gary was in a band and they had a song hit big. He packed up, left without a backward glance. It was as if she was completely irrelevant. She never cried or fell apart. Instead, she refused to love again.

"If it were me, what would you say?" I ask.

She huffs and stands, "I'd tell you what I always do. But you're different. You have a heart. Mine shriveled up and died."

"Oh, Ash," I stand and envelope her in a hug. "You have a heart. A very big heart."

"Who's going to kick my ass when I'm being a twunt?" she asks earnestly.

I look at her with sad eyes, not knowing what to say. We've both relied on each other and seeing her vulnerable leaves me at a loss.

"I'll still kick your ass, it'll just be from across the country."

"Damn, you've got some long legs," Ashton says in only the way she can. "Okay, enough with the heavy shit. Let's go pretend like you're only going on a business trip instead of leaving me alone and depressed."

I shake my head at her craziness. "You'll be fine. Come on, let's get you drunk, Ashypoo, so I have something to make fun of you about." I loop my arm in hers and we head out of the house. We grab the train and head into Manhattan to meet Gretchen.

Let's hope tonight isn't a repeat of the last time the three of us went out.

chapter

twenty-one

"I'M STILL PISSED at you," Gretchen says as she stands outside of the swanky new bar we're meeting at.

"Well, hello to you too," I say laughing at her greeting.

She grabs me and pulls me into a hug. "I can't stay mad at you. It's not your fault you're an idiot. I blame it on you living with Ashton for so long."

I swear, only my friends.

"I resent that!" Ashton exclaims from behind me. "Maybe her stupid rubbed off on me."

"Not likely," she giggles and I wink at Ashton.

"Bitches," Ashton grumbles from behind us as we walk on.

We enter the bar and the music squashes the remainder of their argument. It's a beautiful, new building in the fashion district of Manhattan. I heard about it from a client last week and she got us on the list. She claimed it has the best drinks and hottest bartenders, which was all we needed to hear. I wanted to cancel because of the laundry list of things piling up. But they demanded this was not an optional invitation.

I take in the dark purples and blues, its robust color scheme giving a sexy yet elegant feel. I find myself moving my hips to the bass pumping through the room. But the music is so loud we'll never be able to talk.

"Rooftop?" I ask when we notice it has a VIP rooftop bar.

They both nod and we head over to the bouncer who lets

us pass with a smile. I'm wearing a black, strapless, tight dress with my hair down, Ashton's boobs are barely covered, and Gretchen's ass is hanging out. I'm shocked—or not. The three of us are dressed to the nines for our last night out.

Once we reach the bar, we find a couch that's open and grab a seat.

"This is nice," I say and pull my legs up under me while pulling my dress down.

"So, since you skated the question before, I'll ask. Why did you go see Neil after Gretch said you shouldn't?" Ashton asks.

She's got to be kidding me. This is what she wants to talk about tonight? The good mood I was trying to hold on to evaporates.

"The suit never was filed, all is well in the world. Neil is gone. I think I'm much smarter than you give me credit for." I cross my arms and lean back on the sofa.

"Bitchy much?" Gretchen replies and pokes me in the arm.

"Sorry," I say softening my posture. "I'd much rather spend our night *not* talking about Neil. Plus, I'm beat."

"Of course you are! You're moving, you got promoted, you had a month to get it all done, and you broke up with Jackson. It's been a busy few weeks," she says with sympathy laced in her voice.

This is why I love her. She's the ying to Ashton's yang. When one is hard the other is soft. Good cop/bad cop. But they always seem to tell me what I need to hear. I may not like it, but it's always said with love.

"What are we drinking? It's on me tonight." Gretchen smiles and Ashton whoops, allowing the Neil subject to drop.

We order our drinks and I opt for a glass of wine. If I drink too much, I'll be asleep in the chair. Ashton however is taking full advantage of Gretchen's offer to pay. They're laughing and I'm mostly laughing at them.

"Are we going to talk about Jackson now?" Ashton pipes in.

"Are you trying to piss me off tonight?"

"Better to be pissed off than pissed on," she retorts.

"I'd rather not be either right now," I say, hoping she'll drop this too.

I long for him every night. I've slept with a pillow clutched in my arms just to have something to hold on to. I've cried, thrown things, and memorized that piece of paper to feel close to him.

"Well, I think we should. You've been avoiding saying shit to either of us." She looks as Gretchen for support, who just nods.

I ask myself every day if this job is something worth throwing it away for, but the doubt and lies bring back my resolve. There's no reason for him to have kept this from me, and it leads me to believe there are far deeper secrets he has buried. Then I'm reminded of Piper and how even she knew.

I embrace the rage bubbling up, shoving away the doubt.

"I'm not willing to talk about Jackson, but you two are more than welcome to." I grab my wine and sip it, suddenly wishing it was something stronger.

Sitting here ignoring the two of them, a heavy feeling settles over me. It's hard to breathe and my chest is heaving. All of the energy shifts—it's the same sensation I have whenever Jackson's around. I look around for him as if he's suddenly going to appear. We've never been to this bar, so there's no reason to think he's here, but I feel as if someone's watching me. Scanning the area, I don't see him or anyone I know.

Ashton snaps her fingers in front of my face. "Earth to Catherine."

"Sorry, I thought someone was here."

"I can call him if you want," she says smirking.

My jaw drops as I process what she says. "Seriously?"

Gretchen shifts and taps Ashton's arm. "Enough, Ashton. Okay, let's talk about how I met someone."

Immediately, Ash and I start asking a million questions

about the new guy. Gretchen doesn't date. Her job demands her time and she never wanted to put herself through the arguments that come with having to work. My heart is full for her. She deserves love and happiness. Work won't fulfill her forever.

After another round of drinks, Ashton turns her attention back to me. "Okay, I know you don't want to talk about him, so let's talk about how you're about to take over the world with your bad ass self."

"Are you getting excited?" Gretchen asks.

"Yeah, I really am. I'm going to miss you guys, don't get me wrong, but the idea of running an office and getting this opportunity ..." I shrug trying to downplay my emotions.

Gretchen smiles, "I'm really proud of you."

"Thanks. The apartment I found is really amazing. It's a little further away from L.A. than I wanted. It's in San Clemente, but it's close to the beach." I start to let the excitement build. My company believed in me and I'm definitely the youngest in CJJ to ever head an office. Even Sean, who helped start the company, pointed out my age. He said they have absolute confidence I'll be up to the task.

"It sucks that even being here—on an island—we never go to the beach. And when we have two feet of snow you'll be in a bathing suit."

I feign sympathy. "Yeah, that's really going to suck," I pause, "For you."

Ashton slaps my arm and we all start to laugh. It feels good talking with them about everything and allowing myself to really be happy about this opportunity.

"What about your dad's house. Did it sell?" Gretchen asks.

"The realtor said the buyer is good to go and we're going to close the day after the memorial."

"You're going?" Ashton's eyes widen in shock.

I've gone back and forth over the right thing to do. I could skip it but I promised Jackson a while ago, and I promised

Natalie. While Natalie might understand, I won't do that to her. It took her this long to do the memorial, so I'm not about to cause any undue stress. We spoke the other day and she sent me pictures of her gorgeous daughter. She said they'd both really like to meet me. So, I'll go.

Biting my lip I look at them both. "I have to. I don't know how the hell I'm going to get through it but I'm going."

"I'll go with you," Ashton says without question.

"Really?" I ask, unsure if she really wants to be there since she never met Aaron or Natalie.

"Of course, Cat. You're going to need me more than you think. You'll see Jackson. You'll be around his friends. I think you've been great at pretending when you don't have to deal with him. In person though ..." She trails off and I suddenly feel nauseous.

My eyes prick when I think about how much this is going to be hard for everyone. "What if he doesn't want me there?"

"It doesn't matter. I do think you should talk to him beforehand though."

That's the last thing I want to do. They're watching me, but I don't respond. My heart says to call, but my head says no. The hairs on the back of my neck raise and I glance around again.

"Why do you keep scanning the crowd?" Gretchen asks looking around.

"I keep getting the feeling I'm being watched."

Ashton stands up and looks around.

"Sit down!" I exclaim and pull on her arm. "I'm probably being silly."

"Or G.I. Joe decided he's tired of being shut out and is coming to get his girl." She leans back with a shit-eating grin, piercing me with her blue eyes.

"Fuck off, Ash. Do you want me angry at you? I'm leaving for California. Even if I could go back to him, it wouldn't work. I'm not about to enter into a long distance relationship that already has issues. Christ, let it go!" I storm off and head to the bathroom before she can reply.

I look up at the mirror and attempt to fix my makeup before going back out there. I know I lost it on her, but I'm tired of everyone and their unsolicited advice. What ever happened to being supportive?

The door opens and a pretty blond enters smiling. She looks familiar, but I can't place her.

Before I can give it too much thought, Gretchen enters. "Cat," she says sympathetically, "You know how she is."

"Yes, I do." I sigh and my head falls back. I get why she's acting like a bitch, but I wish she'd cry it out and move on. "I'm tired, Gretch. I wanted our last night together to be fun, and I don't want to fight. Between work and the move I just want a night to myself. Will you hate me if I head home?"

"Of course not! I'm sure you're exhausted. Promise me you'll find a way to see me once more before you go."

"I'll do my best." I wrap my arms around Gretchen and she kisses my cheek.

"We're being silly girls. But I'm going to miss you."

"I'll miss you more."

She smiles and gives me another hug, "Oh, I meant to tell you ... my lawyer friend, who was going to take on Neil's case, called me. She said since he got back the property he was looking for he no longer needed her."

"Yeah, I think it was really about money."

"I think so too ... anyway, I'm going to come see you, and you'll come back and visit."

"You better," I reply.

Gretchen laughs and grabs my hand. "Let's go, I gotta pay Ashton's insane tab."

We head back out to the seating area and get Ashton. When I turn around to leave, I stop dead in my tracks. Across the room is the figure of a man I'd know anywhere.

"Oh my God!" I grab Ashton's arm and pull her down.

"What?" she asks looking around to find whatever I'm

hiding from.

I keep my head low and try to point to the man making out with the blond from the bathroom. "Look, it's Neil."

She looks and when she spots him, her hand clasps over her mouth and she starts laughing. "Funny, that's not his slut of a girlfriend."

I sit there shell shocked watching him with another woman—who is not Piper. Then it clicks when I see her profile. She's the reporter, Linda, from Raven's press conference. It seems Neil has moved on to one of Piper's friends. My lips turn up at this very interesting turn of events. "Well, this is quite entertaining," I laugh and Ashton snorts.

Pulling my phone out, I snap a few photos of the happy couple. When he turns his head I have the perfect shot.

We sneak out and catch up with Gretchen, showing her the photos. "Well, if the dickface decides to come after you again, we have leverage." She winks at me.

Who thought we'd be here laughing at the fact that he's once again kissing someone else and I had to see it. Last time it destroyed my world, this time I couldn't care less. He has no hold on me and it feels fantastic.

Stick that in your pipe and smoke it, Neil.

I head home as Ash and Gretch continue to another bar. As much as I'd love to go to sleep there's one task I need to handle before I collapse. I need to hire an assistant before I get on that plane. Grabbing the folder of resumes, I thumb for the one I set up to speak to today.

I grab my phone and call. "Hi, is Tristan there?" I ask into the receiver as I walk around my empty room.

Thankfully, this is the last of the interviews I need to do over the phone before I arrive in California. Tristan is the one candidate I'm most excited about interviewing. He has some executive assistant experience along with acting and public speaking.

"This is." His deep voice is gruff and sexy.

Well, hello there. Now that's a voice I could listen to all day.

"This is Catherine Pope from CJJ Public Relations. We emailed and I informed you I'd be calling regarding your application for the assistant position."

"Yes, hi!" Tristan exclaims as he perks up a bit. "I'm very excited about the office opening and was waiting for your call."

"Your resume was great and I'd like to go over a few things." I grab my notepad and sit on the floor. "Is now a good time?"

"Yes, Ms. Pope. Definitely." Tristan's voice is warm yet rough. It reminds me of another man, but I shut that thought process down quickly.

"Can you tell me a bit about yourself and why you're looking to make a move?"

Tristan and I spend almost an hour going over the job, expectations, and possibilities the company has for him. I have a great feeling about him. He's easygoing, articulate, and has a good background for the job. Honestly, he'd be fabulous as a publicist, but for now he'd like to learn as much as he can from me. As long as his references check out, I'll have myself an assistant.

Feeling good about where we leave off, I lie in my bed hoping I can fall asleep, mentally running over the goodbye with my mother tomorrow and the last minute stuff at my dad's house.

chapter

twenty-two

TODAY IS THE memorial. The day I'll say farewell to two men. One man who meant the world to many. A father, a hero, a husband, and a friend who died leaving a gaping hole in so many people's hearts.

The other is a man who left a hole in *my* heart.

I hate this dress.

I hate this day.

I hate the makeup I'm not able to wear because I can't stop crying.

I woke up this morning a mess. The idea of having to see him has been too much. I received a package last night of more lilies, and this time I allowed myself to open the card and read it.

I've never cried so hard in my entire life, but there's no going back in time.

After my heart was already completely ripped from my chest, I grabbed the other notes he sent with the gifts to my office. I figure I'll get it all done in one fell swoop and allow the pain to take over so I can get it out.

Dear Catherine,

Today, I hate myself. I don't deserve you. It's been less than twenty-four hours since I last held you. One day, and I feel worse than I ever have. I saw this lighthouse and thought

of you. It reminded me of the magic we shared up there. How you made me want to live again. You give me that. I'll tell you everything, just give me a chance.
    All of my heart and soul,
    Jackson

The tears stream and I sob, but Ashton ignores the sounds of my breakdown if she hears me. I open the next card that came with the Battleship game.

Dear Catherine,
    I've lost track of the times I've picked up the phone. I can't sleep in our bed. Everything in this fucking house reminds me of us. Be my anchor, Catherine. I hate myself. I hate what I've done to us. Call me and we can work through it. My heart is yours. It's up to you if it sinks.
    All of me,
    Jackson

There's no changing the fact that I'm leaving for California in four days. I want to forgive him, to run back to his arms, but it doesn't erase the doubt and the three thousand miles that are about to be between us. I know I should stop myself from reading the rest of the notes, but I owe him.

My Catherine,
    Love notes are dumb but I should've written them to you. Then you'd have known what was inside of me the entire time. You wouldn't have questioned anything because it would be there in black and white. My proof to you when you felt doubt and you'd know how much you mean to me. I don't even know if you read these but if you do ... I miss you. I went to work today and everyone asked about you. I broke two things because I was fucking mad. I'm mad now too. If you love me, how can you walk away so easily? Don't answer that. I'm

pretty sure I'm talking to myself. I talked to Mark and my mother today, told them about what happened. I'm sure you can imagine the things I heard. But one thing my mom said that stuck:

"Above all, love each other deeply, because love covers a multitude of sins." – Peter 4:18

I love you deeply. I love you with every breath I take. I've made mistakes. I've fucked up. I know this, but love me.

Don't give up on us.

Jackson

My eyes are puffy, my heart is heavy, and the idea of seeing him has made me sick. I allow myself to read the final letter one more time.

Dear Catherine,

I know now it's over. I know you don't want to talk to me, or hear my side and I respect your decision. I hate it, but I can't push you anymore. I know I hurt you. I don't know how to live without trying to win you back. I can't think. I can't sleep. I hurt so fucking much, Catherine. Every day I look at this godforsaken apartment and I want to sell it and move— but then I'll have lost the only thing I have of you. You were the only woman to ever sleep in this bed. You were the only woman to touch this house. Nothing here matters because you're gone. I'd go back in time and tell you everything. But I can't do that. I can't fix this and it's killing me. I call and you don't answer. I text and you won't respond. I can't fix this without you. I meant every word I ever said to you. I love you and I'll love you until my last breath.

You're it for me.

Jackson

How can someone hurt so much? The depths of my heart are hollow, my eyes are burning from the onslaught of tears. I feel like I've been torn apart and when I was put back together, they forgot some pieces. But I won't quit my job. I can't walk away from this opportunity, and we can't work. So it's my turn to save him. Allow him to move on with a clean break.

I know when I see him today, I'll have to put on the show of my life. If I thought the launch party was difficult, this will be a thousand times worse.

I should've left the damn cards unopened. But I couldn't.

So today I'll somehow handle looking at the man who's no longer mine. The one who forced me to love again, to give my heart to him—then forced me to be alone. He's gone from my life and I can't get him back. I have to let him go—for good.

I'll need a miracle to get through this.

He took everything from me with that damn letter.

CHAPTER TWENTY-THREE

JACKSON

"**Y**OU READY?" MARK asks from behind me. He's wearing his full dress uniform, white gloves and all. With a little help I was able to get my dress blues on. The only time I've worn this uniform since I got out was for the last team member we lost a few months ago. I hate how once again I'm putting it on for the same reason. In fact, this is pretty much the only time I wear it. I'm going to fucking burn it after this, and then maybe we'll stop having to go to funerals.

I straighten my belt and huff. I can't do this. I can't bury another friend. "Fuck. I can't do this. Just go without me," I say looking away.

Next thing that registers is his fist connecting with my bad shoulder.

"What the fuck?" I ask while trying to get rid of the stinging in my arm.

"You're going. I'll punch you in the fucking face if you even try to say it again. You shut your mouth and listen. Maybe when you were taking your little nap you didn't hear me, maybe your tiny brain can't retain it, but I've had enough of your goddamn bullshit. You're going! I swear to fucking God you're going today," Mark rages and runs his hand down his face.

I've never seen him so pissed—well, not at me at least. "I

don't know what the hell you're talking about."

"Of course not! You weren't the only one in that village, asshole. You weren't the only one who watched Aaron go and handle the issues in Afghanistan that either one of us could've dealt with. *You* didn't fucking go to Natalie and tell her that her husband was dead. No, fucker, I did that. I had to knock on her door, catch her in my arms as she lost it. So kiss my fucking ass."

"Keep it up, dickhead," I warn.

He turns as if I didn't say anything and mocks me, "'I'm not going.' My fucking ass you're not. You're not the only one who's ever lost anyone!" he yells and punches the door. "I fucking lost them too! They were my friends too, Muff. *You* aren't the only one who lives with guilt!" Mark chokes on the last part.

"I know that!" I yell back at him. "But I sent them to their deaths! I live with this every fucking day."

"You *still* don't get it. We were a fucking team. I left the Navy after you did because where you go, I go. I followed because you, me, and Aaron—we're a team." Mark balls his fists up and steps toward me. "You aren't the only one in this team. I've watched every single fucking one of them die. I watched you die too, you son of a bitch." He points his finger and jabs me in the chest. I push him back away from me. And he stumbles.

"Don't fucking push me," I say strained.

"You want to fight me? Today? You want me to fucking lay you out?" Mark says taunting me and throwing his hands up.

"Fuck you!" I don't want to fight him but he's about to push me there.

"No, fuck you! I'm not sitting around acting like I'm the only person who suffers. It's what the job is. You know this. I know this. When we became SEALs we knew we could die but it's what we lived for. Losing him though—he wasn't supposed to die."

The words I want to say to him won't come out. I want

to tell him to fuck off, but I can't. He's lost as many friends as I have. As much as I want to say something, he's right. Mark and Aaron worked together every day. They spent more time together than I did in the last year while I was cleaning up my mess of a life.

After a few minutes of us pissed off with our fists ready to strike, we both take a step back. "He was a brother to me," he says. I look up and he shakes his head. "He was a better man than me or you. He didn't deserve to die."

"I know. It should've been me," I say, feeling devoid of any emotion.

"It shouldn't have been any of us."

"I don't ever want to wear this uniform again," I say, fixing my jacket from the near fight with Mark.

He looks over and grips his neck. "I'm tired of attending these funerals. The next one I plan to go to is my own. And I won't give a fuck what you wear."

There are times when I wish we were back eight years ago, young, dumb, and ignorant to the world around us. We thought we were invincible. Who the fuck was going to bring down a group of SEALs? No one. We lived in this idealistic world that we could live dangerous and not pay for our sins.

We weren't married, no kids, just money to burn and tails to chase. The missions were, in our minds, fun. The deployments were what we looked forward to. I couldn't wait to be away, because Virginia was fucking boring.

"Dude, I—" I start to say but he cuts me off.

"Not today, Muff." He shakes his head. "I'll kick your ass another day, but not today. Come on, let's go."

Today is going to be hard on everyone, but especially Mark.

We get to the funeral site without further incident. I'm able to put pressure on my leg now as long as I use a crutch, but today I won't be using it. I'll stand through the pain because it will be my reminder. I'll fight through the hurt because Aaron deserves it.

There's a tent set up, and Natalie and her family are sitting while the color guard stands guard of the urn. There are a few of the team guys here along with some of their wives. I say hello to everyone and stand off in the back.

Natalie comes over to me hesitantly. "Jackson, thank you for doing all this." She bites her lip and a tear falls.

"Nat, you don't owe me anything."

She gives a sad smile. "Aaron loved you like a brother."

I ball my fists and stand up taller, "I'm sor— "

Natalie puts her hand on my arm and cuts me off. "Don't you dare say it. You didn't kill him. I hate everyone telling me they're sorry because I can bet you a thousand dollars if it were you or Mark, he would wish it was him."

Her mother comes up behind her and hands her Aarabelle. She's a beautiful baby with dark hair and Natalie holds her close. Natalie turns to me while I gaze at the tiny infant in her arms. "I have a piece of him," she says as she rocks back and forth.

I look up and she kisses Aarabelle's head. Mark and I stand there together watching her walk over and talk to the other team guys who are here.

The feeling in the air shifts and my body registers Catherine's presence. My heart pounds harder in my chest as I scan the area looking for her.

"Dude," Mark grips my shoulder and points over at our former Senior Chief as he approaches. "Look, it's Wolf."

I don't respond because I know she's here. Finally, I catch a glimpse of her. She's even more beautiful than I remember. The pictures I have of us don't do her justice. Her hair blows in the wind and I fight the urge to go to her, fall on my knees, and grovel. I want to wrap her in my arms, beg her for forgiveness, and bury myself in her and never leave, but I know it'll do no good. She's made it clear that she's done. Her sunglasses hide her eyes, but the way she's holding on to Ashton leads me to believe she's upset.

I see her nod and look over at the crowd, but she doesn't see me—or at least doesn't acknowledge in any way that she does.

Every part of me is pulled toward her. But once again she shuts me out.

"Cole, it's good to see you. I wish it was under better circumstances," Senior Chief Wolfel says.

I shake his hand. "I agree, Wolf, but it's good to see you as well."

"I hear the company is doing well."

I nod, trying to keep my eyes on Catherine as she approaches with her head down. I'm willing her to look at me, but her head stays firmly downcast and she maintains her distance. "Yes, I'm focusing on growing the firm. Mark and I are looking at doing some bigger bids."

The priest who begins to speak halts our conversation. His voice is somber and the mood within the tent shifts. He talks about Aaron's life as a kid, his heroism as an adult, and the absence his loss brings. There's no comfort because the pain will never completely fade. Sure, it will lessen in time, but Natalie is a widow, Aarabelle will grow up without a father. She'll suffer the loss of a great man and she'll never know why.

I gaze at the woman I lost. She wipes her cheek and her body shakes. My feet move without permission. I can't watch her suffer and not go to her. She's falling apart. One step closer, then I feel Mark grip my shoulder, holding me in place. He shakes his head and I stay where I am, but my eyes stay locked on Catherine.

"Today, we remember a hero who lost his life too soon. We remember the man who fought through wars and protected those who couldn't protect themselves. We remember a husband, a son, a father, and a friend." The priest looks up and I hear Natalie cry louder while people wrap their arms around her.

My shipmates stand off to the side and begin the military

funeral honors. The bugle plays "Taps" and the sounds of people crying grow louder. The sound of that song haunts me.

Two sailors accompany our former Senior Chief who's presenting the flag to her. He kneels and says the words every woman never wants to hear. The apology that should never come. A grateful fucking nation my ass. How about telling her we'll kill the fuckers who made her have to hold that folded flag.

Mark and I stand watching her sob, holding the baby to her chest. The echo of her cries breaks our stance. We push forward at the same time and each put our hands on her shoulders. Letting her know she's not alone and we're here. Even with the throbbing radiating from my leg, I refuse to move. Fuck the pain, because it's nothing compared to what she's feeling. Her chest heaves as we stand guard behind her.

I hear the people crying behind me but one sound breaks my hold. The person who matters most to me and the only one I'd be willing to move for. I look over and see Ashton pull her close. I look over at Mark who nods once and puts his hand on Natalie's other shoulder relieving me from my position.

Walking up behind Catherine, without thinking, my hand drifts up her back and rests on the skin of her shoulder. A jolt runs through me from being this close to her. Within seconds, the feelings I'd managed to push away come barreling forward. I need to touch her and feel her against me.

"Catherine," my voice is low and full of emotion.

She sobs, falling forward, and Ashton catches her. She shakes in her arms but I won't move my hand. I can't stop touching her. I won't stop. She's mine and I *will* protect her. Looking at Ashton she closes her eyes and gives a small nod.

It's all the permission I need. I grab a hold of Catherine and pull her into my arms. I hold her once again and my world shifts. Her touch, the smell of vanilla hits me, and I can't fucking breathe. Everything that matters is in my arms and I won't let go of her again.

"Catherine, it's okay," I say softly, running my hands down her hair. I pull her close not allowing any space between us.

She clutches me and pulls me even closer as she buries her head in my chest. This insanity will end. She'll know everything today, and she's not leaving me ever again.

"Jackson," she cries and takes a deep breath. "Please," she pleads, but I don't know what the hell she's asking for.

Catherine starts to pull back, but I tighten my grip and shift on my leg trying to balance. "I'm not letting go. I need you right now," I say unashamed.

She nods into my chest as the funeral goes on. Just her being here gives me the strength I need. It allows me to say farewell to my brother-in-arms.

People filter out, but we stand here clutching each other.

Mark removes his pin from his chest and walks to the urn. He closes his eyes and places it down. The moments pass as he stands there saying goodbye silently. After a few minutes, Ashton walks over and places her hand on his shoulder. He grips her hand and they walk away.

It's my turn. I release Catherine and remove my trident. I grip her face and stare into her eyes. I see all the hurt and pain in her, and I swear I'll never be the cause of that look again. Once she knows everything we can move forward.

"I have to—"

Catherine's hand touches my lips silencing me. She leans in and places her lips to mine. I don't want to fucking move. I want to stay with her like this forever. When she leans back, I instantly feel her absence.

Without a word I walk over to the urn. I stand there alone for a moment and tell Aaron everything I need to say.

"I'm so sorry. I'll make sure she's okay. I'll be there for Aarabelle and remind her of the man you were. You'll never be forgotten," I say quietly hoping somewhere he hears me. I'll never break the vow I made to him.

I place the pin next to the other five that lay there from members of our team who came to pay their respects. When I turn to grab Catherine's hand, I see her heading to the car.

The panic sets in. I'm going to lose her.

"Fuck," I say, trying to move quickly.

Ashton stands there arguing with her, and I pray it gives me enough time to stop her.

She sees me coming and grabs the keys and closes her door.

I stop moving and stare at her as she rushes to get away.

"Get your head out of your ass and fix this mess you've created. If you love her, fight like a man. I'm tired of watching you act like a bitch," Mark says and throws his keys at me. "Follow her."

I move as fast as I can and get in Mark's car, ready to chase her. This isn't over. Not by a fucking long shot.

chapter

twenty-four

Catherine

KEEP DRIVING. KEEP your foot on the gas and don't stop.

I tell myself over and over. Don't look in the rearview mirror because it doesn't matter. It's behind me. I have to keep moving forward and pretend that I didn't allow myself to feel again.

One touch was all it took.

One word crumbled the walls I'd rebuilt.

If I'd stayed there he would've broken me down. I could see it in his eyes. He wasn't going to let me go. So I did as I promised myself before I went—I let him go first. I protected myself from yet another round of heartbreak. Which is all that seems to come from Jackson and I. We hurt each other whether it's intentional or not. The damage is still the same and I've had enough to last me a lifetime.

The drive to the house in Scotch Plains is shorter than if I had to head back to my apartment, so I brought an overnight bag since Mark and Ashton made arrangements for her to get home. As soon as Jackson let me go, I had to get out of there.

I needed to get the hell away from him because he'd consume me. The pain remains though.

I wipe the tears that continue to stream down my face. I can still feel him around me, his scent clings to me and I inhale it. I'd give up everything to go back in time and never have given in to him. If I'd saved myself then it wouldn't hurt so damn much right now. There's nothing more I want to do than turn this car around and run back to him. His touch sent my entire world into a tailspin. In his arms I felt it all. The love, the hurt, the agony of our reunion, knowing it was the finale too. It was the last time Jackson would ever hold me, ever touch me, his lips, his face will never be mine again.

I look in the rearview mirror wanting to go back.

Keep driving.

Pushing the accelerator faster, I fight my heart's wants. It doesn't change the circumstances we're in. My clean start is in California and I leave in four days.

Keep your foot on the gas and don't stop.

I pull up to what was my father's house and drop my head on the steering wheel. Now what? Drawing a deep breath I lean back while the ache washes over me. I remember how it felt to find out everything. How devastated I was during that press release and what it felt like to find out the love I thought we shared was built on lies.

Removing myself from the car, I open the back door and grab my bag.

"I wasn't done," I hear Jackson's voice.

My entire body freezes at the sound of his deep voice and my legs go weak. I grab on to the frame of the door to stay upright. "What are you doing here?" I ask on the verge of sobbing.

He takes a step closer, gripping my wrists, and his voice softens. "No more running. We're going to talk. Now."

I look into his eyes and the storm rages across his face. Allowing myself a minute to take him in. He's dressed in his dark blue uniform and if I ever thought he was sexy in a suit, this just put that image to shame. I watch as he smirks when he catches me looking him over.

That sexy grin infuriates me. "You don't get it," I say exasperated.

Jackson's hands move up my arms slowly. I start to draw short breaths and shake. Why does he do this to me? Why can't I fight him? I'm weak against his touch.

"I know that I love you," he says as his fingers move against my neck. "I get it, but I don't care about giving you space anymore."

"You don't care?" I push him back and he leans forward, trapping me in his arms. "God, do you hear yourself? Why are you here if you don't care?"

"If we're really done. Why the hell should I care?" His lips graze my ear. "If you don't love me and you're done with me, then I have nothing left to lose." The heat of his breath against my neck causes me to shiver. "So, we're going to talk because I," his lips touch the skin of my neck, "Don't," another kiss, "Care."

He pulls me against him and presses his lips to the base of my neck, lingering and moving slowly while he holds me close.

I melt into his embrace like always. But this is our dance. He breaks me down, and I break more. Only I'm not sure I'll be able to seal the cracks from this one.

"It doesn't matter," I say pulling out of his arms. "None of it matters anymore. You should go."

"I'm sure I should, but I won't. Please, come home. Let's talk." Jackson looks around and takes in the street we're standing on. "Or have you found a new home?"

My eyes close and my heart pounds against my chest. "Not that I owe you any explanations, but no, this was my father's house. Tomorrow I'm selling it," I say as I walk to the door. I need him to go now. "I have a lot I need to do, so please get back in your car and go. Goodbye."

Jackson grabs my arm and I turn to face him, but before

I can say a word he slowly presses his lips against mine. His hands grip my neck and hold me at his mercy. Every part of me comes to life. The heart that has been beating out of rhythm just found its cadence. My breath comes easier from one solitary kiss. Needing to be closer, needing this feeling to remain, my hands grip his neck as I pull him closer. Jackson pushes my back against the door and I give myself over to him for a moment. I allow myself the feel of his weight against me. The way he ignites my body because this will be the last time.

Jackson pulls back and his blue-green eyes are solid and he struggles to catch his breath. "There are no goodbyes between us." He grabs the keys and I stand here dumbstruck.

This is not going according to plan.

Jackson fiddles with the keys until he gets the door open. Standing off to the side with his arm outstretched he waits for me to enter.

"You're not staying," I say defiantly.

"I'm not leaving, so either you're coming with me to New York, or I'm staying here until you hear me out. You pick."

"Neither of those works for me. So you can leave or I'll call the cops."

He shrugs, "I'll be right here."

"I'm not kidding."

"Be my guest, baby."

"I'm not your baby anymore."

Jackson takes a step forward and his eyes are steel. "Get in the fucking house. I'm done playing."

I stand there with my arms crossed. He's lost the right to boss me around.

"Always have to do things the hard way, don't you?" he asks before grabbing me around my waist and placing me in the house.

"Put me down!" I yell and he kicks the door shut. "God! You don't have a clue, do you?"

He laughs, apparently finding this amusing, before he

winces and grips his leg. "Did you get my gifts?"

"You hurt yourself, didn't you?"

"I'm fine. Answer the question."

"I burned them," I say completely full of shit, but I hope if I can piss him off enough he'll take the hint and leave.

"Mature," he scoffs. "Did you read the cards or did you burn those too?" His brow rises in question.

I blink repeatedly while my jaw falls slightly ajar. I can't lie to him about this. His heart was bared in those letters. "I read them," I say softly.

I read them and fell apart. I lost a part of my heart in those letters, but I won't tell him that.

"But they didn't matter to you?"

"You lied to me, Jackson!" I say infuriated that he continues to neglect this fact. "I told you my deal-breakers. I gave you every chance to tell me about your *wife*." I throw my hands up and start to pace. "I can't have this conversation with you now. I'm not angry, or upset, I'm not going through this again. You promised me. You fucking promised!" I yell and push against his chest. "You promised. Of course those damn letters mattered, but they don't change anything!"

"I know."

"You weren't supposed to break my heart," I say, clutching my stomach.

Jackson pulls me to his chest and his voice is thick with emotion. "You weren't supposed to win mine. I was dead inside. I refused to ever love again, yet here we are."

I look up and plead with him. "Please, let me go."

His jaw sets and he releases me. "I can't. Sit down. No more games, no more lies."

"Jackson," I say drawing a deep breath. "It doesn't matter. Nothing matters. Things have changed."

"Not for me they haven't! I'm fucking dying without you, Catherine. My entire fucking world doesn't make sense anymore. How is that possible? How even after the absolute hell

I've lived through does that make sense? Because it does matter. We matter, goddammit." He drops to his knees in front of me.

I look at his face and see it. The bags under his eyes, the pain in his eyes. He's a mess. So am I. I sink to the couch and we continue to look at each other. I ache. I physically ache for him.

"Love shouldn't hurt like this," I say as he grips my hands.

"I was married for six years to a woman named Madelyn."

"Please don't do this."

Jackson continues as if he didn't hear my request. "I met her when I was active duty. I fell in love with her. She was beautiful, alluring, and I was a twenty-two-year-old idiot who thought he was invincible. The world was at my feet. I was a Navy-fucking-SEAL and she doted on me."

I close my eyes wishing he would stop and we could say goodbye.

But he doesn't.

"She was born into a wealthy family. Her parents gave her anything she wanted because she was born with a severe heart condition. I married her after two years thinking it was the next step. Maddie and I had everything even though we couldn't ever have kids. Losing her was pure fucking torture." Jackson looks at me and tears fill my eyes.

"I'm sorry you lost someone you loved." I don't know what else to say.

"I didn't lose her. I was the reason she died," he says as he grips the bridge of his nose.

My jaw falls slack. "I don't understand."

"This isn't going to be easy for me. I know you think you fought feeling anything for me but you have no idea how hard I fought against you. I didn't ever want to love again. There wasn't a part of me that ever wanted to feel this again." Jackson's gaze bores through me. "If I didn't love you, then I wouldn't have to lose you. I wouldn't have to feel the fucking pain and torment again. You were never supposed to get to me."

I look at him as he traces his calloused thumb across my palm. "Jackson, we can't do this to each other."

"Maddie and I enjoyed our life together as long as I kept her needs first. She hated the deployments, training exercises, and most of all she hated how much I loved it. There were times I had to miss her doctor's appointments because of the Navy, but I loved being a SEAL. We knew from the beginning we could never have kids. I was fine with it because I was gone so much." Jackson's eyes glaze over and he grips my hand harder.

"Her family demanded she take over Raven. The Elliotts built it from the ground up. They urged me to leave the service because I should be home to care for Madelyn. After the mission that went wrong, Maddie demanded it too. I wanted to re-enlist, but we barely saw each other as it was, and now she was going to be in New York. She hated being a military wife and I loved her, so I gave it up. We fought and argued, but ultimately her happiness came first for me." He looks at me for the first time with tears building in his eyes.

"You don't have to ..." Watching him cry is too much.

"That last mission happened four months before my contract was up. I was on limited duty anyway, so I said fuck it and I quit. She was happy and I thought that's all that mattered. She gained complete control of the company and we bought out her brother. I had a lot of money saved from my missions. My only request was that I start the security company. She supported it—I think she knew there was a part of me that felt dead. I hated the messages from Mark and the guys about what they were doing. I fucking wanted to crawl out of my skin staying in New York, so I made Cole Securities bid for contracts so that I could still use my skills. Of course, it meant I was gone from her again."

"Why are you telling me this?" I ask as a tear falls from my face. I don't want to hear about how much he loved his wife.

"Because I should've told you before. But I was terrified it would make everything real. It was the only piece of me I had left to give you. If you knew about her then you would see how fucking wrecked I am." He trembles as he speaks and another tear falls from his eyes. "I would've sold my soul to have the rest of this story not happen. I was flying between New York and Virginia constantly. We were trying to make it work. She was getting sicker, so I couldn't leave as often and she had to resign from Raven. None of the doctors were sure why her medication suddenly wasn't effective. There was a problem with something in Virginia and I had to handle it ... she begged me not to go. She said she felt sicker than usual, but Maddie was dramatic. She said fine, go, that she'd call her mother. So I left. What kind of man leaves his wife whose heart was starting to fail?" he asks rhetorically before beginning again.

"As much as I knew I shouldn't go, I couldn't stay. I got on the plane and when I landed, I had thirty missed calls. Madelyn had collapsed and was in a coma."

I gasp and he looks up. "See, we couldn't have kids, Catherine. I knew this, she knew this. But she must've come off her birth control or I don't know, but she was pregnant." Jackson's hand covers his heart and he grips at his chest. "Her heart failed because she couldn't carry a baby. I killed her and I killed our baby. Knowing I was the reason she died is beyond anything I can describe." Jackson's tears fall silently as he relives his grief.

He looks up at me and I sink on to the floor with him and wrap my arms around him. He's so broken. My heart drops and I join him with my own tears as I see the anguish on his face. This isn't what I was expecting. I thought he was divorced, not that she'd died. And he lost a baby too. How much loss can one person handle? He's lost so many people in his life by some form of tragedy.

"I'm so sorry," I say with tears streaming.

"The doctors said she was about four weeks, but the increased stress on her heart was too much and she never woke up. Her family blamed me for being careless and hated me for a long time. But no one can hate me more than I hate myself."

"It wasn't your fault, Jackson." A tear falls down my cheek at how much pain and death he's dealt with. "You didn't kill your baby or your wife. It was tragic and awful, but you didn't know. You didn't do it on purpose."

"In a matter of a year, there was five people's blood on my hands. I was terrified of failing you too, and I did it anyway. I couldn't have you look at me like that. It was my job to protect them and I failed every one of them."

My throat aches and I try to get the words out. "Do you know what I see?" He looks up and then his eyes close. "I see a man who needs to forgive himself for something he couldn't control. You didn't purposely put anyone in danger. Bad things happened, but you didn't kill anyone. You're not capable of doing that."

"I can't lose you, Catherine. I couldn't tell you. I didn't want you to see me that way. I left her, and she died." Jackson's hands cup my face. "I lost my wife and child and the last words I said to her were how I wished I was fucking deployed again so I didn't have to deal with Raven. I vowed after she died I wouldn't ever give myself the chance to hurt anyone else. Then you fell into my lap—literally. I tried not to love you. I tried to keep at a distance, but when I'd see you ... I wanted you more."

"Our entire relationship has been one thing after another," I sigh as his thumbs rub my cheek.

It's been a lot of hurt, but we did have good times with laughter, playfulness, and love. I wish there was more of that because the bad times make those feel minimal. Watching our relationship fall apart has been agony, but Jackson taught me a lot. I learned how to love again when I thought I couldn't.

"In the six years I was married to Madelyn, I never in my dreams imagined loving anyone as much as her—then came you. You make me feel alive. You give me hope that I can be more of a man than I was then. You showed me how to love again. I never felt like I did after you walked away. Doesn't that say something?"

My heart sinks because as much as I understand him, I'm leaving. I move in four days and here is the man that I loved and still love, but now what? Everything's different. Those weeks changed the course of my life and I don't know if I can go back. It doesn't negate the fact that if he'd told me all of this I wouldn't be faced with this choice. Or if I was, we could've navigated this together. If I give everything up for him, then what? If in four months something else happens and our worlds fall apart, can we handle it then? All of the questions swirl around in my head, but I already know the answers.

He looks into my eyes and pulls me close, pressing his forehead to mine. "Give me tonight. Don't say anything, just give me tonight," Jackson says before pressing his lips to mine.

The desperation rolls off of him in waves. He coaxes my lips apart and I allow him entry. Gently tilting my head, he kisses me deeply and reverently. I feel his hand lower to my back and he lays me down. My brain ceases to exist. I want to feel. I want to have him in my body and my soul because I don't know if I'll ever find a love like this again. And even with all that was exposed tonight, I can't give up everything for him. I can't give up my dreams. So I'll give him tonight, and pray tomorrow doesn't kill me.

chapter

twenty-five

EVERY MUSCLE IS tight as if someone is pulling me apart from the inside out. He kisses me languidly and ardently. All I want is more. I want aggression and roughness because the tenderness is breaking me. I want to forget. I need to get lost in him and for the world to fade away. No jobs, no loss, no sadness ... only us.

His lips leave mine as he kisses from my neck to my collarbone. "I've missed you so much," Jackson says quietly as he pulls the strap of my dress down, exposing my shoulder.

I close my eyes and memorize the way his lips feel against my skin.

He lowers the zipper of my dress. "We don't have to do this," I say unsure of what I'm feeling. He bared his soul, told me about the loss of his wife and child—it feels wrong knowing tomorrow I have to leave.

Jackson turns me to him, cups my cheeks, and waits for me to look at him. "I need you. I need every part of you. You make me whole."

My chest is weighted by his words because I'm going to hurt him. I know I am and I think he knows it too. "Just for tonight," I say hoping he understands. "You have me."

Without answering he lowers his lips to mine, stopping all conversation. I close my mind off. If I think about what this is, it'll kill me. The loss that this man has endured, the pain that we've caused each other, is too much. But if he needs this, then he can take from me. I've taken enough from him.

"You're so beautiful," Jackson says letting me know he in no way takes this moment for granted. My dress comes off. He leaves on my heels and I lie here as he admires me while taking off his uniform.

"Let me," I say, sitting up.

Each button that I undo I lose a part of myself—a part of us.

Trust. I trusted him. I trusted us—but we failed.

Another button.

Hope. We shared hope that we would be enough for each other.

Another button.

Security. He made me feel safe, loved, adored.

Another button.

He stops my hands from moving and he removes the tears I try to stifle. "Stay with me."

I nod as his shirt falls. He removes his undershirt and my eyes fall to the scar on his chest. It's no longer red and angry, but it serves as a reminder of how close I came to losing him forever. The scar marks a time that I will never forget. But I don't want to remember any of it because it'll make telling him about the job that much harder. My stomach churns and I struggle to hold it together.

"Jackson, make me forget," I plead. I need to do anything but feel.

His lips crush mine and he lays me down. I relish in the way his tongue dances with mine, volleying for control. When his hands softly graze against my body I shiver. The weight of him on top of me holds me together. His arms press me against him and I'm whole once again.

Releasing me, he never breaks eye contact, forcing me to stay in the moment and not retreat into my head. Jackson's eyes swim with emotion, but he slowly moves his lips to mine while he removes my bra.

"Every part of you belongs to me," he whispers against my lips.

"Take me."

Slowly his tongue glides to my neck as he makes his way to my chest. When his mouth latches on to my nipple, I cry out in pleasure. Jackson's tongue circles it slowly and then he licks his way to my other breast, lavishing it with the same attention.

"I love you," he says as he makes his way to my stomach.

Every part of me wants to tell him how much I love him. Every cell in my body is crying out to give in to him, but I fight it. I resist it because I know it doesn't change the position we're in.

"Please," I beg so he'll stop talking.

Jackson slips my panties down my legs and his fingers brush against my clit and my back bows off the floor. "Jackson," I sigh as he spreads my legs apart and I feel the scruff of his cheek against my thigh. The roughness sets my body on fire. All I want is to stay in this moment forever. Just the two of us tonight, because I don't want this night to end. I want to freeze time and live right here forever.

When his tongue touches me, I grip his hair. He inserts a finger and my body moves of it's own accord. Jackson's tongue enters me and he holds my hips fucking me with his mouth. "Oh, God," I cry breathlessly as his thumb presses on my clit.

He's barely touched me and I'm already teetering on the edge.

Jackson stops and I look at him. "If I only have tonight, we're going to take our time," he says answering the questions in my eyes. "Now flip over."

Again I stare at him, biting my lip, trying to figure out his plan. His hands travel up my body, and when he reaches my hips, he grips them and turns me over. I feel his weight and warmth disappear. Looking over at him, I see him remove the rest of his clothing. He's even more magnificent than the last memory I have.

He returns to my side and I feel his hands on my shoulders, pushing down, working out the tension. "I'm sorry," he says as his lips press against my spine. "I shouldn't have kept things from you."

I close my eyes and attempt to halt the tears. "I know. I'm sorry too," I say.

I'm sorry for the fact that this is where we are. To love someone so much but not be able to be together.

Jackson continues to massage my back without a word, stopping only to place a kiss every few minutes. After he's content with loosening my muscles, he turns me back over. The look in his eyes stops my heart. There's so much emotion in that single moment. The most dominant is despair. He's breaking and I'm already broken.

As we hold each other's gaze, Jackson enters me. It's like coming home. We fit like two pieces of a puzzle. My body welcomes him and he sighs.

"I need you," he says as he slides back and forth. "I hate who I am without you. You have no idea how miserable I am. Please, come back to me," Jackson requests, but I don't respond. "No more secrets."

"I miss you too." It's all I can say because I can't make promises. I'm miserable without him too, but I was living. My life was working out, but now I want to lock myself away with him and never leave.

Jackson grinds his hips and my body climbs higher needing release. I moan and close my eyes.

"I need to see you," he says through gritted teeth. "Let me see you when you come."

I open my eyes and try to keep them on him while he continues to hit the spot that's driving me to orgasm. "So. Close," I gasp in between thrusts. I grip Jackson's face and pull him to me as my tongue delves into his mouth. I lose myself and my body rockets into another world.

Jackson continues milking every ounce of pleasure I'm capable of feeling before he loses it. "Fuck, Catherine. I love you," he says as he orgasms.

We lay here, both spent emotionally and physically.

After we both clean up, I see him in my father's office. "Is this him?" he asks, finding a frame I missed during the packing.

"Yeah, that was my dad," I say looking at the photo.

"You look like him."

"Jackson we should talk," I say softly.

"Not tonight. We've done enough talking. Tonight, I just want to pretend," he murmurs and pulls me against his chest.

I sigh and wrap my arms around him. As much as I want to pretend as he's asked, I know it'll only leave us both in worse shape tomorrow. "I don't want to hurt you."

He rubs his hands up and down my back and sighs deeply. "I know." He places a kiss on my forehead. "Let's go to bed."

My lips press against his scar on his shoulder.

We move into the bedroom and he hands me his t-shirt. A smile spreads across my face as I remember how much he likes seeing me in his clothes.

Today has been overwhelming and heartbreaking. I think about how strong Natalie is, how she lost the man she loves and can't ever get him back. I have the man I love in my arms and I'm going to let him go willingly. I wish I could be mad again. Mad didn't hurt so much. It made leaving a little easier because it was his fault. Now, it's a choice.

Jackson's arm slides under my shoulder and he pulls me against his chest. "Is there anything I can say to change your mind?"

I look up at him and a tear falls. "No."

He nods once and pulls me tighter. "I'm not going to give up. You're mine and I'm going to win you back. I'm just warning you."

"Jackson ..." I start and he brushes the tear running down my cheek.

"No tears."

"It hurts so much."

His eyes stay focused on the ceiling. "I won't hurt you anymore. Nothing heavy, I just want to hold you, talk to you, love you."

"How?" I ask because I don't see how we can pretend.

"Easy. How've you been?" His fingers run up and down my arm as we lie in each other's arms.

This will last a few questions before we find a way back to the conversation we should be having.

"I'm living. How's your leg?"

"Today I overdid it, but it was worth it. I wasn't going to be on crutches for the memorial. Did you get to see Aarabelle?"

I smile thinking about how beautiful that tiny baby was. I promised Natalie we would see each other before I leave for California. "She's perfect."

"Yeah, she is. Natalie asked me and Mark to be her godfathers."

"She told me. I think you'll spoil her and do all the things you're supposed to as a godfather."

My mind drifts to how Jackson would be a father right now. He'd have his own baby to love but he's lost that chance.

"Jackson, this is too hard. It's going to hurt even more in the morning."

"It can't hurt any more than it already has," he says quietly and adjusts himself to be more comfortable. "Go to sleep, baby."

I was a fool to give him tonight. To think I could ever give him one night and it wouldn't ruin me. Allowing him back in my heart even if only for a little bit reminded me all the reasons I loved him. His heart, his hurt, the way he loves are all there buried beneath a lot of guilt and pain. Jackson's lived through hell, yet never let it destroy him.

Tonight I'm in the arms of the man I love. Tomorrow I won't be. Selfishly, I close my eyes and allow the exhaustion to take over so I can pretend tomorrow isn't coming and I can dream of Jackson like I do every night.

I wake up overheated and I can't breathe. Trying to get air, I realize it's because Jackson has his entire body wrapped around me. His legs are tangled with mine and his arms are steel cages around me, ensuring I can't go anywhere.

He begins to stir and I try to disentangle myself, but he shifts and somehow pulls me closer. "Jackson, I can't breathe," I mumble, trying to move him.

"Shhh, it's not tomorrow if we sleep."

"Let me up."

Jackson pulls his leg tighter around mine. "No."

Glad to see he hasn't lost his defiance. "Please, you're smothering me."

"I'll smother you in another way if you want," Jackson says groggily.

"Not until we talk. Now let me up, I need to pee."

He groans and lets me up reluctantly. "I'll be here in case you change your mind about the smothering."

"I've got the closing in a few hours. I need to get up and get ready. But thanks for the offer."

He laughs and gets out of bed while I hop in the shower.

This conversation is happening and time isn't on my side. All I want to do is wrap my arms around him and hold on. My heart aches when I recall everything we shared last night. I hate how his fear of thinking I'd see him at fault kept him from telling me. Our paths might have been different than they are at this moment. My dream job is in California but my dream man is in the other room. I can't give either up but I have to choose.

I clean up in the bathroom and when I come out, I smell coffee. Making my way into the kitchen, Jackson is standing there in his boxers and I can't hold back the appreciative sigh.

The cocky smile spreads across his face when I'm caught admiring him, but he doesn't say anything.

Once I have my cup of coffee we sit at the table. "We should talk," I begin.

"I'd rather not," Jackson says as he leans back in the chair.

"I'm sure, but I need to get this out."

He grabs my hand and laces his fingers with mine. "I need to say something before you start. I never wanted to keep secrets."

"But you did."

"That night Aaron died, when we sat on the couch, I had it all planned out on how to explain about Madelyn." His grip tightens slightly. "Then I got the damn call from Mark. I couldn't think straight. I was responsible for someone else's death. Then I was shot and I wanted to forget about it and be with you. Here's the thing," Jackson pauses and runs his hand through his hair. "Even if Maddie was alive, I don't think I'd be married to her. I resented her for making me leave the Navy."

My stomach rolls as I think about the resentment he talks about. It's how I'd feel about him if I gave up my job. I release Jackson's fingers and sit back in my chair holding my hands tightly.

When I look up, he rubs his hand down his face. "I've really lost you, haven't I?"

Looking at the table, the poisonous word is on my tongue. "Yes."

"I saw it in your eyes," Jackson admits and my heart breaks at the sadness in his voice.

I thought he knew but I wasn't sure. If I could go back in time and rewrite our history I would. I'd do so many things differently, but this is life and love is messy. There's no pretty bow on the box.

"I know yesterday was a lot for you and for me. I can't begin to tell you how sorry I am for all you've lost. No one should have to go through that. I know you weren't trying to hurt me by not telling me about your wife."

"But it doesn't change anything for us, does it?"

Oh, how I wish it did.

"No. Things have changed for me."

"Is there someone else?" Jackson asks and he gets up out of the chair.

"No, there's no one else."

"Then what? Just say it so I can fix it," he says hurriedly.

I close my eyes and say the words I don't want to tell him, "I'm moving to California."

"What? When?" He starts to pace around the kitchen.

"I leave in three days," I say looking down, not wanting to see his face.

Jackson sits back in the chair and doesn't say a word.

"I was offered a large promotion in CJJ. It happened a few days after we broke up. Anyway," I say as the pain lances through my chest. "I was offered to head up the office they're opening out there. It's a huge opportunity for me, and it's what I've dreamed of." I look up and he closes his eyes.

"Funny," Jackson pauses and let's out a shaky laugh. "Here I sit with the shoe on the other foot and all I want to do is beg you to stay with me. I want to say anything to make this not happen, but I can't ask you to give up your dream job. I fucking hate this."

A sob erupts from my chest and Jackson's arms are around me in a moment. "I knew I shouldn't have let you in last night. I knew this was going to kill me today," I cry against his chest.

"I'm not letting go, Catherine."

I grip his shoulders and hold on, not knowing when I'll ever feel his body against mine again. "You have to."

Sure, we could try and make it work long distance, but who knows how long that would last for. Jackson runs two companies and travels, and my job is going to be extremely demanding.

"We'll see," he says and releases me. Jackson stands there

for a minute before heading into the living room as he collects his uniform.

I sit here feeling desolate and numb.

When he returns, he pulls me from my chair and holds me one last time. "Can I call you?" Jackson chokes out.

I look up and see the emotion in his eyes. "I'd like that," I say as my heart shatters.

"I love you, Catherine."

The tears stream like rivers down my face. "I love you too, Jackson. So much. I wish ..." I trail off unable to say what I wish because we both know.

"Me too, baby. Me too. I'll call soon."

I close my eyes as our lips meet. He holds my head and we both pour everything we're feeling into each other. Jackson pulls back from my lips too soon. He kisses my forehead once and turns, walking out the door. I hear the door close and I crumble to the floor.

Love is messy and life sucks.

chapter

twenty-six

THE HOUSE IS sold, my things are packed, and I'm finally taking care of some last minute stuff before my last day of work tomorrow. My emotions are all over the place. I'm sad that I only have a few tangible things to hold onto of my father's. I'm excited for the new venture my life is about to embark on. Most of all, I'm broken over losing the love of my life. I go from one extreme to another depending on the hour.

It seems like the only part of my life that I have any control over is my work. Tristan and I have planned out the first week and he's already setting things up with new employees. Already he's proven himself to be valuable and reliable.

My phone rings and it's Natalie.

I swipe the screen to answer. "Hey, Nat," I say with a big smile.

"Hi, Cat," she giggles softly. "Aren't we the rhyming names?" Natalie muses.

I laugh with her, "I'm glad you called me back. I'm so sorry I left so fast."

"It's fine. Honestly, the memorial was a blur. I would've talked to you and probably not remembered. I thought being so far out from his death it wouldn't have been so hard for me."

"I don't know anyone would ever fully get over it, do you?" I ask.

"Probably not," she pauses. "I heard you're leaving in a few days."

I sigh and run my hands through my hair. "Yeah, I leave in two days."

"The last thing I expected to hear was you were going to California. Why didn't you tell me?" She chuckles but I hear the hurt in her voice.

"Sorry, I don't have any excuses. I didn't want him to know." I feel bad because I didn't want to be deceitful but at the same time I didn't want to risk it.

"I get it. Listen, I'm leaving New York and I'd love to come stop by on my way back to Virginia. Are you around?"

"Yes!" I practically yell. "I'd love that. I have some stuff I need to finish up around here, but I'd love to see you and Aarabelle."

"Great. Text me your address and I'll head over."

I send it off and try to clean up a little more before she gets here. I'm excited to hold the baby and get to spend some one on one time with Natalie. Our entire relationship has been only through phone calls. Then there was the memorial, but it really wasn't the time for a big friendly chat.

The doorbells rings a few minutes later and I rush over to open it.

I swing the door open and she stands there holding Aarabelle. "Hey, come in! Come in." Aarabelle is beautiful. Her pretty pink dress and white frilly shoes melt my heart. You can't help but want to smile around babies.

"Thanks," Natalie smiles and enters the room. It's amazing how someone who just had a baby is already as tiny as she is.

She places the baby in the car seat as she puts her long blond hair into a quick braid. Natalie's bright blue eyes narrow and she looks me over. "You look like I feel," she chuckles.

"That bad, huh?" I ask.

"No, not bad at all, just tired of it all."

We sit on the couch and I fight back the emotions bubbling up. This woman has truly lost it all. The man she loves is gone and she will never see him, touch him, or hear his voice. Jackson isn't dead, but there was a time where that could've been the outcome. I sat there watching and wondering if he would make it.

"I guess you know everything?"

Natalie places her hand on mine and smiles. "We'll talk boys later, let's talk about the job."

"Only if I can hold that beautiful little girl." I grin and she laughs.

"Of course!" Natalie says as she grabs Aarabelle. "I swear, she hasn't been put down once in her life." We both laugh as she hands her to me.

Her tiny frame fits in my arms as I delicately hold her.

We talk a little about the job and the move. Before I finally turn the tables onto finding out about her. "How are you doing?" I ask Natalie.

"Some days are good. Some days are awful. Post-partum doesn't help but she grounds me. She makes me get up and live. Plus, either Mark or Liam, Aaron's swim buddy, call or stop by daily. They drive me absolutely insane," Natalie says with a soft smile as she gazes at her daughter in my arms.

"I'm sure Mark can drive anyone nuts."

"Well, then there's Jackson, who calls me practically every damn day. I know they're all worried, but honestly, Cat, I knew this was going to be my life. The reality was that one day this could happen. I was built for this. I entered a marriage with Aaron knowing he could die. Does it hurt any less? No, but it was the chance I took when I loved him."

"You're so strong," I say looking at her and then at Aarabelle.

She lies sleeping, oblivious to all the pain in this world. She'll grow up very similar to me. I know what it'll feel like for her to have no father for a father-daughter dance, how she'll feel sad when other girls in her class talk about their daddies. Aarabelle will never know what his hugs feel like, what it's like to have an in-house protector from childhood on. I remember the pain and hurt of not knowing that kind of love. Although this little angel will never really be without a man because of Aaron's military family, but it won't ever be her daddy. When she's ready to give her heart to the man she loves, she won't have him there to give her away.

"Strength isn't measurable, it's inside of each of us and we need to find it when we feel weak. I refuse to break. Besides, I'm no different than you are right now."

Natalie's statement snaps me from my internal pain. "I'm not half as strong as you are."

She leans forward and fixes Aarabelle's dress. "I see it differently. At least from what Jackson explained."

"I'm not sure what he told you."

Natalie smiles warmly and her head tilts to the side. "He told me everything. About how he's an idiot and never told you about Madelyn. How he lied and hurt you. He explained it all."

"I wish he would've told me before."

"When she died, it destroyed him. I've seen these guys low, but he was beside himself. It was like he shut off every part of him that could feel. Plus, if he had told you, you have no idea what path your life would've taken. I think all the choices we make are a road we were meant to veer off onto." Natalie absently coils her hair around her finger. "I loved Aaron more than anything. We were together since we were nineteen. I was there with him when he signed the papers and left for boot-camp. I watched the bus drive away with him on it. I was there the day he graduated and then went through BUDs. My life was always his. Even when he got out," she laughs softly. "My life has never been my own. Everything we did, everywhere we went was always Aaron's choice. Now I have to choose and I don't know what to choose." A tear rolls down her face and she catches it.

"You have so many people who love you and Aarabelle. I know Jackson would help you in any way."

Aarabelle begins to stir in my arms and then settles.

"I know. He's kinda a good guy."

"Yeah. Kinda." I laugh and Natalie joins me.

"Okay, no more heavy crap. I think I've had all I can take. Tell me about California."

We spent the next hour chatting about life, California, and all the things about being a mom. Natalie was stationed in San Diego for years and tells me all the places I need to go. We talk about how much she loved it out there and how she'd love to come visit.

"I'd love to keep chatting, but Aara and I need to get our butts on the road," Natalie says as she puts Aarabelle in her car seat.

"Thanks for coming over. I know we never really saw each other, but I'm going to miss you."

Natalie smiles and pulls me in for a hug. "If things hadn't happened the way they did, we wouldn't have met," she pulls back and looks at me. "I know he hurt you, but don't give up." I nod and she continues, "I've lost the great love of my life. I know what it feels like to have that taken away. I'm not telling you not to go and follow your dreams, because I think you should go. Sometimes love isn't enough, but sometimes it is. He does love you though, don't ever doubt that."

"I don't doubt his love. And I love him, but our entire relationship has been one thing after another. We've gone from bad to worse to amazing and then plummeted again. I need to rely on myself. I just hate losing him at the same time."

She pulls me back in for a hug, "I'm sorry."

I laugh against her. "I can't believe you're consoling me."

"I'm happy for once I'm not the one blubbering." Natalie laughs and we say our goodbyes.

Unfortunately, this is only the beginning of them.

"Taylor, please come in here!" I ask her once again. My flight leaves tomorrow morning and I don't have a lot of time. She keeps ignoring me and making excuses why she doesn't have time for my "bullshit."

"No!" she yells from outside the door.

I shake my head at her refusal. "Fine. I'll just keep your present or maybe I'll give it to Ash."

She pops her head in the door. "Present? I like presents." Her eyes brighten.

"Dork. Get in here."

"Give me a second and don't you give that to anyone else!" she exclaims and disappears somewhere.

I don't know how I'm going to get used to dealing with a new assistant. Taylor has been my right hand and sometimes my left. I'm not sure I'm half as good as my bosses think I am without her.

"You got a present too." She smiles as she brings in a huge bouquet of yellow daffodils.

"Wow. You shouldn't have."

"Good, because I didn't," she explains.

"Want the card?" Taylor holds it up smirking.

I walk over to her and take the vase. "Yes," I say putting them down admiring how beautiful they are.

Opening the card from the same florist Jackson used the last time.

Great.

I brace myself for another card like the last.

Dear Catherine,

Did you know there are meanings behind each flower? Like I had nothing else to do today but find one that said what I couldn't say to you. I thought maybe this would win me a few brownie points too since I spent an hour googling flower meanings. Apparently, this flower says you're the only one and some shit about sunshine. I thought you should know

that even though you're going to California tomorrow, you're taking my sunshine with you. You're the one for me. I'll miss you and I love you.
   Yours Always,
   Jackson

I grin and clutch the card to my chest. It's hard to picture Jackson sitting around googling flowers but it means a lot to me. We spoke once and he asked to see me again, but I told him it would be too hard for me, so we've texted a few times. I told him when I got to California I'd call, but it hurts and I don't know if I'll be able to.

"Is he being all swoony again?" Taylor asks, trying to read over my shoulder.

"Isn't he always? I swear it's impossible to resist him."

"That's the truth. He's kinda perfect, isn't he?"

I take a deep breath in and then release it. Yeah, he's pretty damn perfect.

"He loves you, Cat. I have a feeling you two are going to find a way."

"I let him go, Tay. He knows there's no way."

As much as I'd like to believe the words I speak, I know it's not completely true. I don't know that I'll ever really let him go. He found a way to penetrate my soul. Jackson fits me in every aspect and if I wasn't leaving for California, I'd be back in his arms. All our secrets were laid out and we would have been happy and in love. Instead we'll live apart, knowing how much we both wish it was another way.

"Sure. Whatever." She gives me the stink eye and then looks around the room. "Okay, where's my present?"

I pull out the bag from Michael Kors and her jaw falls slack. "No way! Thank you. Thank you. Thank you!" she yells after she recovers.

"I'm going to miss you so much. Promise me you'll call me, and I want to hear all about the new job. Especially if that twunt, Piper, gets hit by a bus." I wink trying to keep from getting emotional.

We give each other a long hug and laugh.

Once we finally get a grip, Taylor asks, "Did you hire your new assistant?"

"Yes, he's starting to get things set up. I think you'd like Tristan."

"Probably, but I'll pretend not to. He better be on his game to handle you."

"I'm not that bad ... well, maybe."

A few people stop by the office and say goodbye while I make sure the files I need for California are in order. I look up when I hear a knock at the door.

"I wanted to wish you a *very* safe flight," Piper sneers.

I smile and tilt my head to the side, unwilling to let this bitch ruin my last day in New York. "Why, thank you, Piper. That's awfully kind of you."

She glares at me, "Did you hear? Neil and I are moving in together." Her brow quirks as she tries to goad me.

Not working, but thanks for playing.

It reminds me that Neil was making out with another blond. I wonder if they're all going to live together or if Piper is unaware of her boyfriend's extra plaything.

"No, I missed that news, but I saw you guys at the bar the other day. Did you see us?" I ask sweetly.

"I have no idea what you're talking about."

"Oh, I swore it was you. I mean, Neil was clearly shoving his tongue down a petite blond's throat." I shrug and return to my paperwork, trying to smother my smile.

I've waited months to hand it back to this bitch and I'm going to enjoy every second. She stands there waiting for who knows what while I ignore her.

"Nice. Glad to see you've come over to the other side. You're so full of shit that it's actually pathetic."

I look up with the smile I can't hide any longer. "I was

really sure it was you. I mean, Neil is such a stand-up guy. He would never cheat, would he?" I stand and walk toward her with my phone. "Look, Piper, see for yourself." I open the picture and extend my hand to her.

She glares at the phone, no longer petulant or sure of herself.

Karma.

"It won't bite," I push the phone closer. "How about we take a look together?" I put my arm around her and pull the phone close so we can both see it ... nice and close.

She tries to shrug me off, but she's unleashed my inner Ashton and I'm all too happy to be here to deliver her own worst nightmare.

"Look, that's definitely Neil, but hmmm, that girl ..." I look closer as Piper starts to shake. "Nope, that's not you, but I think she must be a friend of yours. She looks a lot like the reporter that was at the Raven press conference. Strange, right?" I move back and scowl at her.

"Fuck you," Piper replies.

"Nope, fuck you. You thought you were so much better than me. You treat people like they're beneath you, but you're the one who's beneath us all. Once upon a time, you were a nice and decent human being. I don't know what happened to her, but you should work on finding that girl again. In the meantime, get the fuck out of my office and go back to work. I'd hate to have to file a complaint since you're still on your thirty-day probationary period." I return to my seat, ignoring her presence.

I could screw her royally by going to any of the partners and claiming she did something. But I won't because I'm better than her. Knowing that right now she's feeling even an inkling of what I went through is enough. In the end, I'm better off. I got the job and I found real love. I might have lost Jackson, but at least I know what it feels like to really be loved.

"I won't—" Piper starts to say, but I put my hand up and

shoo her out.

"I'm done here. I suggest you be smart for once in your life and get out of my sight. I have work to do." I turn my chair and look out the window.

Vindication. Piper deserves to be alone and miserable. After the hell she's caused in my life, I should only be seeking revenge, instead I *almost* feel sorry for her. She's going to live a sad and lonely life. But ... not my problem.

I hear clapping coming from outside and when I spin my chair. Taylor is standing there clapping. "Bra-fucking-vo, my friend. That was spectacular."

"She had it coming."

"Ummm, yeah, she did. I wish you would've slapped her."

"Who are you and what have you done with my sweet, Midwestern assistant? The one who would've told me I should just pray for her," I ask.

"I killed her," she winks and walks into the office.

The text alert pings on my phone and I open the message.

Jackson: Did you know a one-minute kiss burns 26 calories?

I sit and focus on my phone wondering what is going on and why he wants me to know this tidbit of information.

Me: I did not know this, but thanks—I think.

Jackson: I think you should come over and burn some calories before your flight.

I laugh and look at the phone. He's incorrigible.

Me: You need help. Thank you for my flowers.

Jackson: I mean it.

Me: Mean what? The card or the kissing?

Jackson: Both.

Me: I'm sure you do. I can't ... I wish things were

different.

Jackson: Me too, baby. Call me when you land. I love you, Catherine.

I put the phone away and Taylor sits there smiling at me. I completely forgot she was there.

"Sorry, it's Jackson," I explain.

"I figured as much. Can I ask you something?"

I already have a feeling it has to do with Jackson, but I allow her anyway. "Sure."

"Do you regret choosing the job?" she asks earnestly.

The question I can't really answer because regret isn't really what I feel—it's sorrow. "No, I don't regret it. I think it's more like I wish we could go back in time. Things would be different, but then again who knows? Because if I was offered the position and I turned it down I would regret that. Especially if things didn't work out between us, and let's face it ... my relationship with Jackson hasn't been easy. So maybe us not being together allowed me to follow my dream without having to question what to do about him."

Taylor smiles. "I get that. When I moved here to follow Quinn, I kept thinking what if we broke up once we got here? But then I figured I'd be in New York City and I had the job here so I knew I'd be okay."

"I'm glad we are able to part as friends though. It doesn't hurt any less knowing that we both love each other and can't be together, but at least I'm not leaving thinking there's a wife somewhere. I can think of him and smile instead of wanting to punch him in the junk."

My heart still yearns for him. I don't know if that feeling will ever go away but at least I can have a tiny part of him. If or when he meets someone, I don't know how I'll handle it. The idea of him being with anyone else is too much right now.

"I'm proud of you, Cat."

"Thanks, Mom." I wink as Taylor and I laugh. We finish

up packing my office, then it's time for me to leave. I'm having dinner with Ashton and then my flight is early tomorrow morning.

"Okay," I say and take a deep breath. "Be strong. Don't take any of Elle or Piper's shit. My phone is always on and available to you," I say as my lip quivers. I hate saying goodbye. "You're one of the best people I know and I'm so proud of you."

Tears fall from Taylor's eyes and she nods. "Don't ever doubt yourself, Catherine. You're one of the strongest women I've ever known. I hope you know how much I've learned from you. Thank you for not only being one of the most incredible people to work for, but also one of my best friends. I'm going to miss you so much," Tay chokes out and hugs me.

"I'm going to miss you too but I'll be back to visit." I return her hug and try to stifle my own tears.

"You'll come back for the wedding, right?" Taylor asks.

"I wouldn't miss it for the world."

We embrace again and I leave my office for the last time. When I close the door a part of my heart breaks while another part comes to life at the new adventure I'm embarking on.

Now I have to go home and somehow manage to leave Ashton behind.

chapter

twenty-seven

ON MY TRAIN ride home, I think more about Taylor's question. I don't regret anything because it's brought me to where I am, but it makes me sad to think I would've given up an opportunity like this for anyone. I don't believe Jackson would've asked me to, but I probably would've wanted to stay with him. Which I probably would regret later on and possibly would've resented him instead.

When I get home, Ashton is sitting on the couch in her pajama pants.

"Aren't we going to dinner?" I ask.

"Nope."

What in the hell?

"Okay? I thought that was our plan."

She shuts the television off and stands with her hands on her hips. "I'm mad at you, Biffle."

"For what?"

This should be good.

"I don't know. I just want to be mad at you!" Ashton cries out and falls on the couch.

I sit on the couch next to her and lay on her lap. "I'm going to miss you too. This is so hard, Ashypoo. These goodbyes suck."

Ashton runs her fingers through my hair and her lips purse. "I'm sorry. I know this is hard for you." She puts the mask I know so well up, making sure she protects herself.

After a few moments of silence, Ashton starts up again, only this time her tone is light and playful. "I've decided what I'm going to do with your room."

"Oh, what did you decide? A pottery room or did you decide to make a home gym that you'll never use?"

The first time we talked about what to do with my room I almost peed myself. She had the most insane ideas, but then again, it's Ashton. Last we talked she was leaning toward a meditation room.

"Nope, neither. I'm going to make it into a library!"

"I feel as if you want me to react so I'm just going to say ... okay then, to the girl who doesn't read," I say, shaking my head.

"Jealous much?"

I laugh and snuggle into her. "You're nuts but I love you. Tell me why you look like a homeless person instead of dressed to go out?"

She lets out a long sigh and pats my head like a cat. "I want to spend our last night as roomies drinking wine and eating pizza. You know you won't be able to get Jersey pizza in Cali."

I smile and nod, "I know."

"I still can't believe you're leaving. You're lucky I haven't tied you up so you can't go."

"I might like it."

"You probably would, freak."

"You know it."

"What kind of kinky shit did you and Jackson do?" she asks laughing and sounding slightly scared.

"He didn't need to tie me up." I look up and wiggle my eyebrows.

Ashton smiles and swats my ass while laughing. "Yeah, I wouldn't willingly leave that man's bed either."

I flush thinking of some of the things Jackson and I did together. The way his body was made for mine, the way he could drive me to the end with his words alone. He was my other half in every way. I miss him already. Every night since the memorial he's starred in my dreams. My mind drifts to him during the day, and then he haunts me in my sleep. I close my eyes and hold my arms over my chest. One day. One day it won't hurt so much.

"Hey," Ashton nudges me. "I'm sorry. Let's enjoy our night with fattening food and then tomorrow hopefully you'll be so hung over you won't be able to fly."

A laugh escapes me at the logic in her plan and I decide I need to keep my thoughts of Jackson at bay. I made my choice, now I have to live with it.

"Okay, let's eat so I can be bloated."

"Deal."

The pizza gets delivered and we spend our night curled up on the couch talking about all the things I have to do in California. She demands that if I meet any Hollywood A-listers she's the first to know. Also if I start dating any of them she's agreed to quit her job and become my personal assistant.

Reluctantly we clean up and return to the couch.

"Let's have a slumber party like we did when we were kids," Ashton suggests.

"Okay," I reply and grab the blankets off the couch.

We turn the lights off and wrap ourselves up. I have to be up in a few hours and Ashton promised she'd take me to the airport.

"I'm going to miss you, Biffle." Her voice is quiet but I hear her.

"I'll miss you more," I whisper, but she doesn't respond.

A few minutes later, right as I'm about to fall asleep, I hear Ashton sniffle as a tear rolls down my cheek.

"Let's go!" I yell to Ashton as she drags her feet. We woke up and had coffee and a lot of tears. But now you'd think she just got out of bed. She's moving slower than normal. I swear she's doing this on purpose.

"I'm coming, Jesus. Calm your tits."

"Well, I'm going to miss my flight if you keep screwing around."

"We have plenty of time." Ashton rolls her eyes and walks away. "I'm gonna grab my keys."

This is the last time I'll be in my apartment. The memories besiege me of when we moved in and I smile remembering us fighting over the paint color. Ashton of course won, which is why we have a blue living room when I wanted brown. I smile thinking of the scuffmark on the floor that we covered up with a rug because we dropped a table. Ashton and I arguing over food, which couch to buy, and so many other things happened right here.

This is my home. It'll always be my home.

I glance at the photos on the wall and my chest squeezes when I see the one of me, Ashton, and Gretchen from high school. I know I'll never find friends like them again and even though there's the phone and internet, it'll never be the same. When I need a hug, or to be slapped around, they won't be able to.

Ashton comes up behind me and tackles me to the ground hugging me. "Don't leave me!" she says in an exaggerated panic and starts to tickle me.

"Ash!" I squirm and try to fight her off, but she holds me tight.

"You can't leave if I hold you against your will," she laughs and sits on my back.

"Get off me, you asshole! What are you doing?" I try to wriggle, laughing while she assaults me.

Ashton starts to bounce up and down, not letting up. "This is a struggle snuggle. Don't fight it—it feels better if you let it happen." She giggles and lies on top of me. "Let it happen," she whispers and pets my hair.

She's lost her mind. That's the only explanation. Girl has completely cracked.

"I'm going to give you a struggle if you don't get off me." I laugh so hard there are tears running down my face. "I'm gonna pee my pants!" I burst out.

She laughs and falls off me, lying next to me on her back looking at me. "Ohhh," she sighs and smiles. "I had to make us laugh or I'd cry again, and we all know that's a bad idea if I have to drive."

My heart warms and I return her smile. There's so much history between us, so many times we've laughed or cried together. I'll miss her more than I can fully express. She's my partner in crime and my world will be boring without her.

"You know you'll always be my better half?" I say as I sit up.

Ashton follows and smoothes her dark red hair into a ponytail. "Yup. I know, but one day Prince Charming is going to come along and sweep you off your feet," she pauses and stands. "Hopefully he delivers your ass back to New Jersey. Come on, you've got a plane to catch."

She grabs my hand and pulls me up. We head to the car and Ashton suddenly stops short.

"No more stop—" I start to say and freeze when I see Jackson leaning against a black stretch limo smiling.

Ashton turns blocking my view. "This is goodbye, Biffle," her eyes fill with unshed tears. "I'm going to miss you so much. Promise me we'll Facetime every day. Promise that no matter how amazing these people you meet are, they'll suck in comparison to me." A tear falls on her cheek and my chest tightens.

"I promise. They're no Ashton Caputo." I smile and she pulls me in to her.

"I love you. I'm so fucking proud of you, my friend. You're going to kick ass, take names, and be sexy as hell doing it. Don't doubt yourself, Cat." She wipes the tears running freely down her face. "I never have."

"I'm going to be so lost without you and your craziness."

We hug a little tighter and I hear Jackson approach, "Catherine, we have to leave if you want to make your flight."

I nod and pull her close once more. "Goodbye, Ashypoo."

"Bye, my love pie." We both sniffle and break apart.

Jackson grabs my bag and my hand as I look back once more. Ashton stands there holding her middle with tears streaming down her face. He hands my bag to the driver and helps me in the car. Looking out the window at her standing there, my tears fall faster. This is so hard. I want to stop the car and fix my best friend because she doesn't cry. She uses her sarcasm and wit to avoid hurt, but she's hurting.

Jackson's arms encase me and I take the comfort he's offering. Once again, in the back of a car, this man holds me together. Only this time it feels like it's me who died. There's no doubt that this is what I want, this job is everything I've ever wanted for my career—yet the things I feel like I'm losing are ripping me apart. I want it all. The love of my life, my best friend, and this job—but I can't ask them to come with me and I can't stay here.

"I know this is hard, believe me I know, but it'll be okay," Jackson says as his fingers graze the skin on my arm.

I pull myself upright and brush the tears off my face. "I'm so sorry," I say shaking my head trying to dispel the sadness. "You're here."

"Of course I'm here," he says tenderly, drawing me back against him. "You weren't leaving without me seeing you."

My heart sputters and I take a breath inhaling the masculine scent that is Jackson. God, I've missed his smell. It's comforting and arousing at the same time.

"You okay?" Jackson asks, holding me tight.

"I'll be okay until I have to say goodbye to you," I admit. This is only going to keep getting worse. "I'm surprised Ash let me go with you." I look up and he smirks.

"She's known about this for a while, baby. I called her and

let her know I'd be driving you."

With a shaky voice, I say the only word I can, "Oh."

"Don't be so surprised. I told you I wasn't going to let you go."

Jackson leans in and places a kiss against my temple and I close my eyes. Sometimes his gentleness breaks me more than anything. Right now, I want to beg him, plead with him to come with me. Get on the plane and we'll figure out all the shit later, but I can't. Especially knowing how his wife made him give it all up and how much he resented her. I never want to be the reason he gives something up. I want to give *to* him. This is the conundrum we face. My heart wants Jackson and my head wants to follow my dreams with this job.

Two good things and two broken hearts.

"I knew this was going to be impossible."

"It doesn't have to be."

My face pales as I look at him. "How doesn't it? My job is sending me to California. You're in New York. Sure, we could try, but when would we see each other?" I ask, attempting to keep an even tone.

"I don't know. I want to fucking turn this car around and take you home. Do you know how hard it is to drive you right now? Knowing this is the end. I feel like ..." Jackson trails off and grips his neck. "I'm not going to do this to you. I won't be selfish." He looks at me and I see the agony in his eyes.

"I'm no better. I want to beg you to get on that plane and come with me. But you can't and I won't ask you to do that."

"I fucked this all up."

"If we'd never broken up, I might not be going because I wouldn't want to leave you. So then what? Would I feel like you did about Madelyn?" I wince saying her name.

"I wouldn't have asked you to give it up." Jackson closes his eyes as we have our come-to-Jesus moment.

This is where the truth lies. Nothing would be different, but everything would be. I would either be getting on the plane and feeling the exact way I do now, or I wouldn't and be wondering if I gave up my career for nothing. Jackson's made me strong enough to do this. He's given me the power to get on this plane and while it will practically kill me, I'll survive. I don't know if I would've been able to do this six months ago. If it were Neil, I wouldn't go—and then what? Where would I be? Alone, broken, and jobless.

"How can we want this so much, but not be able to have it?" I ask him, hoping for some brilliant insight, because I don't get it.

"No one said we can't. We just can't right now. But I'm not giving up on you and someday, Catherine, we'll find our way back together."

"I wish today was someday."

"Me too, baby."

"Kiss me," I say breathlessly.

"Any time," he says as his hands encompass my cheeks and he places his lips to mine for a moment. He pulls back and his gaze is locked on mine, and I see my future, my past, and all that could be. Only none of it matters.

We spend the next few minutes of the drive to the airport touching, kissing, and drawing comfort from each other. When the car stops, my entire body locks in place. I can't do this. I can't walk away from him. Jackson grips my hands and I begin to tremble. I knew this would be too hard.

The driver opens the door and a sob breaks through.

Fuck.

I can't do this.

"Come on," Jackson says, brushing my hair off my face with his other hand.

"Dammit," I curse and a tear breaks free. "Dammit, Jackson."

He closes the door and grips my arms. "Look at me."

My eyes slowly lift to his and I see how much this is hurting him, but he's fighting for me.

"I've had to leave more times than I can count. I know what you're feeling. The fear, the excitement, the guilt, and everything in between. But this ... this is worth it. You worked your ass off for this and now you need to go grab it and run. Are you going to miss things? Yes. But, baby, it's all worth it. You're not going to lose the people who love you because *you're* worth it. There are no goodbyes between us. Okay?" he asks and my stomach coils.

Jackson opens the door and we exit the car. I'm splotchy and a mess. His arm wraps around my waist and he tells the driver he'll call him later. I look up in surprise.

"What are you doing?"

"I bought a ticket so I can get through security. I'm staying with you until the last second," he says matter-of-factly.

There's no way he can be any more perfect and completely impossible to resist. I really wish I was still upset with him because then I would get on this plane and not think twice. I'd hold on to the lies and hurt, but it's not there anymore.

We grab our boarding passes and head to the gate. Jackson holds on to me the entire time. He keeps me together while I feel like I'm falling apart. This shouldn't be this hard. I should be excited, but instead I'm totally distraught.

"Why is this so hard?" I ask mostly to myself, but I know he hears me.

Jackson pulls me in his lap, and when I look at him confused, he smiles. "You've been away from me long enough, I need you close."

And my heart melts.

"I don't want to lose you. I've been thinking and maybe we can try this long distance?"

"I don't want this to be it either, but how would that work? You're a busy man, and I'm starting up this office. I'll be inundated with meetings and late nights. You have two companies to run." I shake my head and try to force myself to not get caught up in this idea. "If we weren't on opposites sides of the country ..."

"I have a plane."

"And you have *two* companies."

"I know," Jackson's head falls against my side.

I open my mouth to speak, but they call to begin boarding.

Here is our end. Where there will be our goodbye contrary to what he says.

My eyes close and I tuck my head into the crook of his neck. I feel his pulse, hear his heart beating, and I don't want to move.

"I have to go, don't I?"

"You could stay forever, but I don't think that's in your plan," Jackson whispers from behind me and he helps me stand.

We're eye to eye and I fight hard to form a wall around my heart to protect me—but it's futile. "Forever is a long time."

"It wouldn't be long enough for us."

His eyes well with tears and mine spill over. They call for the next section to board but I don't move. I'm going to stay every second I can and burn this into my memory.

Jackson leans into me and kisses me worshipfully. His lips move against mine in perfect harmony. I lose myself to his touch. My hands grip his shirt and pull him closer. I want to take him inside of my heart and hold him there. They call for final boarding and Jackson breaks the kiss.

"It's time. No goodbyes."

"This wasn't supposed to be us. We were supposed to be together. This was our time," I say angrily.

"Shhh," Jackson puts his fingers to my lips. He clutches my face and breathes the words into me. "I'll find you again."

I close my eyes and hold on to his wrists, "I don't want to lose you."

The black chill of silence surrounds us. I have to let him go.

Our lips meet again and I taste the salt of our sadness.

Unsure of whose pain blurs between us. His tongue glides against my lips and I open to him. With each swipe of his tongue against mine, I break apart from the inside out.

They call once more for final boarding and he draws back and places a kiss against my forehead.

I look up at his turquoise eyes and choke out, "I don't want to let you go."

He's my everything.

"If you love something, you have to let it go. I love you enough to let you go. Go live your dream, baby."

We kiss once more and I hold on to his hand until the absolute last second. When the tips of our fingers disconnect, my chest tightens so much it physically hurts.

The last image I see when I glance back is the door closing as Jackson's head falls into his hands.

Now I know what it feels like to lose your heart.

CHAPTER

TWENTY-EIGHT

JACKSON

I'M A FUCKING idiot.

That's the only thing that keeps rolling around in my skull. I watch her walk away and do nothing to convince her to stay. It's like someone just shot me all over again. Pure agony. I want her to be in my arms, not on a damn plane. I could've asked her to stay, made her see what her leaving was doing to me, but I told her to go.

I *told* her to leave me, but I didn't think she'd go—or maybe I did.

I'm a fucking idiot.

She needed to choose and I can't blame her. Do I wish she would've stayed for me? Of course I do. She belongs with me. Then again, I've screwed up so many times I'm losing count. So I'm glad she got on that plane because I now know what I have to do.

I lived through her walking out the door once, but I won't live through it again.

Fuck that.

It's time to get her back.

Pulling my phone from my pocket, I call the limo driver to have him swing back and get me.

Then I call Mark.

"What up, dickhead?" he answers laughing.

I don't even have the energy to insult him. I have more important things to do. "I'm on my way to Virginia. It's time to get shit done."

"About fucking time. I was starting to question the legitimacy of your man card. I thought maybe you liked playing dress up with your little makeup company and I needed to be concerned with how often you might have stared a little too long after the showers," Mark crows in his condescending I-think-I'm-so-awesome-just-ask-me voice.

"You wish. There'd have to be something to stare at. I need to meet with Carter and if that doesn't go well, I have a guy in New York who I can call." The wheels are spinning in my head.

"You know Carter is going to be a prick. I would call your guy now and start the ball rolling."

"I'll handle it."

Mark gives a sarcastic laugh. "Just like you handled everything else? Let's face it, Muff, you've been fucking up left and right. So for once, listen to me. Call me when you land."

"Yup," I say, already forming a plan.

"It's about time you dealt with all this bullshit," Mark says and he hangs up.

Yeah, it is about time.

Two years ago, I went into a dark place. Losing Maddie and the baby was like nothing I've ever felt. When we lost the team guys, it was horrible, but she was my world at the time. I was so pissed at her for constantly riding my ass and needing me to give her more. Even though she told me to leave that day, I never should have. I lost her because I was selfish, and I won't do that to Catherine. When I found out Madelyn died, my guilt was overwhelming.

Once I get in the car, I instruct the driver to go straight to the other airport.

He looks at me like I'm half stupid since we're at an airport, but I need my plane. I text the pilot and tell him to be ready to leave immediately. I don't have time to waste anymore.

Catherine reminded me it was okay to love and live, and I'll be damned if she's going to live without me, let alone love anyone else. She's mine and I'm going to show her exactly what that means.

I land in Virginia and have an email from my brother-in-law stating if I want to meet him then I can meet him at the bar today or not at all.

I arrive at the restaurant where Catherine and I had dinner.

Being here reminds me of her.

"Jackson," I hear Carter approach.

I nod and I stand to shake his hand, keeping my attitude in check. While our last meeting was pleasant, we've almost come to blows a few times.

"Carter, thanks for meeting me."

"So, what does my favorite brother-in-law want?" he asks as he sits.

"I would really like to talk and be civil. Can we manage that?"

No one loved Madelyn like Carter did and no one hated me more than him either. I understood because I'd kill anyone who hurt Reagan, but I lost a lot that day too. The way Carter saw it was that I'd abandoned her to die.

"It's been almost two years since I've heard more than a word here or there. Let's not even talk about the brush off I got the last time we saw each other. I don't know what exactly you expect from me. What's going on?

"I won't bullshit you, so here it is ... I want you to take over Raven."

He looks at me and leans back in his chair. This was his

family's company and I'd be a total dick if I didn't at least give him a chance at it. When Maddie died, I asked him to take over, but he'd told me to fuck off and fade away.

"When she died, I couldn't imagine going to that office. Now, I have no desire to have anything to do with it. I'm doing well here and I don't want to move Chelsea and the kids."

I give a quick nod and bite my tongue from telling him how I moved because it was what she wanted, but Maddie wasn't his wife. My life was altered more than he can imagine. "I understand. I'll be making some calls today."

"You're just going to walk away from it?" he asks with brows raised.

"I'm making some changes in my life."

"I see. I have a question, since you're here," Carter says as he grabs his drink.

"Go ahead."

"Why did you walk away from the family?"

My eyes widen as I try to decipher the underlying meaning. "I didn't walk away."

"Yes, you did. I reached out to you numerous times. You came to Virginia often, I assume, but you never came and said hi. It was like when Maddie died you disappeared.

"I wish things were different," I pause. "I couldn't see you and the girls. I lost everything. My life was a mess and you hated me."

At her funeral, Carter called me every name in the book. He was distraught and had attacked me. I took it because I understood. It was my baby that killed his sister. It was my fault.

"I didn't hate you." Carter puts his drink down and watches me. "I hated everyone. Her for not being careful. You for leaving her that day. She called me after you left. She was upset, didn't know what to do. She said it felt like she was losing you." He closes his eyes and sighs heavily. "I know you didn't want to leave the Navy and yet you did it for her. I think she knew that too. Anyway, I told her if you loved her, you'd come back. Did you love her?" Carter's question pulls my attention.

"Of course I loved her," I pause. It's about time we have this conversation. "I gave up everything for her, man. I mean, you know how much I loved the Navy. I would've retired from there and even then they would've had to throw my ass out. But Maddie couldn't handle the deployments and the fear of me dying. So I gave it up."

"She used to cry every night that you were gone." He looks up and takes a drink.

I know this. I remember her telling me every time I had to leave.

"We met when I was active duty. She knew what a marriage with me was, but she said she could handle it."

"She couldn't."

"I figured that out. I did right by her so your anger is misplaced, brother. I loved her for a long time, but I didn't kill her. That baby was never planned, and honestly, I wouldn't have let her keep it knowing it would've killed her. I don't know how she got pregnant. We were very careful. *She* was very careful. I know you lost your parents and then your sister, and for that, I'm sorry."

Carter stands and extends his hand. "I'm sorry. I know you lost a wife and a child. That day, I lost a sister, a niece or nephew, and I lost a brother too."

I'm on my feet in a second and I grip his hand and clap him on the shoulder. "I think we both fucked up."

"I'm not proud of how I behaved, but I was fucking livid. At everyone, and you were there to take it."

"You don't have to explain how you handled your grief, but I need to move forward in my life."

Carter nods in understanding and we stand there as the weight of the conversation settles.

I feel like I need to lay it all out. I don't want any misunderstanding in what I'm telling him, and if we can ever move forward, then this will be the deciding factor.

"I'm going to be honest with you. I've found someone, and I can promise you, one day she'll be my wife. She'll never replace Madelyn, but I love her and would like your blessing."

"Is she the girl I saw here last time?" he asks.

"Yes," I reply waiting for him to say something more.

"I think Maddie would want you to be happy, and if she makes you happy then you better marry her before she realizes she can do better." Carter smiles and claps me on the back. He grabs his drink and swallows it quickly, then turns without another word.

"Don't worry, Carter. I'll grab the tab."

He throws his hand up and keeps walking.

Fucker.

I leave the bar and head to the office.

"All right, which one of you dickfaces parked in my spot?" I ask laughing when I enter. Only Mark knew I was coming, so I catch a few of the guys off balance.

"Oh, you work here?" Mark says walking over. "How'd it go with Carter?"

"I need to make a call to Hudson Pierce and see if he'll help me out."

Hudson and I met a few times in New York. If he's not willing, then maybe one of his contacts will be.

"Then what's your genius plan?"

"I'm going to get her back."

"What if she doesn't want you?" Mark asks, taunting me.

"That won't happen, but if it does she's going to find out just how persistent I can be."

He laughs and walks off. "I forgot how stupid you can be."

"I forgot what a jackass you are."

"I never forget that about you." Mark flips up his middle finger and I walk into my office feeling determined.

My phone bings.

Catherine: I landed.

Two words and I could punch a hole through the wall.

Me: I'm glad you're safe.

Catherine: I've got a lot to do in the next few days. I love you and miss you already.

Me: We'll talk soon.

I've got a lot to handle too, and the more time I waste, the more of a chance I have of losing her for good.

chapter

twenty-nine

Catherine

MY APARTMENT IS beautiful, but it feels empty. I feel empty. Around an hour into the flight, the tears stopped and I fell asleep. I was one of those weird girls who smelled her shirt because it made me feel closer to him. When I got off the plane, Tristan had scheduled a car service to pick me up. I couldn't help but think if it were Taylor, she would've been there. Tomorrow morning, we have a face-to-face meeting scheduled, so it's not a huge deal.

I walk around and put some things away. Giving myself a moment to absorb my new home, I sit on the couch and take it all in. The furniture is modern and comfortable. Everything screams upscale, from the cherry floors to granite counters. It has exposed wood beams in the vaulted ceilings and the light paint colors make it feel airy. I open up the windows and inhale the salty sea air. The breeze blows and I let the curtains flap as I walk around into the next room.

Entering the master bedroom, my jaw drops. It has two French doors that open onto a deck. I go out there and hold on to the wrought iron railing. The metal is cool even in the warmer temperature. Going back into the room I look at the huge king size bed that sits against the wall. There's a beautiful fireplace tucked in the corner of the room with light-colored stones that stand out against the deep grains of the wood flooring. As much as I want to love it, it could be a cardboard box for all I care.

I try to make myself feel happy. My choices have consequences and moving here means I had to sacrifice my relationship with Jackson. I knew this, now I need to dust myself off and live. Tomorrow I meet Tristan and we begin getting some staff hired. I need to focus on the task at hand and worry about my lack of a love life later—if that's even possible.

The sun is just now starting to set since I'm three hours behind New York. So while it feels like eleven p.m., it's really only eight here. I see a very early night in my future.

I hop in the shower to wash off the plane and airport smells. When I get out, I throw my hair up in a bun and put on one of Jackson's t-shirts I stole. I feel like I ran a marathon. Even with sleeping on the plane, my entire body is worn out.

Closing my eyes, I sink into the plush sofa, wishing I had someone to hold me close. If I try hard enough I can feel his arms wrap around me, blanketing me with his love and protection. Pulling my shirt up I inhale again, wanting to smell his cologne, but already the smell is fading.

My phone lights up and I smile seeing a text from Jackson on my screen.

> *Jackson: Did you know a female ferret would die if it goes into heat and doesn't find a man to satisfy her?*

> *Me: Good thing I'm not a ferret.*

> *Jackson: If you need some satisfaction, I'm right here, baby. I'd be on my plane before you finish talking.*

> *Me: I'm not surprised.*

> *Jackson: You know I'm happy to be of service. I've been*

known to be equated to God by someone a few times.

Me: She must've been confusing you with someone else.

Jackson: Take it back.

I laugh at the easy banter we have via text message.

Me: Did I bruise your ego?

Jackson: I'm going to bruise your ass if you don't take that shit back.

Me: I'm sorry I can't hear you. Reception is really bad here.

Jackson: Funny, I'll be sure to hold off your orgasm the next time. Or maybe I won't let you come at all.

I begin to respond but I can't type the words. There won't be a next time. Unless I pack up my things and leave right now. And there's a huge part of me that wants to, but that would mean losing what I love to do. Back to square one.

In time, I know everything will fade. The memories, the pain, and eventually our love will cease to exist. It's reality and no matter how hard I fight, our separation in distance will cause a fault in our relationship. I relax into the sofa and hold on to the last touch we shared, hoping we'll find our way back together again. As the exhaustion overtakes me, I close my eyes and see him there in my dreams, waiting with open arms.

"Catherine?" I hear someone calling. "Catherine, are you okay?" I hear a deep baritone voice and open my eyes to a man standing in my living room.

Why is it so damn bright?

Who the hell is in my house?

I leap off of the sofa and shuffle backwards.

His hands fly up and he backs away. "Sorry to scare you, but the door was unlocked. I'm Tristan."

"Oh my God," I grab my throat and focus on breathing. "You scared the shit out of me."

"I called five times and got a little worried that you didn't get here. So I came to check on you this morning. I knocked and then when the door opened, I got nervous," he says slowly lowering his arms.

"I didn't hear anything."

"You should really lock the door at night," he chides as I rub my chest trying to get my heart rate back to normal.

"I don't know if I should thank you or punch you."

"I'd rather the first option if I get a choice."

Tristan smiles and I give myself a second to look at him. He's tall, lean, and has dark brown hair. His eyes are a lighter brown than mine and his smile is mesmerizing. It's obvious that he takes care of himself by the way his clothes fit. The muscles on his arms are impressive. Tristan moves with grace as he looks around the apartment.

"Wow, this place is way better than where I live," he muses.

What time is it?

"Am I late to our meeting?"

"No, I was just worried."

I grab for my phone. Sure enough, I have nine missed calls—five from Tristan, one from Ashton, and three from Jackson. The men in my life apparently don't think I can take care of myself, and one of them doesn't even know me.

"Sorry, I was beat. I must've passed out. Thank you for checking on me though."

He smiles warmly, "Taylor called me and gave me very strict instructions and informed me if I screwed up she'd make sure I paid for it."

A smile paints across my face as I imagine my cute, little, Midwestern friend threatening Tristan.

"She's all talk, but I appreciate it. I'm gonna get changed real quick. We can grab some food and then get to work."

"I'll meet you in the courtyard," he says as he heads out of the apartment.

Looking myself over in the mirror, I'm deeply embarrassed. This definitely wasn't the impression I was hoping to give. I have the lines from the throw pillow across my cheek, my hair is knotted and sticking up in random directions. Quickly, I brush my teeth and hair. Throwing on my capris and a cute top, I hope for 'gym cute' or maybe 'hobo chic,' because right now all I see is 'hot mess.'

Tristan takes me to the restaurant down the street. We grab some coffee and a few things we can eat in the office. The drive from my apartment into the L.A. office is around forty minutes, but I was adamant that I wanted to be close to the ocean and not living in the city.

Once we reach the office, we settle in and start to make a plan. Some of the clients we already secured will be meeting with us this week. There's a lot to do to ensure the space is ready. Tristan already ordered some of the furniture and it'll deliver in the next few days.

"So, how did someone as young as you get so high up?" Tristan asks as we start to put some files away.

"Well, I busted my ass. I started as an intern while I was still in college, then I got hired full time. From there I made sure I was always on top of my game. I worked extra hours, helped without being asked, and became invaluable. At least that was my plan."

"I'd like to be a publicist after I prove myself."

"I'm sure you will." I smile at how he was able to let me know his goals without being uncomfortable about it. "I had a fantastic assistant in New York and she's now running accounts on her own. I don't believe in holding anyone back." As the words slide out, I'm brought back to Jackson. One day I'll be able to talk without somehow circling back to him.

"Must suck though, not really having time for anything other than work."

"I made time for friends and life outside of work. But yes, being a workaholic comes at a price."

A very great price for me.

"So there *is* a guy?" Tristan's voice rises in surprise.

"There was. What about you? Anyone special?"

"Are you asking me out?" he asks smirking, and then laughs.

I blink repeatedly and shake my head. "No, no, I was—"

"Catherine, relax. I'm kidding. You're missing a key part to my engine, if you know what I mean."

"Huh?"

Tristan pauses waiting for me to catch up.

"Oh!" I say as it clicks. "Sorry, the coffee and time difference are slowing me a bit. Well, he's a very lucky guy. Have you been together long?"

"Two years, and I'm sure this is going to floor you, but he's an aspiring actor."

I sit here enjoying how I can feel comfortable around him and not have to worry about a sexual harassment suit. It was one of the things Taylor warned me about, since there were plenty of times I had to have her come over late at night, or we were traveling alone.

"Is this something I'm going to hear a lot?"

"This is L.A., honey. You're going to be shocked when you don't hear it. Now tell me about this guy you gave up."

The next week passes without incident. Tristan and I work extremely well together. He's funny, smart, witty, and it's as if we're lifelong friends. Ashton and he spoke on the phone last night and she's in love with him. I'm pretty sure he feels the same.

Today the rest of the office starts work, and I'm both excited and nervous. There's a lot we need to do and I heard from Sean letting me know they'd be coming out later this week to see the set up.

"Cat, there's a delivery for you," Tristan says strolling through the door.

"He's never going to stop," I say more to myself than anyone.

Sure enough, Tristan is carrying in a large photo wrapped in brown paper.

"Is this from my favorite sailor?" he asks, trying to peel the paper back.

I slap his hand and start to open the gift. "Probably. He's been texting me and calling, but with the time difference it's really hard."

I rip the paper off and start laughing so hard I have to hold my stomach.

"What is that?"

Jackson sent a huge photo of my time from the obstacle course. However, in true Jackson fashion he added one question across the top: REMATCH?

"It's a long story, but let's just say Super SEAL lost and apparently isn't over it."

I pick up the phone and dial his number.

"Hello, baby." Jackson's deep voice vibrates through the line and I fight the urge to sigh.

"Hello, Muffin."

Jackson chuckles, "Oh, we're going to play that way?"

"Whatever do you mean, my dear?" I say playing coy.

"So what do I owe the honor of your phone call, Kitty?"

I purse my lips at his jab toward the nickname I hate so much.

"I got your present," I say looking at it while Tristan tilts his head as if he'll find some hidden meaning in the photo.

"Did you now?"

"I did."

Jackson clears his throat and muffles the phone, "I only have a minute, babe. I'm about to head into a meeting."

My lips turn down. This is the exact problem we'll face if

we tried for anything other than friendship. "It's fine. I have a really busy day too. My client is due here in a few minutes."

"I miss you," Jackson says and my chest tightens.

Tristan comes back in and taps his finger on his wrist letting me know we have to go. I pull the phone from my ear, "Okay."

"Okay?" He sounds instantly pissed.

"Not you. I was telling Tristan okay," I explain.

"Who the fuck is Tristan?" Jackson's voice no longer holds any tenderness.

"Jealous much?" I taunt him playfully. After a second of his silence I realize he's upset. "Relax, Muff. He's my assistant."

"You hired a guy?" Jackson doesn't sound any less pissed than before.

I huff and organize the file on my desk. "I did. And if I remember correctly you have women who work for you."

"Yeah, but they're old or ugly."

"Danielle isn't either of those," I gently remind him.

"Is *Tristan*," Jackson sneers his name, "old or ugly?"

"Well, he's definitely not old," I joke and he growls.

Jackson smothers the phone but I can still hear him. "Hold the fuck on, dude. I'm dealing with a pain in the ass on the other side of the country."

"Jackson," I call but he doesn't answer.

"Jackson!" I yell and I hear the phone clear.

"You can hold on too."

"Jackson we're not together and I don't have time to ex—"

"Don't. It's been a week and a half, Catherine. I'm fucking miserable and you're hanging out with some tool."

I roll my eyes as Tristan taps his foot letting me know I really need to go. "As much as I'd love to argue with you, I have to go. Apparently I'm late. Thank you for my present and you can forget about any kind of rematch. I'll never run that shit again. I love you, always," I say and I hear him grumble as I disconnect the call.

Tristan smirks playfully when I approach. "That was like watching a one-sided tennis match. I can only imagine what you just did to him."

I jab him with my elbow and we start walking to the conference room where our first Hollywood client is waiting. "He can handle it."

Tristan elbows me back. "Muff?"

I laugh at how someone who doesn't know Jackson or Mark would hear that word and insinuate what it means. "Not that kind of muff. Come on, we've got clients to sign."

After the meeting, I feel terrible about the way I handled the call. The entire time I wondered how I'd feel if the shoe was on the other foot. If he walked away from me and then taunted me about another woman, I'd be hurt.

I grab my phone and call, but it goes to voicemail.

"Hey, it's me. I'm sorry about before. Thank you for the gift. Give me a call when you get a chance if you want to talk. Miss you."

I set the phone down and feel even worse.

chapter

thirty

"HEY, WANT TO hit the beach?" I look up at Tristan standing at my door smiling. It's still warm and sunny even though it's fall.

"When?" I ask.

"Now? I have this amazing boss, who loves me. And she wants to stare at my luscious body." Tristan's eyes sparkle with mischief.

"I'm pretty sure you crossed about a hundred lines of inappropriateness, but I *am* amazing. Is the schedule clear?"

"Yup! Go home, grab your suit, and I'll meet you at your apartment."

Tristan and I have been spending a lot of time together since he's funny, sweet, and actually cares if I take breaks. Plus, he tells me that Taylor calls him to threaten his life daily.

I still haven't heard back from Jackson, which has been weighing heavily on my mind. I send him a quick text while I'm on my way home.

Me: Hey, I'm sorry if you're upset.

Jackson: I'm not. I'm really busy. There are some big things going on that I'm handling.

Me: I understand.

Jackson: We'll talk soon. I love you.

Me: I know, I love you.

Sometimes you can love someone so much, but it isn't enough. It's been two weeks and already whatever I thought we had is dissolving. There is a part of me that knew all of this was going to happen. Loving someone doesn't mean that it'll work out. Plenty of times I thought love was going to make me whole. Neil for one, I loved him and he showed me how sometimes love is blind, and not in a good way. I loved my father, but that love couldn't conquer his guilt or reasons for staying away.

Then I have the good love. The people in my life who reciprocate love: Ashton, Taylor, Gretchen, and many more. Love shouldn't come with a price. It shouldn't take from you and make you miserable, because then what would you be left with? If I gave up everything for him and it didn't work out ... then what? No matter what the future holds, I know I'm strong enough to handle it.

I get changed and meet Tristan outside my apartment. The beach is within walking distance, so we head toward it on foot. The sun warms my skin and I draw a calming breath. The sounds of the seagulls above and the waves crashing soothe my soul.

"Do you miss Jersey?" Tristan asks after we find a spot and get comfortable.

I close my eyes and soak in the vitamin D. "I don't know. I miss some stuff but it's fall now and I'm at the beach ... that's pretty amazing. I don't miss the cold."

"So I won't be worrying about you skiing in Tahoe?" he laughs and I join him.

"Definitely not. I will be parked right here until the last beach day possible." I smile realizing I have no clue when that will be. I could get the beach for a lot longer than I even realized.

"Sweetheart, you're going to be a California girl sooner than you planned," Tristan teases.

We laugh and he promises to take me around L.A. and we plan a tourist day. The day passes and when I check my phone, I'm brought back to the small piece of me that won't let go of the east coast.

Jackson: Today, I miss you more than should be allowed. Today, I hate California. Today, I want to hold you, kiss you, love you. Today, I found one of your shirts.

I type out my response but delete before sending ... *Me: Tomorrow, you'll be okay.*

Instead I send:

Me: I miss you too.

Today marks a month since I've left New Jersey.

As much as I long for certain things, I'm growing into my new life. The office is now at a functional level, we have some new clients signing on. There are two publicists that work under me and we're in the process of getting the marketing team in place. Tristan is my lifeline. He's fast become my best friend out here. We spend so much time together, he's almost like a little brother—only not.

The only real dark spot in my life is Jackson. Since our last phone call, I haven't spoken to him but we've had an occasional superficial text. I spoke with Natalie last week and she said she hasn't heard much either. Thankfully, she and Mark still keep in touch. I also get random cat texts from Mark, but it makes me smile. I sent him a Twilight picture the other day and I got a nice text back: *Fuck you.*

Tristan is on his way over to have dinner and keep me company. He said we had to celebrate my one-month open office anniversary with wine and man-candy. I'm a little worried about what he means by the man-candy, but I'm going to go with it.

I'm sitting on my couch going over the proposal letters the

new publicist I hired is sending out, when my computer pops up with a video call from Ashton.

"Biffle!" I yell as I accept the call.

"Hello, my gorgeous friend," she smiles and I want to reach through the screen and hug her. "How's my California girl?"

"Eh, you know," I shrug.

"Nope, I sure don't, because you *never* call me, twunt."

"I've been busy and this time difference really makes it hard. Tell me about your life? Miss me?"

I figure if I can get her to talk about herself maybe she'll back off me.

"I made some babies, met some guys, dumped them ... you know, typical day."

"Still breaking hearts. What about Mark?"

"Pffft. Mark is in Virginia." She waves her hands in the screen. "Hello! I mean, you dumped your ridiculously hot boyfriend because you were a few states away."

I roll my eyes and huff. "I think you need to go back to geography if you think New York to California is a few! It's not even a few hours. It's a damn near six hour flight." I throw my hands up and give her the stank-eye.

"You're being dramatic," she smirks knowing she riled me up. "Miss me yet?"

"Not right now I don't." I give a forgiving smile. She knows I do and I know if there was any way I could make her come here I would've done it already.

"Tell me about the new clients." Ashton practically bounces in her seat wanting juicy details.

I laugh and talk to her about the office, how much I'm decorating. All to which she waves her hands telling me to move it along. She should know better than to ask me about my clients. Of course I can't resist taunting her a little bit.

"The new one we should sign this week you would die over."

"Oh my God, Cat! Tell me! I'm dying here."

"Now, you know I can't do that, but I will tell you I'm really happy!"

"Bitch! Show me the apartment and what it looks like outside," Ashton requests and her eyes glow.

"Okay." I smile showing her how close I live to the beach.

We talk about the location and how I've found a few cute shops. In all honesty though, I'm doing well. I've become close with Tristan and his boyfriend, Logan, and one of the girls in the apartment next to me and I had drinks last week. I make sure to rub in the warm weather when she tells me how it's starting to get cooler—but other than that I miss Jersey. The food, the friends, and him—all there.

"I think that's normal," she says with pursed lips. "You spent your whole life here, but it's been a few weeks now. I think you're doing really well. Have you heard from the Muffin Man?"

"No, after our last talk where he got insanely jealous over Tristan, we haven't spoken."

Leaning on her elbows she comes close to the camera. "Wonder why! You know he's all sad you left his ass crying at the airport. Then not even two weeks later you're joking about a guy. Stupid ass. I bet he'll get his shit together though."

"I don't think so. It's why I said it wouldn't work."

"Details, my friend. Well, have you guys spoken at all?" she asks curiously.

I huff and lean back. "I called and left a message, then a text, but I only got a quick text back. I miss him but I'm happy for the most part here. I don't know that I'll date anyone any time soon, but I have the beach, the sun, and I love being the boss."

"You never know, you may meet someone. Just leave your heart open. For fuck's sake, the man has done some pretty big shit. I can't see him sitting around New York giving up," Ashton says with a raised brow.

"I don't—"

I hear a thud at my door. "Caaaaaat," Tristan whines at my door. "Let me in."

"Speak of the devil. Hold on, you can *officially* meet Tristan."

I jump up and answer the door, letting Tristan in. He looks better than he did this morning, but I take pity on him. "Come on, want to meet Ashton?"

"She's here?" he instantly perks up.

I laugh and grab his hand pulling him into the living room. "No, but she's on the computer."

"Tristan!" Ashton squeals when she sees him. "Holy shit! You're hot!"

I giggle and he puckers up to the screen. "You're pretty sexy yourself. What do they feed you girls in Jersey? On T.V. they sure as hell don't do you any favors."

"Do not get me started," Ashton says irritated by his comment. "I hate those stupid reality-my-ass shows. We are not like that. Fuhgeddabout it," she says in her best Sopranos imitation.

"You don't want to get her started." I laugh and shake my head. "However, Ash, growing up we did think your dad was in the Mafia."

"Yeah, I'm still not sure what he does for living," she shrugs and we all laugh a little.

Tristan, Ashton, and I talk for a while and it's the first time I think I've laughed this hard. The two of them would drive me absolutely insane if we lived close. Between Tristan's flirting and Ashton constantly telling him she could flip him I've almost peed myself twice. After a few more minutes Ash has to go since it's midnight her time and she has to be in the lab early. Since Logan is filming a movie in Seattle, Tristan's been over here more. Might as well be lonely together.

"Movie?" Tristan asks after we go over a few things we need to get done this week.

"Sure, you pick something. I'm going to grab some popcorn

and candy—and pee." I hop up and head into the bathroom while Tristan looks for a movie.

"Someone's at the door," he yells to me.

"Can you answer?"

"Sure thing, hot stuff."

CHAPTER

THIRTY-ONE

JACKSON

KNOCK.

"Someone's at the door," I hear a fucking dude's voice say.

No motherfucking way.

"Sure thing, hot stuff."

I'll kill him.

My whole body locks up ready to beat the ever-living fuck out of whoever is in her house. I don't give a fuck if she's happy with him. He's done.

Time's up.

He opens the door and I puff myself up taller. His eyes widen as he looks up.

Yeah, that's right, douchebag. Now test me. I fucking dare you.

"Can I help you?" He smiles and I push forward through the door. "Hey asshole!" He calls to me but I couldn't give a shit.

"Catherine!" I yell and he grabs my arm.

Without a second thought, I grab him and push him up against the wall. Holding him there with my forearm.

"Where is she?" I ask and he holds on to my arm trying to make sure he has access to air.

"Can't. Breathe. Dying," he barely gets out.

I lean in and my voice is cold as ice. "If I wanted you dead, you'd be dead. Where the fuck is Catherine?"

"Fuck you," he says and I push harder on his neck.

The questions swirl in my head. Did he see her naked? Has he seen her face when she comes? Has he known what it's like to sink into her and bury yourself so deep you don't know where you begin and end?

My eyes narrow into slits as he tries to push against my arm.

"Jackson!" Catherine calls out and is already at my side trying to pull me off. "Put him down! Now!" she screams and pushes me.

"You're fucking kidding me." I let go and he slumps to the floor, gasping for air.

"You idiot!" She pushes me and goes to his side. "He's my assistant!"

Ohhh, so this is her "not old" assistant, Tristan.

I stand there seething, ready to punch something, someone. I can't fucking believe this. It's been *one month*. One. Not a year, but a month and she's already moved on. She's already fucking someone else.

"Seems you moved on pretty easily."

I'm too late.

"Unreal. You're unreal," Catherine says as she stands up after checking on him. "I haven't moved on, you asshole!" She pushes me forward and her touch wakes every part of me. "He's my assistant. Not my lover. You haven't called, or anything, in weeks, and then you show up and almost kill my only friend here."

"There's a fucking guy in your apartment! What did you expect me to think?" I ask as she pushes me back again. I stumble, walking backwards, as the rage practically steams out of her head.

Nice. I'm retreating from a five-foot-two woman. I'm a pussy.

"Wait, this is Jackson?" the *assistant* says from the floor. He's not a small guy by any means, but I'll lay his ass out if he touches her.

Catherine glares at me and turns to him. "Tristan, can you give me a minute with my *friend*?"

"Can I watch?" he replies but his eyes stay fixed a beat too long. My fists flex unconsciously.

"No!" Catherine yells.

"Damn, he's hot. Be careful, hot stuff, and call me in the morning." Tristan kisses her cheek and I growl.

This woman is going to be the death of me.

Tristan smiles at me and then looks at Catherine. "Logan's going to love this story." He turns to me and extends his hand. "I'm Tristan, by the way. Her assistant. Her very gay assistant."

Motherfucker.

I suddenly feel like I'm going to be laid out.

Or she's going to kill me.

I extend my hand and grip a little too tight. I may have figured out what an idiot I am, but that doesn't mean shit. "Jackson. Her ..." I trail off not knowing what to call myself.

"Dead ex-boyfriend," Catherine replies and glares at me.

"Nice to meet you." Tristan looks me up and down, but I'm smart enough to keep my mouth shut and nod.

She walks him out the door while I stand there waiting for the wrath to begin.

Five.

Four.

Three.

Another two heartbeats pass and I anticipate her fury.

But instead she stands there with her back against the door. Waiting for God knows what.

Not sure if I should speak or keep my fucking mouth shut, I just wait.

"Want something to drink?" she asks sweetly lifting her brow.

I'm so fucked.

"No, I'm fine. Look ..." I start to backtrack. "Think about how this looked for me."

"Hmmm," she says as she pours herself a glass of water.

"You've been gone a month. I fly here and some guy opens the door." I keep going because if my foot is this far in my mouth, I might as well lodge it all the way in. "He's calling you 'hot stuff' and I snapped."

"Mmmm hmmm," Catherine hums as she puts the glass to her lips and looks at me over the rim.

I start to make my way over to her. There's no way I can keep standing here without touching her. "You would've lost it if I was with another woman."

"Would I?" she asks, standing her ground as I stalk her.

I smile at this game we're playing, stepping forward. "I think you would."

Her lip slips between her teeth and I'm instantly hard. I need to get it under control.

"Why are you here?" she asks and her eyes drop to her glass.

Moving quickly, I'm in front of her in an instant. My finger pulls her chin up and my world stops. She doesn't see it.

"For you."

"Jackson," she sighs and tries to step away, but I grip her and pull her closer. I breathe her in, and when her hands grab my arms, I feel her tremble.

"I had this speech planned out but nothing with us ever goes as planned." I chuckle and she looks up.

Her brown eyes pin me and I need to touch her, taste her. I crash my lips to hers.

They mold to mine and I kiss her like a man dying of thirst. I need more. My hands move up and hold her neck in place. She sighs and my tongue delves into her mouth.

Heaven.

Every piece of her is heaven.

Catherine moans and I forget about everything but her. The sound she makes leaves me desperate for more. I want to taste her skin and sink deep inside her. I want to make love to her for hours until neither of us can move and then do it again.

She breaks the kiss and pulls back. "I can't do this again. I can't go through losing you anymore."

Good, because that's not happening ever again.

"I'm here for you. I'm not leaving."

She looks up and narrows her eyes, "I haven't heard from you in weeks."

I walk towards her as she takes another step back. She's not running from me ever again.

"I couldn't hear your voice and not hop on a plane. So I'm here now and I'm not leaving. I love you."

I need her. Right now. Lacing my fingers in her hair, I take hold of her again. I push her back and lift her onto the counter. When her legs wrap around me, I feel her heat and I lose it.

Every part of my brain detaches and all I can think about is feeling her. Her small hands glide up my arms as my lips press against hers. I graze my tongue at the seam of her perfect mouth, waiting for her to let me in. She opens them slightly and it's all the permission I need. My tongue pushes against hers and I pull her closer to me as she whimpers.

I pull back and nip at her ear. "I fucking need you. Tell me you want this." She has to tell me before I fucking erupt.

"I-I," she stutters, and my mouth covers hers again, pushing her to give me the damn answer I need. If I can keep her from overthinking, we might be able to get through this.

"Do you want me, Catherine?" My lips brush over hers, and every part of me is rock hard.

Her breathing increases and I take my tongue and sweep it across her lips. Per-fucking-fection.

"Jackson," she moans my name and I cover her mouth with mine again.

Fucking hell.

"Answer me. Do you want me?" I kiss her swollen lips, needing her again. "To keep going?"

"Yes!" she cries out as my hand finds its way up her shirt where I find she doesn't have a bra on. *Nice.*

"I'm not going to stop, so you better be absolutely fucking sure, baby." I don't know how or why I'm still talking.

She grabs my shirt and our eyes lock. Her pupils dilate and the fire burns through them. "You better not."

Hell yes. Don't have to tell me twice.

As much as I'd love to tease her and make her beg, I don't have the patience for it. I want to claim her. I want to feel her wrap her perfect legs around me and fuck me until all I can see, hear, feel, taste, and smell is her. I hope she's ready because I sure as shit am.

Releasing her perfect tits, my hands glide down her sides and pull her shirt off. I tease her with my tongue before sucking her nipple in my mouth as she writhes in my arms.

"You missed me, baby? Want me to fuck you now?" I know how much it turns her on when I talk dirty to her.

"God, yes."

I break away and smirk. I'm a cocky bastard but I can't help it. "I told you I was compared to God."

Her head falls back and she laughs. When she looks back up, she smiles. "Your humility is astounding. Now," her eyes harden, "Do you want to talk or do you want to show me how much you missed me?" She winks and pulls my head close.

There's my sex kitten.

Catherine takes hold of the kiss and I give her the control for a minute. She needs to feel the power and I'm willing to give it up for her. Plus, it's hot as hell when she gets aggressive. Her fingers weave in my hair and she pulls—hard. I almost blow my load right there.

I pull back and her eyes are liquid. I lift her and slide her shorts and thong off. I'm completely unprepared when she hops off the counter and backs me against it.

She's completely bare and she hooks her finger in my belt loop and pulls me against her. My hands glide across her delicate back to her round ass and I grip it roughly, lifting her up. Her hands fumble with the button and my jeans fall around my ankles.

With her mouth fused to mine, I shake my jeans off and grind down against her as she tries to line herself up with my dick.

"Not yet, baby," I manage to choke out as I try to find the bed or a couch.

"Hurry," she moans and then pushes her lips to mine.

Not able to see where the hell I'm going, I walk into the table.

Perfect.

"I'm going to fuck you so hard right now, but I promise I'll be sweet next time." I give her warning because the very thin thread is about to snap and I can't control myself.

Her hand wraps around my dick and I almost drop her. "I don't need sweet. I just need you."

Jesus Christ that feels fucking amazing.

"You've got me, baby."

She glides her hand up and down and I'm harder than I've ever been.

"Promise?" she asks, placing a kiss on my neck.

"Oh yeah, I promise." I lay her on the table and pull her hips close.

Before she can say another word, I push inside her.

Home.

I'm home and I don't plan on leaving again.

Her eyes close and I lift her hips and sink deeper. Wet, hot, and mine.

She moans and I wrap her legs around my back and lift her up. I can't get deep enough. I want her to feel me everywhere. I'm like an animal needing to possess her. There will be no doubt when we finish how I feel.

"Catherine," I say through gritted teeth. "Look at me." When her deep brown eyes meet mine, her hands cup my face. "Take me."

I snap. The words I need to hear from her. With her back on the table, I take this time to plunge into her again. I ride her in and out, allowing her to milk my cock as I lose my fucking mind. She's every breath I breathe, every beat of my heart, and I never want it to stop.

"Fuck. I'm losing it."

Needing her to come, I put my thumb on her clit and rub in circles. I feel her clench and I have to bite my tongue to stop from finishing right then. Her hands find my arms and she holds on while I pound her relentlessly. Each thrust I lose myself in her. I claim her each time I slide in and out. The need to protect her, keep her safe, and ensure she never runs from me again surges through my body.

"I fucking love you. You're mine."

My fingers press harder into her clit and I feel her thighs tighten around my hips. I fuck her harder and as her eyes stay locked on mine, I can feel her get closer, her nails digging into my forearms. She scrapes them down my arms as she falls apart. I can't last much longer.

My hands grip her thighs roughly and she screams my name over and over.

"Catherine!" I call out as I slam against her harder and lose myself over the edge while her pussy squeezes around my cock draining every ounce of me until I'm empty.

My head drops and rests on her breasts as our breathing calms.

That was intense.

I close my eyes and focus on her heart beating beneath me. Catherine's hands slide slowly up and down my back when she lets out a deep breath.

If she pulls away, I'm gonna lose my shit.

"How long are you here for?" she asks, already sounding

defeated.

"Forever."

She huffs, "I don't think that's funny."

"I wasn't kidding."

Why does everything with this woman need to be so damn complicated?

"Jackson, be serious."

Standing up, I put my hands on her sides and look at her. I need to make sure she sees everything in my heart when I get this out. Considering she seems to need me to spell it out, it's best I give myself little room for misinterpretation.

"I sold Raven."

Her eyes go wide. "You what?"

"I sold it. It's gone."

"Why?" Catherine's mouth falls open.

"Because I love you. Because a life without you isn't the life I want. Because every day I think of you. Every moment I want to be with you. So you being in California and me being in New York isn't working. The day you left me, I made a choice."

"But, Jackson, you can't."

"I did."

"This is crazy," she says and starts to shift under me.

"Goddammit, Catherine," I say, growing frustrated as I pin her down from getting away.

She tries to slide out from under me and can't. Trying to hide from me, she puts her hands over her face.

Here we go.

"Why don't you get it?" I ask pulling her hands away.

"Get what?"

I take her hands in mine and pour my heart out. "I'm not leaving. I choose you. You're it for me. I love you—infinitely."

"But you can't give everything up for me. You'll resent me."

I rub small circles on her tiny palms. "Catherine, I didn't give everything up *because* of you. I gave it up for me. For us. I loved you enough to let you go, but I love you enough to give up everything *for* you. You didn't ask me to do this. I did this because my life without you doesn't work. This is your dream and I won't ask you to choose, but you, you are my dream."

She gasps as tears fall from her eyes. I've laid it all out for her. I let her up, and she sits on the table as I wait.

"I guess the question is, do you feel the same?"

Her beautiful eyes lock on mine as the word I want to hear falls from her perfect lips. "Yes."

"Yes?" I ask needing her to tell me again.

She hops down and wraps her arms around me. Her eyes glimmer and are filled with love. "You're it for me. Always have been and always will be."

EPILOGUE

JACKSON

Seven years later

"**O**KAY, YOU READY?**"** I ask her with that glint in her eye as she stands there with the timer.

"No cheating this time. I swear," she vows. I glance at Catherine as she smiles.

Yeah, I know that look. She's already scheming.

"Mommy, push the button!" Erin yells as she starts jumping up and down.

"I thought you were on my side?" I ask the little traitor. She looks up with her big brown eyes and bats her eyelashes quickly. Her dark brown hair is in pigtails that she keeps making slap her in the face when she turns.

"Sowwy, Daddy. Mommy said we could have ice cream if she wins. If you win, we have to eat spinach. Yuck!"

Her puppy dog eyes melt me. Damn girls.

I look at my wife who shrugs with a shit-eating grin on her face. I make note to wipe it off later.

"Kennedy, whose side are you on?" I ask the other half of the demon spawn. Her blond hair is covering her face as she tries to do the same thing her sister is. She may only be three, but surely she wouldn't leave me for ice cream. She's honorable.

"Mama!" she calls out and puts her hands up.

Or not.

Catherine walks over as we stand in front of the obstacle course in California. "What's the matter, Muffin?" she asks coyly. "You ready to lose to the girls today?"

"My ass, Kitty."

"Butt," she corrects me but lets the nickname slide. I'm sure she'll punish me later—which I might like.

Erin spins in circles in the sand pit and Kennedy runs over to her sister. "They can't hear." I grab her waist and pull her against my side. "Besides," I whisper in her ear and she shivers. "You know I like your ass and I know you like it when I swear. You had no problem telling me to fuck you harder last night."

My dick stirs at the images, how hot she looked when she fell apart in my arms.

"You may want to get yourself ready since I'm about to kick your butt—*again*."

"Over my dead body." I snake my hand up her back and run my tongue along her neck.

"Girls!" Catherine calls over and they come running.

"Low blow, Catherine."

"No blowing anything, baby. Other than you're about to get blown out of the water," she says as her fine ass starts to walk away.

"I'd rather you blow something else." I give her a knowing look.

Her head whips around and she smirks. "You'll pay for that."

"I'm sure I will."

She knows the three of them rule my world. Kennedy looks just like her mother—she's tiny and has the biggest brown eyes I've ever seen. Her pout can melt me, and I'm pretty sure she's figured out all she has to do is turn her lip down and I'll cave. She has the same tiny cleft in her chin, which is why most people say she's her mother's child. I think it's her feisty attitude and quick wit.

Erin, on the other hand, is pretty much all me. She's tall and slender but has her mother's facial features. I love that I can look at any of them and see Catherine. They ground me and give me a love like I've never known.

Even with Catherine running her own P.R. firm and my traveling, we find a way to make it work. When we fight, we have a lot of fun making up. When I found out Catherine was pregnant, I was obsessive over everything. What she wore, what she ate, if she took her prenatals, doctor's appointments, pretty much everything she did I was on top of. Needless to say, she really hated me by month two, but she understood. With Kennedy we were much more relaxed. I actually enjoyed my very horny wife.

"Daddy, we're ready to run the os-tickle course," Erin calls, clearly screwing that name up.

I think my cadets need a little extra training.

"Fall in, girls!" I command and they all stand there giggling.

Fine. We'll do this the hard way. I lift each of the girls and put them in line. Kennedy starts to draw in the dirt while Catherine crosses her arms and covers her mouth trying not to laugh.

"Kennedy, you need to stand at attention." I huff as she shakes her head back and forth.

"This should be good," I hear Catherine from behind me.

"Zip it, woman."

"I'll give you 'woman.'"

I turn and wiggle my eyebrows and she rolls her eyes. Some things haven't changed and I hope they never do.

"Okay, Muffin. Let's see how a SEAL loses to his wife—who doesn't exercise—and his two daughters under the age of five," Catherine taunts. "This time if I win, I want something big."

"How big? I've got a big prize for you." I raise my brow and she slaps my chest.

"Idiot. Well, first I want to hear your terms."

My cadets are now doing ring-around-the-rosey. I need a full out boot camp for these two. "Girls ... you're killing me. Killing me." I look back at Catherine and I need to kiss her.

So I do.

I feel someone little pulling on my shirt. Looking down, I see Erin. Little cock blocker. "Is Uncle Mark coming? He always lets me win."

"No, because he doesn't want to lose to your amazing daddy!" I say a little too excitedly.

My beautiful, sweet, perfect daughter laughs at me. "Daddy, you're silly. Uncle Mark always wins."

"Do you want to ever get a present again?" I ask her. "Because I'll make sure you never see another Barbie." I purse my lips and she laughs harder.

I swear I was drunk when I wished for girls.

"Are you done threatening the kids with things they know you'll never do and ready to lose?" Catherine asks from behind me, holding Kennedy in her arms.

Arguing with her is a full-time job. "Sure, baby. Let's set the terms so we're crystal clear on what I get when I win."

"Let's hear it."

I steeple my fingers and try to make this good. When I win, I want to be sure I really come out with what I want. After the fucking play from hell, I still had to send her to a spa in Napa when I moved out here—and fly Ashton out. It's payback time.

"I want a guys' golfing weekend. In Bermuda. With Mark, Tristan, and Logan."

"So you want to take all my help?" she asks.

"Fine, you can keep Tristan. He sucks at golf anyway."

Tristan and Logan live down the street from us. Logan had a breakout role in a major film and now Catherine represents him. Tristan stays home and does ... well, nothing.

"Okay," she agrees.

Immediately my spidey senses kick in. She agreed way too easily.

"That was too quick. What did you do?" I look around and put my hand out. "Give me the stopwatch, dear."

Catherine's eyes widen and she smiles. "Here ya go,

pumpkin," she says sarcastically. I almost prefer "Muffin"—almost.

I look at the timer but it's still at zero.

"I don't trust you," I narrow my eyes before turning around. "Erin and Kennedy," I call them over, "Did your mommy do something?"

They both smile and shake their heads no.

"Fine. You ready to watch me teach your mommy how it's done?"

They both give me a blank stare.

"Okay, good."

"Ready, Muffin?"

"Sure thing, cupcake."

"Go!" Catherine calls out and I sprint off. I get over the logs and halfway to the tunnel when I hear Kennedy start screaming hysterically.

I stop immediately and rush to her. When I get there, she stops and looks up at Catherine. "Like that, Mommy?"

Catherine looks up and tilts her head to her shoulder.

"You're using the kids?" I ask incredulously. This means war.

"A girl's gotta do what a girl's gotta do. You should probably get back to it, old man."

I growl, "I'll show you an old man." I turn and run faster hoping she doesn't try anything else. I leap back over the logs and get through the tube quickly.

Ha! I'm not even breaking a sweat.

I climb the rope, but when I get to the top of the wall, Erin is sitting at the bottom where I would land.

"Catherine!" I practically snarl her name.

I look at my oldest and give her a knowing look. "Sweetheart, can you move so Daddy doesn't crush you?"

"Sorry, I was told I would get to go to Toys R Us and pick out anything I want. Grandma Nina also said if I stayed extra long she'd send me money."

"What? She's in on this too?"

They're all out to get me. Next thing Reagan will somehow be involved.

I leap onto the other side and hear Catherine yell out, "That's an extra minute, babe. You're clearly cheating."

I get through the next four parts of the course and make it down the tower.

Now it's time for my wife to pay for her transgressions.

"What was so important that you wanted to win? You know I'd give you everything."

She smiles and places her hand on my chest. "You already have."

"Does this involve a play? Because I really don't want to sit through that horse shit again."

"No, but you will get to star in it." She smiles and my mind starts to race. "I have conditions though."

"Of course you do," I shake my head and already regret this.

Catherine smirks and wraps her arms around my neck. "Yes, I don't want anymore presidents. I just want one thing."

Now she has me thoroughly confused.

"And that would be, my love?" I question while kissing the tip of her nose.

"A boy."

The End

acknowledgements

This is always the hardest part. I have so many people who make this journey what it is. The book wouldn't be what it is without the help of those who are close to me. Whether you helped me work through a scene or you just messaged me to say "hello", you were a part of this. If I leave you out please forgive me, I literally hate this part.

To my readers, thank you isn't enough. You took a chance on a debut author and the love and support was beyond anything I could ever imagine. Thank you for leaving reviews, messaging me, joining the group, and spreading the word. You'll never know the difference you've made in my life.

Mandi Beck- my sweet, supportive, amazing, and fantastic friend. You're the glue that keeps me together. There's not a word you don't read, or a call you decline. Your love of Jackson has never waivered, even when you were pissed at him. I don't know how I would've made it through this journey without you.

Jennifer Wolfel— as much as you scare the crap out of me, I couldn't wait to send you the next chapter. You push me. You make me work hard on every paragraph, sentence, and word. Your wisdom made me fight through the scenes and the fact that I made you cry...makes me happy. I love you and thank you immensely.

Melissa Saneholtz – there are people who come into your life and make things brighter. That's you. I can call you anytime I need you, trust your guidance and you keep me in check (which is no small feat.) Thank you for the countless hours you spend with me, the laughs we share, and your friendship. I couldn't imagine doing this without you!

My betas: Roxana Madar, Megan Ward, Linda Russell,

and Ninfa Maisano – Thank you for taking the time to read over and over and give me all your feedback. My early readers: Alison Manning, Lara Petterson, and Susan Rayner – you're the first people to see it and give me the best idea on how it flows. I can't thank you enough.

Christy Peckham – You my Stabby Jr. are so important to me. You'll never know how much I love and appreciate you!

Stephanie, Ninfa, Julie, Carla, Melissa, Jennifer, Amy B., Jillian, Debbie, Tanya, Jessica, Annette, Robin, Michelle, Sherry, Mindi, Amy C., Laura, April, and Wendy... You are my lifeline, my friends, and my heart.

Pam Carrion – I'm giving you a face right now... did you smile? You've been a saint! A godsend! No matter what crazy idea I came up with you were there to help. You're an amazing blogger and I'm fortunate to have you as a friend.

Linda Russell – Woman...no freaking words. Just THANK YOU! You were the first person to read Beloved and I'll never forget the way you rallied behind me. This book wouldn't have been half of what it became without you.

Sharon "Satan" Goodman – Oh, my love. You are so far from being Satan...you're more like an angel...that might be pushing it. I love you so much. Thank you for keeping me on track by being afraid of Maleficent and not allowing us to have tangents. You're one of the best people I know.

Crystal Pugh – My giant pain in the ass. If it weren't for you the cover wouldn't have happened. Thank you for being my friend. You know the ugly and you still find the beauty. Thank you for driving me insane but then turning around, making me laugh, and offering to make out with me.

Laurelin Paige – You're constant support is invaluable. You keep me grounded and make me laugh when I need it. The world is a better place because of friends like you. If you never encouraged me, this would've never happened. Thank you for changing my life.

Claire Contreras – You'll never know how much your

friendship has changed my life. You're an inspiration to women and me. #FYTTMCC except I would say #ILYTTMCC.

Katie Stankiewicz – My graphic slave. You come through for me every single time and I don't know how I'd do it without you. You're not only an amazing artist but you're an even better friend. Thank you for everything. Love you!

FYW – I'm so blessed to have you all in my life.

Lisa, my editor, thank you to for fixing my words and your endless support. You forced me to dig deep and fight hard to give them the story they deserved.

SG4L – You are my sisters, my friends, and I can't imagine life without you.

Bloggers, without you I wouldn't be here. You always give your time, thoughts, and support. Thank you for taking a chance on me and telling your readers. You are truly some of the best people I know. Thank you!

Danielle and Alex – You made this cover more beautiful than I could've imagined. Thank you both for in the midst of your move doing the photo shoot and gracing the front of this book.

My family, thank you all for supporting my dream and encouraging me. Even if most of you will never read, I still appreciate you. To my mother: Without you, none of this would've been possible. You'll never know how much I love you and appreciate all you've done for me.

My husband, a long time ago I fell in love with you. I pushed you, pulled you, and sometimes I ran from you...but you were always there. You love me no matter what and I can only pray our children find a love like ours. Thank you for putting up with my crazy and showing me I'm enough.

My children, you're my biggest cheerleaders and I love you more than my own life. You both make me smile at your praise (even though you'll never read.) I love that you tell your friends parents to read and you are the best things I ever did.

about the author

Corinne Michaels is an emotional, witty, sarcastic, and fun loving mom of two beautiful children. She's happily married to the man of her dreams and is a former Navy wife. After spending months away from her husband while he was deployed, reading and writing was her escape from the loneliness. Beloved and Beholden conclude The Belonging Duet and she's currently working on three spinoffs.

connect with corinne

www.corinnemichaels.com

Connect on Facebook
www.facebook.com/CorinneMichaels

Connect on Twitter
https://twitter.com/AuthorCMichaels

Connect on Goodreads

Connect on Instagram
http://instagram.com/authorcorinnemichaels

CPSIA information can be obtained at www.ICGtesting.com
Printed in the USA
BVOW01s0605020816

457652BV00024B/239/P